L J MORRIS

Legacy of Guilt

A Logan Palmer Thriller

To all those still on patrol.

Prologue

The armoured limousine turned off the main road and stopped at the security barrier of the conference centre. The driver rolled down his window and handed his passenger's ID documents to the guard who scuttled back inside his hut, out of the rain. Inside the security cordon, at the entrance to the building, the security detail switched to a high state of readiness as the risky part of the operation approached. All vantage points that overlooked the road had been checked. Offices were cleared and locked, roofs were searched and parked vehicles moved to a different part of the campus. The team on the ground talked into hidden microphones as they scanned windows and rooftops, alert for any possible threat. Everything was covered. The guard at the gate handed the limo driver the checked documents and raised the barrier.

Logan Palmer rode in the front seat of the limo staring through the windscreen, but the visibility wasn't good. He used a cloth to wipe condensation from the inside of the window, but the problem was outside. The weather was getting worse, and it worried him. Rain gave people a reason to wear bulky coats that might conceal a weapon. A reason to pull up their hoods and hide their faces. He would have preferred an entrance through the underground car park and had told them that, forcibly. The car park was easily sealed off and he could get rid of the reception committee. It was safer, more secure, logical. The hierarchy, however, had other ideas; this was a publicity opportunity that couldn't be missed.

Palmer was an expert at what he did. He had been in the private security game since leaving the Royal Marines. He had provided close protection for high powered businessmen who were convinced they were a target. None of them were. He'd guarded celebrities who used him to enhance their VIP status. The more security they had, the more important they were. It was easy money, but he gave every client the same protection. He was a professional and took his job seriously, even if the threat was only in the VIP's head. Today was different. Today, there was a very real threat, and having his security arrangements overruled for the sake of a publicity opportunity, was putting lives at risk.

The company he worked for, Greenline Solutions, had been hired by the United Nations to provide close protection and security for one of their most high-profile scientists. Yvette Duval was the head of the UN Environment Programme. Initially, it was an organisation ignored by the world's main polluters. The major industrial nations of the G7 only paid lip service to the problems of global warming. Behind the scenes, they carried on with their unrestrained use of fossil fuels and plastics, unwilling to risk their economies. The smaller nations pointed to the larger economies and rightly said, 'If they don't do it, why should we?'. But, in the last two years, there had been a groundswell of protest, a wave of rising anger. People were asking questions and demanding that something be done. The world needed someone to stand up and challenge big business. Yvette Duval was that person.

Duval regularly had much publicised meetings with governments and chief executives. She made high-profile speeches at Davos, the UN and the G7. She was lauded by presidents and prime ministers, but, beneath the surface, it was all show and she had upset a lot of powerful people.

When she called for petrol and diesel cars to be banned immediately, she upset the car industry. Her plan to implement restrictions on air travel pitted her against the airlines and aircraft manufacturers. Food and drink producers complained about the extreme cost of not using plastics. But, without any shadow of a doubt, the reason Palmer was in the limo was Duval's push to set up a global environmental organisation. An authority with the real power to force through legislation and boycott all companies that supported fossil fuels. She wanted the ability to remove government contracts from all companies that didn't fall in line. That was why she had received death threats. There were some unscrupulous groups that made billions out of the oil industry. Not just private companies, but governments; and they wanted her stopped.

Palmer had spent every waking hour with Duval over the last month, getting to know her, her routines, her habits. If he was going to provide her with protection, she needed to trust him implicitly. She needed to do what he said without question or hesitation. Her life could depend on it.

Duval and Palmer got on well from day one. They were from similar, working class backgrounds and had a lot of the same likes and dislikes. They often chatted into the small hours about music and literature. Away from the glare of the spotlight and the intrusions of the press, they had become quite close. Close enough for rumours of a relationship to start being whispered within Palmer's team. Rumours that Duval did little to discourage, a relationship that some wouldn't allow to flourish.

The limo slowed as it approached the entrance. Palmer and the driver were hyper vigilant, constantly checking in all directions. Palmer spoke into the microphone that was concealed in his hand. 'Delta Two, Delta One, over.'

There was no response.

'Delta Two, Delta One...OVER.'

Still nothing.

'Delta Three, where is Delta Two?'

'Delta One, Delta Three. Two is checking one of the rooftops opposite your position, over.'

The limo drew to a halt at the end of the red carpet which had been rolled down the steps from the conference centre's ornate entrance. 'Delta Two, this is Delta One. Where are you? Over.'

'Delta Two. Keep your hair on, Logan. We're good to go.'

Palmer lowered his mic. 'Prick!'

Duval leaned forwards in the back seat. 'Is something wrong, Logan?'

'Nothing I can't deal with. Be ready to go, but don't move until I open the door. Okay, Yvette?'

'Okay. I still think it's a lot of fuss over nothing.'

Palmer opened his door and climbed out. He looked around at the small gathered crowed of dignitaries, checked the rest of the team were in place and scanned the rooftops. 'Delta Three, Delta One over.'

'Delta Three clear.'

'Delta Two, Delta One, over.'

'Delta Two clear.'

Palmer took hold of the handle, had one last look around him, and opened the door.

Duval climbed out, opening a small umbrella over her head as she did. The crack that Palmer heard wasn't the sound of a sniper's weapon, it was the sound of the bullet hitting Duval in the chest.

Palmer stepped forwards and caught her as she fell, pushing her back into the car. The second bullet carved a groove in Palmer's shoulder as he closed the door. 'GO, GO, GO.'

The driver put his foot down and sped off as people scattered all around them.

Palmer looked down at Duval. She was staring at him, eyes wide. The Kevlar vest she wore wasn't thick enough to stop the high velocity, large calibre round. The damage was massive. Duval struggled to breathe; blood pouring from her mouth.

Palmer took off his jacket, balled it up and held it over the wound. 'Stay with me, Yvette.' He pressed hard to try and stop the bleeding, but he knew it was too late. He had seen wounds like this before and they were always fatal.

As the limo sped back under the security barrier and skidded out onto the main road, Palmer looked down at Duval. 'Yvette.' Her eyes were still wide open but there was no response. She stopped breathing and slumped in his arms. She was gone.

Chapter 1

The Dharma Café sat at the end of a row of shops in the Forest Gate area of London. It wasn't as big or as cheap as some of the larger coffee chains, but it was becoming more popular with the younger generation who were now moving into nearby flats and houses. The area was far enough outside central London for rental prices to be affordable, but close enough to easily commute to the city when necessary. With its small village like feel and varied green spaces, it was on the verge of a boom and local business were enjoying a renaissance. Times were getting better.

The Dharma was a Buddhist café that had been open for just over five years. Struggling at first and almost going under on two occasions, it was now tapping into the millennial appetite for fair trade products and the trend for vegetarian and vegan diets. Its whole menu was ethically sourced and there was no plastic packaging in sight. When it came to the current demand to protect the environment, The Dharma Café was ahead of the game.

The décor, both inside and out, was faux Tibetan. The colour scheme was dominated by maroon and yellow as the owners tried a little too hard to enforce their Buddhist credentials. The sign above the door was bright red with gold lettering in a font that mirrored Sanskrit writing.

Inside, long bench seats and settees were arranged around an eclectic collection of handmade tables. Brightly coloured prayer flags hung around the walls, and, in one corner, an incense burner filled the air with a fragrant aroma that was spread across the room by the slowly turning, wooden blades of a large ceiling mounted fan. The counter was built out of reclaimed wood, in various colours, and the menu was handwritten on a chipped blackboard. It gave the whole space a recycled feel.

Its clientele wasn't the usual collection of people who sat alone and stared at laptop screens while their skinny latte went cold. Instead, customers of the Dharma Café sat together and chatted. Some carried yoga bags and water bottles, on their way back from early morning meditation sessions. Others, on their way to the office, hid their laptops under tables or cushions, they would be looking at them for long enough during the day. The customers of The Dharma Café were, in the main, young people who valued their health. People who knew the value of taking time out to relax and refresh. There were exceptions, of course.

Sitting in an alcove on a small mustard coloured armchair, Anna Riley stirred her green tea and did her best to be invisible. She didn't come here to make friends and she wasn't in the mood for a chat. Her head was pounding, and her eyes were gritty and bloodshot. She couldn't remember the last time she had anything to eat. It wasn't that she couldn't afford to eat or that it had been a long time, she just couldn't remember. She was living her life through a haze of half remembered conversations and blurred images. All the pictures in her head were randomly jumbled up in a mess of snapshots that were

7

pinned to a wall with no timeline. The memories could have been just a few hours old, but, then again, they could be from days or even weeks ago.

For the last few months, each day seemed worse than the last. A broken relationship and a string of unfulfilling one-night stands had plunged her self-esteem into a pit she was struggling to climb out of. By anyone's standards, she was a mess, and she knew it. She had tried to straighten herself up many times, but it always ended with another night she couldn't remember, another day of headaches and bitter regret.

A tear ran down her cheek and she wiped it away quickly, unwilling to share her problems with the world. She took off her jacket, sank back into the chair and closed her eyes.

Riley's eyes snapped open at the sound of the chair opposite hers scraping across the tiled floor. She sat up. A smartly dressed woman in her forties placed her coffee on the table and sat down. Riley didn't think she had fallen asleep, but it was hard to tell. She hadn't heard anyone approaching her and was caught off guard. She looked around, checking for anyone who was watching them or who didn't fit in, some of her MI5 training was still buried in her subconscious. No one in the café was paying them any attention, it looked like the woman was alone. Riley tried to recover her composure. 'I'm sorry, someone's sitting there.'

The woman smiled and pushed her glasses up to the top of her head where they nestled in her long blonde hair. 'Hello Anna. I'm Victoria Thomson. You can call me Vicky.'

The shock of being ripped from her hangover induced meditation had set Riley's heart pounding. Who was this woman? How did she know who Riley was? 'I think you've got me mixed up with someone else.'

Thomson took a sip of her coffee. 'How's your head? You had a heavy night last night.'

Riley didn't even know what she had done the previous night. The pain in her temples was getting worse. 'What? How the hell would you know what I did?'

'I was there, Anna... Remember? Oh no, you wouldn't, would you?'

Riley's memory was a blank. All she knew for sure was that she had walked into a bar and ordered a drink. As usual, everything that happened after that was a mystery to her. 'Who are you? What do you want? Are you following me?'

Thomson cleared her throat. 'I work for Edward Lancaster, I'm sure you know who he is. He asked me to check up on you, see if you're okay.'

Riley knew the name. Edward Lancaster was the new head of MI6, a legend amongst the security community. But Riley didn't work for him, she worked for MI5. At least, she used to. Before all this. 'Why would someone like Lancaster care about me?'

'We've been watching you, Anna. We want to know if you really are a burned-out wreck ready for the scrap heap, or whether you are still capable of doing a job for us.'

Riley was still trying to make sense of what was happening. If she woke up screaming and found out this was a dream, it wouldn't have surprised her. 'What kind of job? Why me?

'I'm not going to go into details here.' Thomson slid a small card across the table. 'Be at that address tomorrow at 10 o'clock. If you're up to it, we'll give you the details.'

Riley looked at the card. 'What if I'm not ready?'

Thomson leaned forwards and lowered her voice. 'Trust me,

Anna, I know what it's like. I was once where you are. It was Edward that brought me back in. This is your last chance at a reprieve, no one wants to work with you, you're a liability.'

'If I'm such a problem, why do you and Lancaster want me?'

Thomson finished her coffee. 'Call it a hunch, call it sympathy, call it whatever you want, but, if you don't take this job, you're fucked.'

Riley knew she had to go back to work, no matter how anxious she was. She couldn't carry on like this. Her behaviour, her addictions, were getting worse. Turning this job down would undoubtedly lead to one outcome. An increasing downward spiral that ended with her dying alone in a grubby bedsit, choking on her own vomit. She put the card in her pocket. 'I'll be there.'

'Good. You won't regret it, Anna, I didn't.' Thomson stood up. 'Don't tell anyone about this. Oh, and do yourself a favour, try and stay sober until then.' She turned and walked away.

Riley looked at her watch, it was one o'clock already, there wasn't much time to get herself sorted out. Some smarter, cleaner clothes would help, a bit of makeup to hide the black rings under her eyes, and her hair could really do with a trim. She couldn't afford to blow this and wanted to at least look presentable. Checking out Victoria Thomson was also high on the list; they would expect her to do that. But first, before the clothes shops and the hairdressers, she needed to get something substantial to eat. Her hangover was wearing off and the possibility of getting back to work had given her a burst of nervous energy, she realised that she was starving.

She drank the cold remnants of her green tea, grabbed her coat, and left the café.

Chapter 2

Riley's flat wasn't much to look at. One bedroom, shower room, and a combined kitchen and living space were all she could afford, but she liked it and was happy living there. It was small but all she needed and a step up from the bedsit she had when she first came to London. The kitchen cabinets looked a little grubby and a coat of paint and some new carpet wouldn't have gone amiss, but it was okay. In the bedroom, her clothes for the meeting the next day, freshly ironed, hung from a hook on the back of the door along with a new coat. One with fewer stains on it.

When Riley got home from the coffee shop, feeling optimistic about the future for the first time in months, she had decided to clean the flat. It took a while. It had worried her just how far she had let things go, how quickly what was left of her life could fall apart.

During the clean, she found four pizza boxes with half eaten contents, three empty bottles of various spirits, and a plastic bag, with some kind of kebab in it, strewn across the living room floor. Her laundry basket contained some mildew-stained clothes that looked like they had been in there for months and the kitchen cupboards were full of out-of-date food. The bedroom wasn't too bad, but the less said about the state of the shower room, the better. The rubbish filled three large, black, bin bags that she'd taken down to the wheelie bin outside. There was still work to do, but it was a start. The start of a long, hard, climb back to normality.

Riley had bought a takeaway on the way home. Not the healthiest option, but cooking was something she was going to have to work up to. At least, this time, she hadn't just left the empty containers lying on the floor.

She made herself a cup of tea and now sat on her worn sofa tapping at her freshly cleaned laptop keyboard. This was what she lived for. Only now did she realise how much she had missed it.

Since she was a teenager, she had lived her life online, learning to travel around the virtual highways as easily as jumping in a car. By the time she left university, she was writing her own programs and was able to bypass sophisticated security measures with ease. The cyber security position she accepted as a graduate gave her real world experience and it wasn't long before she outgrew her job and had other offers coming in. One of those offers came from MI5, and it was an opportunity that she grasped with both hands. That was ten years ago, and a lot had happened since then, some good, some bad. The last three months had been bad, and she hadn't opened her laptop once.

She picked up her cup of tea and looked at the face that stared at her from the screen. Victoria Thomson was an army nurse whose talent for languages led to her being recruited by military intelligence. She was a front line operative. Confident and fearless, but sometimes reckless and complacent. She was taken prisoner by insurgents during a messed-up operation in Afghanistan and held hostage. The details in the file were sketchy, but her treatment in captivity sounded brutal. Many people wouldn't have survived and the fact that she did was a testament to her mental strength. Her subsequent breakdown, however, saw her cut off from the security services. It is a sad reality that far too many people within the hierarchy see broken soldiers as an embarrassment. A legacy of conflict that they would simply rather not deal with.

Thomson's mental health had understandably suffered and her ability to work in the field was in doubt. Frequent missed days due to breakdown and substance abuse left her labelled as a liability, a dead weight, someone to be cut loose. As she hit rock bottom, it was Edward Lancaster who saw her potential. He was the one who made sure she got the treatment she needed, who brought her back into the fold.

Her recovery was nothing short of miraculous. Now, she was Lancaster's most trusted lieutenant, a confidant with access to the top that few people enjoyed. For anyone outside the security services, speaking with Edward Lancaster often meant getting past Victoria Thomson first.

It was getting late, and Riley needed to get some quality sleep before the meeting, but she was wracked with nerves that would only get worse as the time grew nearer. Her mind, as it always did these days, threw up a thought. You'd feel better after a drink, just one won't hurt. She screwed her eyes tightly shut, it had only been a few hours since her last drink and she was struggling already.

She went to the kitchen and looked inside one of the cabinets, fishing out a bottle of sleeping pills she had been prescribed months earlier. She took two out, swallowed them with a large glass of water, and went to bed.

Chapter 3

The address Thomson had given Riley didn't look anything out of the ordinary. It was a small, slightly shabby looking terraced house in Stratford. Riley had taken two buses to get there and now stood behind a row of parked cars on the opposite side of the road to the house. She had been there for twenty minutes, and no one had arrived or left in that time. She had planned to impress them by keeping a log of what time they arrived and from which direction. It hadn't worked. Lancaster and Thomson were old hands at this kind of thing and Riley didn't know what she was doing. As the hands on her watch ticked round to ten o'clock, she couldn't wait any longer. She crossed the road and walked towards the door.

Before Riley had the chance to knock, the door opened, and she walked straight in.

Victoria Thomson closed the door and checked that no one had been watching from the street. 'Good morning, Anna, I'm glad you made it. Please, go through to the kitchen.'

Riley walked down the hallway to the back of the house where a man in a dark grey suit stood at the kitchen table. Edward Lancaster looked every inch how people would expect the head of MI6 to look. Tall and slim with slightly greying hair, he was well groomed and exuded confidence. Anyone looking at him knew instantly that he was in charge. He held out his hand. 'Good morning, Anna.'

Riley shook his hand. 'Good morning, sir.'

'No need to call me sir. None of this is official.' He gestured towards a chair. 'Have a seat.'

Riley pulled out the wooden chair and sat down. She looked back down the hall. Thomson was still watching the street through the net curtain that hung behind the door. She turned back to Lancaster. 'What's this all about?'

Lancaster sat down. He had his hand on a brown cardboard folder that was on the table in front of him. 'How are you feeling, Anna? Can I trust you?'

Riley wasn't sure what she was being asked. Was Lancaster asking about her security clearance or did he mean her mental state? She thought this was going to be an assessment to see if she was sober enough to bring back in, or if she should just be put out to grass. 'Well... I... I'm sure you know that I've been a little bit... out of sorts lately, but I honestly think I can turn it around. I'm ready to come back.'

'I'm glad to hear that you want to turn things around, that's always the first step. I don't need you back, Anna, not just yet, not officially anyway. I need you to assure me that you can cut out the drink, and whatever else you've been taking. I need you to make the right decisions, to stay clean.'

Riley shifted in her seat. 'I'm determined to do everything I can to sort myself out. I know I've run out of chances.'

Lancaster paused, observing Riley's discomfort, assessing whether she could be trusted. 'This is an important job, Anna. If you can do this for me, I'll do what I can to bring you back in. I have a bit of a reputation for picking up those that have

15

been discarded.'

'If you give me this job, this chance, I won't let you down. I promise.'

'Excellent.' Lancaster slid the folder across the table. 'As I said before, none of this is official.' He looked around at their surroundings. 'This isn't an MI6 safe house; it belongs to a friend of mine who happens to be out of the country at the moment.' He gestured down the hallway to where Thomson stood. 'Vicky and I are officially on our way to an event at a security conference in Manchester. We'll be a little late, but no eyebrows will be raised by that, we'll just blame the traffic.' He pointed at the folder. 'Everything in that folder, everything about this operation is, and must remain, off the record. If that's a problem for you, walk away now.'

Riley wanted this. She needed something that would drag her back into the real world. Her life was spiralling out of control. She couldn't bear to imagine what depths she could plunge to without something to focus on. She opened the folder.

Several photographs lay on the top of a bundle of printed sheets of paper. One showed a man in a Royal Marine uniform. Riley recognized the broad shoulders and angular features of someone she had met a few years before. 'That's Logan Palmer.'

'You have a good memory, Anna. I believe he was part of your security detail when you spent some time in Iraq.'

'That's right. He was a nice guy.' She looked at the second photo. It showed a man with unkempt, shoulder length hair and a straggly beard standing on a desolate hillside. He was carrying a shotgun and had a brace of dead rabbits slung over his shoulder. Riley held the picture up. 'Who's this?'

'That's Logan Palmer now. That photo was taken last week.'

The difference between the two images was stark. 'What the hell happened to him?'

'I'm afraid that's a long story that we don't have time to go into. Let's just say he decided to retire. What I want you to do is bring him back. I want you to recruit Logan Palmer.'

Riley looked up from the images. She was a hacker, not a field operative, she liked working alone. To be honest, she didn't play well with others. 'But I'm not...I mean...don't you have people who do that sort of thing?'

'Yes, you know we do. But they have something that you don't. They have jobs, they can be traced directly to us. The reason I want you to do this is because you are, if anyone checks, currently under suspension. No one expects you to return, they all believe you'll be sacked. In fact, quite a few people think you already have been.'

Riley was starting to sweat. This was feeling more like a reprimand. 'What if they check why I'm visiting Palmer.'

'You have a history with him. You aren't working and you decided to look up an old friend. That should be your official cover.'

It made sense to Riley. 'Okay, that would probably work.' She still wasn't sure if she trusted herself to do this.

'There's also the fact that you're not in a relationship and you don't have to explain to anyone where you're going or why. No awkward questions.'

Riley didn't like being told, once again, how messed up her life had become. 'I take it you want Palmer for the same reasons.'

'Partly, but, like you, he has something that we need. We want him to go in undercover, and he has the links to get him

17

in fast.'

Riley turned over the printed sheets in the folder. 'Get in where?'

'I assume you're aware of the plane that crashed in Iran a few months back.'

Riley looked up. 'The one that the Iranians said the Americans shot down?'

'That's the one. Well, they were right. It was shot down, although not by the Americans.' Lancaster pointed to another photo that Riley was looking at. 'That is Sergei Chernov. He's one of the lead engineers at Russia's rocket launch and development site at Kapustin Yar near Volgograd. He was a passenger on the plane.'

Riley studied the photo. The text underneath the image said Chernov was fifty, but he looked older, he looked exhausted. Maybe the pressure was getting to him. 'Why would a valuable Russian nuclear engineer be on a civilian aircraft flying out of Tehran?'

'Chernov was an expert in nuclear weapons development, one of the world's finest minds in missile technology. He was also deeply disillusioned with the current Russian government.'

'He was defecting.'

Lancaster nodded. 'He contacted us two years ago during a reception at the embassy in Moscow. He said he wanted to come to the west, live a better life, retire in comfort.'

Riley looked up from the file. 'What was he offering in return? There must have been something.'

Lancaster smiled. 'We weren't going to risk pissing off the Russians without some reward. He was delivering details of the latest developments in hypersonic nuclear missiles at

Kapustin Yar.'

Riley nodded. 'The inside info on the Russians' latest weapons, I can see how valuable that would be, but it doesn't explain why the plane was shot down. Do you think it was the Russians?'

Lancaster paused for a second. 'We have no idea who shot it down or why. It may have been the Iranian Government, but I think that's unlikely. It may have been rogue elements in the Iranian security services, maybe it was the Russians. We think it was done as a distraction. A cover up for something else.'

Riley was stunned. 'Someone killed all those people as a cover up? Who would do that? Cover up what?'

'It wouldn't be the first time that that has been done. In nineteen eighty nine, Pablo Escobar blew up a civilian airliner and killed over a hundred people just to kill one man. A man that, as it turned out, wasn't on the plane. We have evidence that Chernov wasn't on this plane either. Chernov is now in the hands of someone else. The Russians don't have him, neither do the Iranians, and we certainly don't. So, where is he?'

Riley shuffled through the other papers in the folder. 'If you were just looking for a missing defector, you wouldn't need me or Palmer. You'd have MI6 and GCHQ on the case. There's something else. Isn't there?'

'I knew I'd picked the right person, Anna. You're right, there is more to this. In two thousand and three coalition forces invaded Iraq based on a report into Saddam Hussein's weapons of mass destruction. As we all know, none were ever found. That led to recriminations and accusations of an illegal war that persist to this day.'

Riley nodded. 'When I was in Baghdad, they were still looking for traces of WMDs. Trying to justify everything that happened.'

'Last year we were contacted by an asset we had inside Iraq. He was a contractor working for one of the private military companies that inhabited the Green Zone. He gave us the coordinates of what he said was a shipping container buried in the desert. A shipping container with a nuclear warhead in it.'

'So, there were WMDs?'

Lancaster shook his head. 'As much as some authorities would like that, it's unlikely it had been buried there since the invasion. It could have been bought on the black market by someone within the Iraqi regime or even Al Qaeda. Maybe they were originally considering a dirty bomb attack but realized how difficult it is.'

'Surely someone noticed a missing Nuclear warhead?'

'You'd be surprised, Anna. There was a great deal of confusion during the collapse of the Soviet Union. Some nuclear weapons may have been unaccounted for and then their absence covered up. All we know is, by the time we got to the coordinates we'd been given in the Iraqi desert, there was no warhead, and our asset was dead.'

Riley couldn't believe what she was hearing. 'If there's a missing nuclear weapon, why aren't we spending all of our time and resources looking for it? The consequences of terrorists or a rogue state getting hold of it don't bear thinking about.'

'It isn't easy to put together a nuclear weapon, Anna. That's one of the main reasons why terrorists haven't done it already. Having the warhead isn't enough. Any electronic circuitry in it would be decayed by now, and then you have the problem of delivering it to a target. Someone would have to be an expert to turn the warhead into a viable weapon.'

Riley's eyes widened. 'An expert like Chernov.'

Lancaster took another photograph from inside his jacket. 'After Chernov got out of Russia, we didn't want him wandering around Iran on his own, so we hired two operatives from a private security firm in Iraq to babysit him. The same company that our asset worked for.' He slid the photo over to Riley. 'That picture is from CCTV in Malaysia. It shows Chernov along with the two bodyguards. That is two weeks after the plane went down.'

Riley looked at the grainy image. 'So, we have a defecting nuclear weapons scientist and a missing warhead that can both be linked to a team belonging to the same private security company.'

Lancaster nodded. 'Greenline Solutions. Logan Palmer's old team. We need him to get back in and track down the warhead before Chernov can turn it into a nuclear weapon for whoever has him.'

This was sounding worse by the minute. Riley considered closing the folder and going to the pub. 'Has there been a specific threat? Do we know what the target might be.?'

'As always, the target will be a major western city. London, New York, Washington DC, maybe Paris. GCHQ have picked up chatter about a supposed spectacular attack taking place over the Christmas period.'

Riley was speechless for a moment as the implications sunk in. 'That only gives us a few weeks to recruit Palmer, get him in, find the warhead and take down whoever has it.'

'Precisely. You see the problem we have?'

Riley's heart was pounding. This was a lot of pressure to deal with. What if she failed? 'Why would Palmer agree to work for you, against his old team?'

'We're hoping he'll realise the danger to us all and that will be enough for him but, if all else fails, he used to be a mercenary and we can offer him a substantial amount of money.'

Riley wondered why they weren't offering her a substantial amount of money. 'Okay, I'll go and see him. I'll do everything I can to get him on board... I will get him.'

'You should know that we've already lost three operatives trying to track down Chernov and the warhead. Some of these private security companies have influential contacts and everyone we've put in so far has had their cover blown. We can't risk a leak on this operation, this is our last chance. We can't afford to fail.'

Riley put the paperwork in a neat bundle and closed the folder. 'When I was in Iraq, Palmer was known as a bit of a loose cannon. Are you ready for the fall out of letting him loose?'

'I'm aware of his reputation, Anna, but at this point, he's exactly what we need.'

Riley put the folder into her bag. 'I won't let you down.'

'Outstanding. There's a phone number in the folder that will get a message to Vicky. Don't use any names, just a contact number.' Lancaster stood up. 'Now, we need to get moving. If we're too late for this conference, it'll look suspicious. You go out the front and we'll leave through the back.'

Thomson checked the street. 'All clear.'

Lancaster held out his hand again. 'Keep us up to date, Anna. Good luck.'

Riley took his hand. 'Thank you. I'll be in touch as soon as I've got Palmer.'

Thomson opened the front door and Riley hurried out of the

house and into the street.

Chapter 4

L ogan Palmer lay motionless, his breathing shallow and controlled. The vegetation from the local hills that he had woven into the fabric of his camouflaged ghillie suit blended in perfectly with the colours of the stark Cumbrian landscape around him. Even an observer who knew where to look would have trouble spotting him, he was almost invisible.

Palmer was in his element. He had a natural ability, built upon by his military training and fine-tuned by years of experience. The time he had spent tracking down insurgents in the mountains of Afghanistan and the deserts of Iraq, the countless missions, alone and surrounded by the enemy, had turned him into the perfect hunter. His ability to blend in, not just into the landscape, but into any environment or set of surroundings, made him a valuable asset to any organisation. But that was years ago, before Geneva, before he retired. Now, he had a different quarry.

The remote gamekeeper's cottage Palmer lived in came with his job. His employer paid him to control the animals on the estate. He, routinely, took care of any problems with vermin, repaired fences to stop sheep wandering onto roads, and made sure poachers didn't take any of the wildlife. There were no shooting parties on the estate anymore, the new landowner was against hunting for sport, but animals still needed to be controlled. The most important aspect of Palmer's job, the role he was uniquely equipped to do, was as a stalker. It was his job to manage the deer population. He was employed, primarily, to cull the animals and make sure their numbers didn't get out of hand.

The deer he was watching through his scope was old, possibly sick. In many other parts of the world, it wouldn't have lasted this long but here, in England, it had no natural predators. Palmer had been following the old stag since dawn. Four hours and he still couldn't get a safe line of fire. Behind the animal's current position was a line of trees, a stone wall, and a narrow, country road. Although Palmer was confident in his own ability and unlikely to miss, he couldn't shoot and risk hitting something, or someone, accidentally.

As he watched, the deer's head sprang up. It looked around, ears twitching, then set off in a slow gallop further away from him. Something had startled it. Palmer kept his scope trained on the road in the distance. A car came into view and drove slowly behind the trees. Perfect timing. He wouldn't be catching up to that buck again today. Palmer stood up, slung his rifle over his shoulder, and set off back towards his cottage.

As he walked across the undulating landscape of the Cumbrian fells, he looked around at his surroundings. Although he had grown up here, he had moved away when he became a Marine. This part of the world could be harsh at times, but it was always beautiful. Even on misty, rain-soaked days like today, he was glad to be back.

The population here was sparse and people tended not to bother him. If he felt like company, there was a country pub less than three miles away where he was always welcomed. Most days he just liked to be left alone. The peace and quiet gave him time to think, time to remember the ones he loved, and time to forget those who had caused him pain. Today was one of the days when he would be remembering loved ones. It was his son's eighteenth birthday; his little boy was now a man.

Palmer had spent most of the last eighteen years away from home. Serving in the Royal Marines and, later, as a private military contractor, he had lived in hastily erected compounds in the mountains and fly-infested holes dug into the desert. His time in the close protection industry had earned him good money and he had always done what he could to support his son, but he hadn't been there, at home, when he needed him.

Palmer stopped and closed his eyes, pushing the bad thoughts out of his head. This was supposed to be a day for celebration, and he was going to make sure nothing spoiled it. He opened his eyes and looked up, through the trees. He could just make out the whitewashed walls of his cottage, but instead of joy at almost being home and the birthday get together he would be getting ready for, his heart sank. The car that had startled the deer was now parked in front of his house. He considered waiting until whoever it was had given up and gone away, but he didn't want to be late. He adjusted the shoulder strap of his rifle and trudged towards the cottage.

Anna Riley stood beside the car and watched as Palmer approached. She remembered the good looking marine she had worked with in Baghdad. He was always smartly turned out, well dressed, and well-groomed. This guy looked like he had slept under a hedge, it couldn't be the same person. As Palmer clambered over the dry-stone wall, Riley took a step towards him. 'Logan? Logan Palmer?'

Palmer stopped several feet from the car and looked past it to the house. There was no one else in sight, the woman seemed to be alone. 'Whoever you are, get back in your car and leave me alone. I'm not interested in whatever you're selling.'

'Logan. It's me, Anna Riley. We were together in Iraq. You were part of my security detail.'

Palmer remembered Riley. She had seemed pleasant enough, although a little aloof and timid. 'I remember you. Now, get back in your car and leave me alone.'

As Palmer headed for the house, Riley rushed after him. 'Please, Logan. I need to talk to you. It's important.'

'Whatever it is, I've got more important things to do today.

'Yes, of course. Your son's birthday.'

Palmer stopped dead and spun around. 'What do you know about my son? Who sent you?'

Riley was taken aback by Palmer's reaction. She was supposed to be recruiting him, not pissing him off. 'You can't be surprised that the security services know about you. The fact that you've got a son isn't exactly a state secret. Please, Logan, just give me some time to explain and if you aren't interested, you'll never see me again.'

Palmer, once again, looked around to check for anyone else who might have been in the car with Riley. 'Okay. Make it quick.' He walked to the door and went inside the house.

Riley followed him through the door. 'Thanks.'

From what Riley could see, the inside of the cottage could best be described as rustic. The room they now stood in seemed to be a combined kitchen and living room. Not in the same way as some modern houses have an open plan layout but simply because there was only one room. The walls were rough

27

sandstone and at one end she could make out an open fireplace that surrounded the ash and glowing embers of a dying fire. Next to it was a single, threadbare, wing-backed chair that looked like it was at least as old as the cottage itself. It was well-worn and had stuffing poking out at the corners. Many people would have consigned it to a skip long ago, but it suited the décor it now sat in.

At the other end of the room, a medium sized oak table stood in front of a Belfast sink and a handful of shelves and storage cupboards. A gas-powered range, as worn out and in need of repair as the rest of the house, completed the kitchen.

Palmer closed the door behind them and flicked on a light switch next to the door. 'Have a seat.'

Riley looked up at the single bulb that hung just above the low oak beams and cast shadows across the room. 'Looking at the place, I wasn't sure you had electricity.'

'I put a solar panel on the roof. It feeds a couple of big batteries. Enough for the basics, I don't need anything else.'

Riley liked the simplicity and solitude of the cottage. She had often thought of escaping the rat race in London. She imagined what it would be like to curl up in front of that fire with a good book while the wind and rain did their worst outside. She was fooling herself though. She couldn't live like this full time; she would miss her coffee machine and laptop too much.

Palmer took off his coat and hung it by the door with his ghillie suit to dry. 'I'm going to have a shower and get ready for my son's party. Put the kettle on, I won't be long.'

Chapter 5

By the time Riley had figured out how to work the bottled gas stove and made them both a cup of coffee, Palmer was back in the room. His hair was now swept back away from his face and his beard had been trimmed. Dark coloured jeans and a polo shirt completed the new smarter image. Not quite ready for the boardroom, but a vast improvement.

Riley put the two mugs of coffee on the table and sat down. 'You scrub up well.'

Palmer ran his fingers through his beard. 'Got to make the effort for my boy.' He took the chair opposite Riley. 'So, let's get on with it. What is it you want?'

Riley took the folder out of her backpack. 'I've been asked to approach you with a proposition.'

Palmer had worked with the security services long enough to know when they were behind something. 'Who by?'

'Officially? It's just me, a potential client, asking you to do some work.'

'What about unofficially?'

'Well, take your pick of organisations. I'm sure you can figure it out.'

Palmer tapped the folder. 'Whatever's in here, I'm not in

the security business anymore. I'm retired. Happy where I am.'

'Please, Logan. Just let me take you through it. You'll understand how important this is.'

Palmer sat back in his chair. 'Okay, give it your best shot.'

Riley gave Palmer the same briefing she had been given by Lancaster, though probably not as well. She told him about Chernov's defection. The disappearance of the warhead and the death of the asset. She even made sure to include the asset's possible link to Greenline Solutions to give Palmer a personal connection to the events. When she was finished, she pushed the folder across the table, sure that she had done a good job.

Palmer turned the photo of him in uniform round and leaned forwards to look at it, smiling. 'You say you've got evidence that Chernov wasn't on the plane?'

'Yes. That's where you can help. Chernov got out of Russia by getting a boat from Volgograd to Astrakhan then a ferry to Iran. He was on his own for that part of the journey as he thought it was the easiest way to get away from Russian territory.'

Palmer raised an eyebrow. 'I can think of countries easier than Iran to get him out of.'

'Yeah, me too. But, like I said, that part of the journey was up to him. Once he was in Iran, he was given two bodyguards. They were private security out of Baghdad, working for Greenline. They sneaked across the border with fake travel documents for Chernov and themselves. You might recognise them.'

The pictures that Riley pointed to also showed men in military uniform. Palmer picked them up and studied them.

'Yeah, I know them. Old acquaintances of mine.'

'They were supposed to get Chernov on a flight to Turkey, then we would take over.'

The next picture that Palmer looked at was one of several that showed the site of a plane crash. Twisted metal, luggage and broken seats littered the area. A burning engine, what was left of the cockpit and, here and there, bodies of passengers. The bodies weren't shocking to Palmer; he had seen destruction on this scale before. What was shocking to him was the final photograph. It showed a child's soft toy. A dog with a shiny black nose and long floppy ears. Its fur had been scorched by the blast and one eye was missing. Somewhere, in the wreckage of the plane, was the body of a child. An innocent killed for reasons that had nothing to do with them. After all the operations that Palmer had taken part in, the idea that he could have done something that led to the death of a child still haunted his dreams.

He studied the photo more closely. Behind the dog was a piece of metal that could have been easily missed amongst the other wreckage. For anyone who knew what they were looking at, it was obvious. He was looking at part of the casing of an anti-aircraft missile. 'This wasn't a crash. Unless this aircraft was carrying military hardware, it was shot down.'

'That part of the story was never released. The Iranians and Americans spent all their time blaming each other. We think it was done by whoever has the warhead. Done to cover up Chernov's disappearance.'

Palmer was still looking at the missile. 'You know that Greenline has access to weapons like this?'

Riley nodded. 'The coincidences just keep piling up.' She slid the CCTV photo across the table. 'This is Chernov and his

31

bodyguards in a hotel in Kuala Lumpur two weeks after the plane crash.'

Palmer looked at the image. It was black and white, and of poor quality. 'What were they thinking? If you're supposed to be dead, you don't book into a plush hotel. You sure this is them?'

'Yes, we are, but don't forget, no one is looking for them. They had no reason to hide. You need to find them, find them and destroy the warhead.'

'What about Chernov?'

'Obviously, we'd like him back here, but the warhead is the target.'

Palmer smirked. 'People are never the priority with you lot. Look, I can give you three or four names off the top of my head who would be interested in this. Guys who are still in the business. This would be right up their street.'

'We already know all the names you could give us. The problem is, they might be involved, they still have contracts with Greenline. We know you aren't. We know you severed all ties with them after Geneva. If you try to infiltrate their organ-isation, it will simply look like you've come out of retirement. If it makes a difference, we can pay you a substantial amount of money.'

Palmer emptied his cup and stood up. 'I need to go. I don't want to be late.'

Riley's head dropped. She knew this wasn't going to be an easy job, but she had hoped for a little more success than this. She had to try and appear as if she was Palmer's friend. Let him know that they were on the same side. 'Where are you going? I could give you a lift.'

'It's a pub called The Coach and Horses. Other side of the

village.'

'You won't believe this, but that's where I'm staying tonight.' She got her car keys out of her coat and shook them. 'Shall we?'

Chapter 6

The Coach and Horses was a typical Lake District country pub. The kind of thing depicted on postcards along with sheep and, of course, lakes. The main, two storey, grey stone building was over two hundred years old and was originally a stopping off point for horse drawn coaches between Liverpool and Glasgow. After falling into disrepair when the brewery dumped it in the nineties, it sat empty for almost a decade until the current owners bought it at auction for a knockdown price. Instead of turning it into a luxury country house or several flats as everyone expected, they decided to keep it as a business.

The addition of a large extension at the rear of the property turned it into a viable bed and breakfast that quickly became popular with locals and tourists alike. The front entrance of the pub was left as original as possible, and a beer garden added. A handful of oak picnic tables gave patrons a spot to soak up the scenery, when the Lakeland weather wasn't soaking them.

Riley pulled into the car park and stopped as close to the entrance as she could. The rain was now torrential and hammered down onto the car. Riley peered through the rain splattered windscreen. 'I'm sure it's a lovely building when you can see it.'

'You get used to this kind of weather up here. It's why we have so many lakes.' Palmer reached over and grabbed a golf umbrella from the back seat. 'You ready?'

Riley fastened her jacket. 'It's only water. We won't melt.'

They hurried past the picnic tables and through the door into the pub's entrance hall. In front of them was a staircase that led to the bed and breakfast rooms and, at the end of the hall, a counter which served as reception. Palmer shook the water off the umbrella and rolled it back up. 'I'll leave you to check-in. My boy's birthday do is in the function room at the back. Maybe I'll see you later.'

Riley looked through the double doors that separated the entrance from the bar. She could really do with a drink. One wouldn't hurt. 'Yeah, maybe.' She walked to the reception desk and rang the bell.

When Palmer entered the bar, a few of the regulars greeted him with a nod or a friendly wave. It was a small community, and they all knew each other. Palmer gave a nod to them and the bartender on his way through to the pub's function room.

During the day, this space was a breakfast room for guests, but, at night, the tables were rearranged, and it was hired out for small parties. It was a recent addition and looked more like a large conservatory than an extension. From waist height to the roof's eves, the walls were virtually all glass with vertical hanging blinds in front of each window. Adjacent to the door was a bar that connected to the main pub and could be served by the same staff. On the opposite side was a small stage where a band or DJ could set up to entertain the partygoers.

Palmer looked through the glass door at the entrance to where his ex-wife sat with their son and her current husband.

Meetings between them were always awkward and occasion-ally descended into a heated argument that never ended well. Palmer's ex-wife wasn't the real problem, he could handle her, it was her second husband. He and Palmer had history. Tonight was going to be a struggle, but Palmer had to try. He grabbed the handle and stepped in.

The room was quite dark and full of youngsters who were obviously waiting for the oldies to leave so that the real party could get started. Palmer wasn't planning to hang about. He just planned to stay long enough to wish his son a happy birthday and have a pint with him. He wanted to be gone long before the inevitable argument. When Palmer entered the room, his ex-wife waved to him, it always started amicably, while her husband glared at him over his pint.

Palmer and his ex-wife, Debbie, first got together while they were still at school. By the time they were 18, Debbie was pregnant, and they rushed into an ill-advised marriage that was destined to fall apart right from the start. They were little more than kids themselves and had a lot of growing up to do. Palmer had always wanted to join the Royal Marines just like his father and wasn't willing to give up that dream. Looking back on it, he realised that that was the point when he showed he wasn't committed to the marriage.

After his basic training, the cracks were already showing, and he did nothing to prevent their relationship from falling apart. The time he spent on foreign tours, many he had volunteered for, didn't help. After eight years, he and Debbie split up and the inevitable, acrimonious divorce soon followed.

Debbie got re-married, a little over two years later, to a man Palmer knew, an ex-marine he had served with. There had always been rumours of an affair between Debbie and Connor

Harris. Their marriage, in Palmer's mind, just confirmed it. Although they served together, Palmer never thought of Harris as a friend, there was always something about him that Palmer didn't like, something he didn't trust. Now, he knew why that was.

Palmer often wondered if things would have been different if he had committed more to his relationship with Debbie, but they wanted different things from life. Ultimately, the marriage broke down because Debbie was unhappy. If Palmer hadn't joined the Marines, it would have broken down because he was unhappy. They should never have got married in the first place. His son, Nathan, was an innocent who got caught in the middle.

When Nathan spotted Palmer, he stood up, a broad smile across his face. 'Dad, I knew you'd make it.'

Palmer gave his son a hug. 'I can't stay too long, Nathan. I'm sure you and your friends would have a better time without your parents hanging around.'

Nathan was genuinely disappointed, but he was old enough to understand the acrimony between his parents. 'You can at least buy me a pint for my birthday.'

Palmer gripped Nathan's shoulder. 'Order whatever you want, son, I'm paying.'

The two of them walked up to the bar and ordered their drinks. While they waited, Palmer took an envelope out of his pocket and handed it to Nathan. 'Happy Birthday, Nathan. That's some cash to add to your university fund.'

Nathan took the envelope. 'Thanks, Dad, but I'm not sure I'm going to go to uni now.' He glanced over to where his mother and stepfather were sitting.

It was only when Nathan turned his head that Palmer noticed

the bruise on the side of the boy's face. 'What have you been up to?'

Nathan raised his hand to the bruise as if to hide it. 'Oh, nothing.'

Palmer could tell there was something wrong, something that Nathan wanted to tell him but couldn't. 'What's wrong? Why wouldn't you go to uni? You were always excited just by the thought of it.'

Nathan shuffled the envelope around in his hands. 'Well, things change. Mum needed money and I had it, so...?'

'Your mum needed money? You mean that arsehole's gambling debts got out of hand. Did he do that to your face?' Palmer pointed across the room at Nathan's stepfather.

Palmer's raised voice caused a hush to settle across the function room. Harris stood up and took a step towards the bar, but Debbie grabbed his arm and held him back. 'Don't, Connor.'

If Harris had stepped back and Palmer had walked away, that would have been the end of it, but that was never going to happen.

Palmer took two steps towards Harris; his fists were clenched. 'Sit down, dickhead, before I put you down.'

There was a pause and a moment of silence as everyone watched Harris, then it was as if someone had fired a starting pistol. Harris rushed at Palmer, arms outstretched, but Palmer was too fast for him. He drove Harris headfirst into the door of the gents. When Harris staggered backwards, Palmer grabbed his shirt and dragged him out through the fire escape.

The two men stumbled down the steps outside and into the car park, followed by Debbie and Nathan. The rest of the party guests watched through the function room's windows as Harris and Palmer stood toe to toe in the rain and threw punches at each other. Harris was no pushover, but Palmer was bigger and stronger, and it wasn't long before he had the upper hand. A short jab to the rib cage followed by a crunching uppercut to the face put Harris on his knees, spitting blood and at least one tooth onto the tarmac.

Palmer grabbed him by the throat. 'How much is it this time you fuckin' waster?'

Harris knew he was beaten, and, underneath the bravado, he was a coward anyway. 'It isn't gambling this time, I swear.'

'Then what is it?'

'I took on a private security contract abroad. Things got messed up. They want their money back.'

'Where's the money they paid you?'

Harris wiped the blood away from his nose and mouth. 'I invested it.'

'Invested? Blew it on a fuckin' horse more like. How much do you owe?'

'They want a hundred grand, or they'll hurt Debbie and Nathan.'

Palmer threw another punch that tipped Harris over onto his back. 'Wanker!'

Debbie stepped in and threw herself across Harris. 'Leave him, Logan. This won't help anyone.'

'It'll make me feel a whole lot better. Why do you stay with him? He's a tosser.'

'At least he was there when I needed him.'

Nathan grabbed Palmer's arm and pulled him away. 'Please, Dad, just leave it.'

Palmer wiped a trickle of blood from his cheek and stared at Harris. 'This isn't over. If you ever touch Nathan again, I'll slit your throat and bury you in the fuckin' woods.' He turned and walked away.

Back inside, Palmer took Nathan to one side. 'I'm sorry about that, son. If he ever touches you again, you let me know and I'll sort him out, okay?

'It's okay, I'm eighteen now, I can take care of myself.'

Palmer lowered his voice. 'It sounds like he's mixed up with some dangerous people. I don't want you getting hurt because of that.'

'I'll be fine, Dad. Look, when school breaks up for Christmas, I'll come and stay with you. How would that be?'

Palmer put his hand on Nathan's shoulder. 'I'd like that, Son. I'm going to leave now; I think I've caused enough trouble. You enjoy the rest of your party and I'll speak to you soon.'

Nathan gave Palmer a hug. 'Love you, Dad.'

'I love you too, Son.' Palmer left the function room and went back into the main bar.

The manager of the pub handed Palmer a towel. 'You okay?'

'Yeah. I'm sorry about that. I'll be on my way.'

'It's okay, Logan. Stay and have a drink. That guy was being a dick to my staff anyway.' He poured a fresh beer and placed it on the bar.

'Thanks, mate.' Logan looked across the room and noticed Riley sitting in a corner cubicle nursing a glass of fizzy water. He walked over and put his glass down. 'Mind if I join you?'

Riley gestured towards the seat opposite hers. 'Please, I could do with some company.'

Palmer sat down then leaned forwards, his voice low. 'Can I talk to you, about our discussion earlier? The work you have?'

Riley was surprised that Palmer had had a change of heart so quickly. She checked for anyone within hearing distance. 'I

40

don't think this is the place for that right now. I think it would be better if we talked about it tomorrow.'

'Okay, I'm cool with that.' He pointed at her fizzy water. 'Do you want a real drink to go with that?'

This was one of those times that Lancaster had warned her about, when Riley had to make the right decision. A time when she should turn down a drink and stick to water. But now that she had Palmer on side, she didn't want to lose him again. She could have one drink, one wouldn't hurt. 'I'll have a glass of red wine please.'

'No problem.'

Outside in the car park, Harris had only just managed to drag himself to his feet. Debbie supported him as they made their way back to their car. They decided that it would be best for everyone if they just went home. Besides, although he didn't admit it, Harris didn't want to risk running into Palmer again.

Debbie opened the car door and helped Harris into the passenger seat. She climbed behind the wheel, turned on the engine, and pulled away from the pub.

At the same time, another car's lights came on. The two occupants of the other car had watched events unfolding with interest. They had followed Harris to the Coach and Horses under orders from their boss. 'Protecting our investment,' was how he put it. They had seen Palmer and Riley arrive and the fight in the rain. They had watched Palmer go back inside and Harris limp away. 'Tell me if anything interesting happens,' the boss had said. Well, this slotted into the interesting category.

The driver turned to the passenger. 'We need to know who

that big guy is. He took out Harris quite easily, we need to know if he is going to be a problem that we need to deal with or someone we can use.'

The passenger took out a pen and wrote down the registration number of Riley's car. 'I'll get our guy on it. He can trace the car.'

Chapter 7

Riley's eyes flickered open as daylight broke through the curtains and crawled across her face. The sudden bright light made her squint as she waited for her eyes to adjust. Her head throbbed, her mouth was dry, and she had no memory of what had happened. She had done it again, the one thing she said she wouldn't. It was supposed to be one drink to put Palmer at ease, but, for her, even one drink was too many. It inevitably led to a second and a third, the result was the same every time.

She lifted her head from the pillow and propped herself up on her elbows, there was no sign of Palmer. Thank God she hadn't woken up next to him, that would have been a nightmare that didn't bear thinking about. She swung her legs over the edge of the bed and stood up. Her head spun, her legs wobbled, and she sat down again. 'Come on, Anna, for fuck's sake.'

The sudden, loud knock made her jump. The last thing she wanted to do was speak to anyone, all she wanted to do was curl into a ball and wallow in self-pity. A second, longer knock echoed around the room. Riley struggled back to her feet and, holding on to the furniture, made her way across the room like a toddler learning to walk. She paused at the bathroom door and threw a towel around herself then peered through the peep hole in the door.

Palmer's distorted face greeted her from the other side, he was smiling. Shit, why would he smile like that? She closed her eyes and searched her memory, but her mind had already erased the events of the previous night. She swallowed hard and opened the door.

'Good morning, Anna. How are you feeling this morning?'

Riley put her hand up to her mouth and ran for the bathroom, vomiting loudly.

Palmer stepped into the room and closed the door. 'I brought you some breakfast. Don't suppose you'll be wanting it now.'

After a few minutes, Riley came back into the room drying her hands on a towel. Her face the colour of parchment. 'God, I feel rough.'

'I thought these might come in handy.' Palmer was sitting next to the table under the rooms only window. He had placed two large plastic bottles, one of water, one of orange juice, on the table next to a pack of paracetamol. 'There's a coffee there too if you can stomach it.'

'Strong and Black?'

'Of course.'

'Thanks.' Riley took a long drink of water then grabbed her overnight bag and went into the bathroom.

When Riley re-appeared, she looked a little better than she had when Palmer arrived. She wore faded jeans and a grey t-shirt, her hair washed and tied up into a ponytail, but her skin was still pale and her eyes bloodshot. She walked over to the table and sat opposite Palmer. 'Sorry about that. I feel a bit better now.'

A mischievous grin spread across Palmer's face. 'You were the life and soul of the party last night.'

'I'm sorry, I must have been really tired, and I hadn't eaten properly and...'

Palmer could see she was struggling. He knew what she would be feeling. The shame and paranoia that came with an alcohol induced blackout was bad enough without someone winding you up about it. 'Don't worry, Anna, you don't need to apologise or explain anything to me.'

Riley took two of the paracetamol out of the blister pack and washed them down with a large swig of orange juice. 'I can't believe it happened. I promised I wouldn't.'

'Sometimes it takes a hold and there's nothing you can do to stop it. All you can do is take one day at a time.'

'Look, my memory is a little blurred. What happened? I mean...did anything...'

Palmer interrupted her. 'It's okay, nothing bad happened. We both had a couple of drinks and a chat then you ordered a bottle of wine and drank the whole thing. That, plus the vodkas you necked, obviously had an effect.'

Riley put her hand up to her head. The tablets were kicking in, but she still felt like there was a very loud party going on behind her eyes. She took another long drink of water. 'How did I get back here?' A sharp intake of breath filled her lungs. 'How did I get undressed?'

'I just brought you back here and made sure you were okay. You don't need to worry, I slept in the car.'

Riley let out a nervous laugh. 'Well at least I've got some reputation left.'

Palmer smiled and slid the lukewarm cup of coffee across the table. 'Oh, I don't know about that.'

Chapter 8

Once Riley was feeling up to it, Palmer drove them back to his cottage and they now sat at the kitchen table with another cup of coffee. Riley took two more paracetamol. 'I almost feel human again.'

'You look much better. At least you've stopped throwing up.'

'Yeah, I shouldn't mix wine and vodka. You'd think I'd know that by now.'

'Funnily enough, you said that last night.'

Riley shook her head. 'Really? Why don't I ever learn? I'm never drinking again.'

'Look, Anna, now that I know, I'll never put you in that position again. If you feel like you're going to fall off the wagon, give me a call.'

Riley smiled. She genuinely appreciated the offer. 'Thanks. So, what did you want to talk to me about before I slipped into a drunken coma?'

Palmer leaned forwards. 'Tell me more about this job.'

'Are you sure? You didn't seem too interested yesterday.'

'Things have changed since then. The people Harris owes money to don't look like they're willing to back off. I don't give a shit about him, but now they've threatened Nathan.'

'I could have a word, see if some police protection could be arranged.'

Palmer shook his head. 'The Police can't be everywhere and there's no proof that any law has been broken. I need a lot of money quickly and I don't see anyone else offering it.'

'Are you sure? This could be dangerous. We've already lost other operatives trying to track the warhead down. You could easily be killed.'

'This kind of work always comes with a risk. All that matters to me is that Nathan is safe. If that involves me putting myself in harm's way, so be it. Besides, aren't you supposed to be talking me into this?'

Riley knew she wasn't cut out for this type of work. She told Lancaster that from the start. She realised that this was the business they had both decided to be in, but she still wasn't happy about it. 'I've never been the one responsible for putting someone at risk. I don't want to get you killed.'

'You won't, I can look after myself. I know the risks and I'm willing to take them. If anything happens to me, it'll be because of something I've done, not you.'

'Okay, let's get this over with.' Riley opened Lancaster's cardboard folder and spread out the contents. 'I'm more used to doing this on a laptop or a big screen, but we don't want any digital footprints. This folder needs to be destroyed once you've read it.'

'Feels a bit like a cliché from an old Cold War movie. You really think it's likely that things could leak out?'

Riley nodded. 'Greenline have some big government contracts, and some powerful backers, even in our own security services. You can never be too careful.'

Palmer took a sip of his coffee. 'The guy that started

Greenline off was a Colonel in the US Marines, Gabriel Wallace. He was a shrewd businessman too and, unlike many of the mercenary outfits that sprung up back then, he had principles. He wasn't in it just to get rich, he wanted to do things right. Unfortunately, he died of a massive heart attack and his son, Kane, took over. Kane Wallace...' Palmer drummed his fingers. 'Now there's an example of an unprincipled shit.'

'Nothing like his dad then?'

Palmer paused. 'Don't get me wrong, he was a good soldier, but was only in it for the money. He didn't care who got hurt along the way. All the decent guys, most of the lads I started out with, could sense he was trouble and started to walk away. By the time I gave it up and retired, I was the only original one of us left in the team.'

'What happened to the others?'

There was a long silence as Palmer remembered his old comrades, his brothers in arms. 'Some of them are still kicking around, although I don't see them very often. I know that two died doing close protection work in South Africa, Jerry runs diving holidays from an island in Indonesia, and one is in prison.'

'Really? What did he do?'

Palmer grinned. 'What didn't he do? He was always a bit of a rogue. I believe he was caught trying to smuggle a ton of marijuana into the country in the lining of a caravan.'

'Sounds like you miss them.'

'Yeah, they were a good bunch, and we had some great times together, but time moves on. Maybe I'll see them again someday. Who knows? Jerry is the one I really miss. We joined up together, he's my best mate.'

'When was the last time you saw him.'

Palmer puffed out his cheeks. 'It's a couple of years at least. I was supposed to go to his wedding when I retired, but things didn't work out. I wasn't good company to be with back then.'

'I've read the report. The one about what happened in Geneva, about the death of Yvette Duval.'

Palmer's expression changed as one of his demons resurfaced. 'Geneva was a fuck up. I had buildings sealed off and people on every rooftop that overlooked the conference centre's entrance. How the fuck did a sniper get a shot off and then vanish. It doesn't make any sense. The old team wouldn't have allowed that to happen, that's for sure. I was there to protect Yvette, and I failed her.'

Riley could see that the memories were hurting Palmer. She made a mental note not to bring it up again. 'Look, Logan, I don't like pushing this, but there's a clock ticking on this job, and it needs to be done as soon as possible. When can you start?'

Palmer stood up and carried their empty coffee mugs over to the sink. He dug a notebook out of his coat, tore out a page, and handed it to Riley. 'The first set of numbers is Nathan's bank account details. I want one hundred thousand pounds paid directly to him. That should get those thugs off his back. I don't want Harris pissing it up the wall or blowing it on some three-legged nag. The other numbers are an old account I have in Switzerland. I want another one hundred and fifty thousand paid into that account to fund the operation. I'll let you know if I need more.'

'What about you, how much do you want?'

'I don't need loads of money, I'm happy as I am. This is all about Nathan. If something goes wrong, if I don't make it back for some reason, you pay him enough to fund his university.

That's what I want, okay?'

Riley folded the note and placed it in her mobile phone case. 'I promise it'll be done. I'll look after it personally. You have my word.'

'Thank you. Hopefully, next time I see you, this will all be over.'

Riley passed a notebook across to Palmer. 'I'll need some contact details, some way I can get hold of you.'

Palmer shook his head. 'Too risky. I'll get in touch with you when I sort something out. I'll get a phone that isn't registered to me and let you know the number. I'll contact you when I find something. You don't need to know the details and I'm sure you can track me anyway, if you're as good with your laptop as people say you are.'

'You've been checking me out.'

Palmer passed the notebook back to Riley. 'I still have some friends in the right places. It just took a quick phone call.'

Riley felt a little uncomfortable that Palmer had found it so easy to dig up information about her. She wondered what else his contact had told him. 'I hope they only told you the good bits about me.'

'Don't worry, Anna, I'm not going to judge you. We all have bad times in our lives. Sometimes we just need a little help to get through them.'

Riley was relieved. She didn't know why, but she cared what Palmer thought of her. Now she felt even worse that she was about to put him in harm's way. 'What will you do first?'

'I'll go and see Nathan, let him know I won't be around for a little while, I'll tell him the money's coming.'

'And the job?'

Palmer pulled the CCTV image out of the folder. 'I'll start

with the hotel in Kuala Lumpur. They must have teams in the area, probably on anti-piracy duties. I can pass it off as a holiday and, if I get caught sniffing around, like you said, I'm just coming out of retirement. Looking around for work.'

Chapter 9

Palmer's taxi pulled up and he handed the driver a twenty-pound note. 'That's so you know I'm not doing a runner. I'll be going to the airport once I've finished here.'

Debbie's house was twenty yards back the way they had come. Palmer had got the taxi driver to go past the house so that he could check that Debbie and Harris weren't out front before he got out of the car. With the coast clear, he walked back along the pavement towards the house but stopped short and stood at the end of the driveway. He didn't want to go inside. It would just cause trouble again. Harris had a knack of winding him up. Palmer was aware that Harris was watching him from the upstairs window but made no attempt to look or acknowledge him. He hated the prick and would have preferred it if he had dropped dead in the car park the other night.

Nathan opened the front door and walked down the drive. 'Hi, Dad. I didn't think I'd be seeing you so soon. It's only a couple of days since my birthday.'

Palmer held his arms out wide. 'Aren't you happy to see your old man?'

Nathan glanced back at the house. 'It's not that, it's just

with... well, what happened. I thought...'

'It's okay, Son, I'm pulling your leg, and if numb nuts doesn't like it, that's his problem.'

Nathan smiled. 'So, what are you doing here? Has something happened?'

'Nothing serious, son. I'm off on my holidays, that's all. Thought I'd take a break, a little R 'n' R. I'm on my way to the airport now.

'Anywhere nice?'

Palmer didn't want Nathan to have any information that might get him into trouble later. 'Oh, here and there, I'll tell you all about it when I get back, maybe send you a postcard. I just wanted you to know that I've arranged for some money to be paid into your bank account. Enough to pay off Dickhead's gambling debts. I want you to make sure that that's what it gets used for.'

Nathan made sure no one could hear him. 'Where did you pull together that kind of money so quickly?'

'Don't worry, your old dad can still earn a buck or two. I didn't steal it or anything, it's all legit.'

'That's not what I meant, Dad. You shouldn't have to lose all your money because of him.' Nathan pointed back at the house.

'Don't worry about it, I've got work lined up that'll more than cover it. I'll call you when I get back, you can come and stay with me, like we said.'

Nathan stepped forwards and hugged Palmer. 'I love you, Dad. Enjoy your holiday.'

'I love you too, Son. Look after yourself. I'll see you soon.'

Palmer got back in the taxi and watched through the back window as it drove away. He had to convince his son to go to university. It was the only way he would get away from Harris and make a decent life for himself. Palmer was going to do everything it took to make sure that happened. He gave Nathan a final wave, watching him until the taxi was around the corner, then he turned to the driver. 'Airport please, mate. Quick as you can.'

Chapter 10

Palmer sat in the bar on the top floor of Traders Hotel and looked out over the Kuala Lumpur City Centre Park to the Petronas Towers. The view was stunning, he could see the attraction of staying there. This was the same hotel that Chernov and his guards had been photographed in. It was a popular, high profile hotel and not somewhere to hide out. Under normal circumstances, Palmer wouldn't have stayed here, but he wanted to be noticed. Maybe the bodyguards had chosen to stay here to meet a contact, perhaps that contact was still here. If Palmer made enough noise, maybe someone would come and check him out.

He had arrived in Malaysia the previous morning and hadn't acclimatised yet. He was wide awake in the early hours of the morning and, whenever he stepped out of the air-conditioned surroundings of the hotel, he sweated like a man in a panda costume doing a spin class. The journey from the airport had been air conditioned all the way. From the arrivals hall to KL Central by train then onward to the station that sat under the KLCC. Up through the shopping centre then air-conditioned walkway right into the hotel. When he stepped outside, he wasn't ready to be plunged into the heat and humidity of Kuala Lumpur.

If he were here on holiday, he would have spent the weekend sorting out his sleep patterns and trying to get used to the humidity, but he didn't have time for that. He needed to get on with it. It was time to do a little digging in the local bars. If any of Greenline's men were here, that's where they would be, blowing their wages before heading back to their day jobs. Maybe Palmer would get lucky and bump into the two idiots who were supposed to be guarding Chernov. He drained his beer, picked up his phone, and headed for the lift.

He was drenched in sweat within a few minutes of leaving the hotel. He now understood why the locals walked more slowly than he was used to. He had bought a few thin, loose fitting, cotton shirts before he left home, but they didn't seem to be making any difference. He might as well have been wearing an Aran sweater.

Palmer stood at the side of the road and checked the map on his phone to get the layout of the city. Unlike the park at the centre of the KLCC, the roads outside were noisy. Dozens of scooters and motorbikes zig zagged in and out of the traffic. The riders, wearing their jackets back to front to shield them from pollution, lined up at red lights like they were on the starting grid of a grand prix. The green light released them, triggering a loud whine from the two-stroke engines as they accelerated and continued their zig zagging off into the distance.

Palmer hated cities. The crowds, the noise, the pollution. He couldn't wait to be away from it, but he had to give it a few days. It would be a lot easier if someone from Greenline recognised him and made contact. If they thought his coming back was their idea, it would look less suspicious.

Fortunately, there were lots of restaurants and bars within

easy reach of the hotel. None of the bars were aimed at locals and some were more up market than others. The bar that Palmer picked was well and truly at the seedier end of the market. It was the kind of place where men who fought for a living went to get drunk and get laid between ops.

Outside the bar, women in stiletto heels and short skirts tried to entice male tourists inside. Palmer wasn't sure that all these women were just being friendly. He suspected that any worse for wear businessmen who fell into the grip of these women would wake up with a considerably lighter wallet than they had started out with. He crossed the road, managed to sidestep the most eager greeters, and walked into the bar.

The inside of the building wasn't as crowded as he was expecting. The décor was more beach front hut than cocktail lounge and the only attempt at air conditioning was several three bladed fans hung from the walls. All the fans really did was move the warm air around and Palmer could still feel the beads of sweat running down his back. He ordered two beers and drank the first without stopping for breath.

The bartender handed him a paper napkin and pointed at his forehead.

'Thanks.' Palmer wiped the sweat from his face and neck. It felt a little better. How the hell did people live in this?

He picked up his second bottle and moved over to a bar stool that was in front of one of the fans. With his back to the wall and a clear line of sight to the entrance, he was in the perfect position to monitor everything that was going on.

After two hours, Palmer had stopped sweating, mostly. He wasn't sure if it was because he was sitting in front of the fan or, somehow, he had run out of sweat. In the time he had been there, nothing out of the ordinary had happened. Nothing to interest him anyway. The bar seemed to be frequented by a mixture of backpackers and businessmen. The younger ones there because it was cheap and the older ones because of the women. He was about to give up and move on somewhere else when something caught his eye.

Two men, a little worse for drink, walked through the door and up to the bar. They were obviously fit, but not overly muscular. Their haircuts and demeanour flagged them as military. US military by the sound of it. The US embassy wasn't far away, and it wouldn't be unusual for off duty marines to be out on the town. Of course, they could just be on holiday, but there was something else that Palmer had noticed. One of them was wearing a polo shirt with the Greenline Solutions logo on it.

Palmer waited for the men to get their beers and pick a seat, then nodded to one of the women hovering around the door. The woman smiled and flicked her hair over her shoulder. She adjusted her dress, what there was of it, and tottered over to where Palmer was sitting.

Palmer pulled out a wad of money and peeled off two notes. 'What's your name?'

'Kim, but you call me what you want.' She ran her hand across Palmer's chest.

Palmer held up the money. 'Kim, I want you to go over to those two Americans and start an argument.'

The young Malay woman was unsure, she didn't want to get into trouble, but this guy was offering her more money than she usually earned in a week. She pointed across the bar to where the two men's raucous laughter seemed to be getting louder. 'But they'll get angry.'

'It's okay. I'll step in before anything happens, I promise.'

Kim paused, this much money could get her off the street for a week. She could spend time with her family. She had been asked to do stranger things. What harm could it do? 'Okay.' She took the two notes and tucked them into a small leather bag that hung from her shoulder, turned, and set off across the bar.

Palmer waited until Kim was almost next to the two Americans, then followed her. The bar was getting more crowded, and the noise level meant that he couldn't hear the conversation, but whatever Kim was saying was having the desired effect. The biggest of the two men stood up and grabbed Kim's wrist. She responded by pulling away and then slapping him. She had a great right hook, and the American took a step back holding his face.

The look that flashed across the big man's face gave away his intent, he meant to do Kim real harm. As he walked forwards, his fists clenched, Palmer stepped in.

The American was at least a head taller than his friend, but Palmer matched him for height and bulk. It was enough to make the man hesitate as he realised that taking on Palmer wouldn't be anywhere as easy as what he had in mind for Kim. The man was a classic bully.

Palmer pulled Kim around behind him and held his hand up in front. 'Whoa, slow down there, mate, no need for anyone to get physical here.'

The man pointed aggressively at Kim. 'She says I owe her money. I've never seen her before.'

'It's okay, I'll take care of it. Obviously, a misunderstanding. We all look the same.' He waved towards the bartender, held up two fingers then pointed at the table. 'Have a seat and a beer, guys. Relax.'

Palmer backed away from the two men, keeping Kim behind him. Once they reached the door, he turned around to check on her. 'You okay?'

Kim nodded. 'I think I hurt my hand.'

Palmer laughed and rubbed the side of his face. 'I'm glad it wasn't me.' He pulled another two notes out of his pocket and handed them to her. 'Here, you've earned it. I'd go home for the night if I were you, just in case.'

Kim took the money and smiled. 'Thank you.' She put the notes into her bag and flagged down a taxi.

Palmer went back into the bar. The two Americans were finishing the beer that he had ordered so he bought three more and took them over. 'Here you go, guys.' He held out his hand. 'My name's Logan, Logan Palmer.'

The big guy introduced himself as Quinn, his smaller friend was Brad. They shook hands and Palmer sat down opposite them.

Quinn held up his bottle. 'Thanks, Logan.' He took a drink and put the bottle back on the table, tracing a line in the condensation that ran down the glass.

Brad eyed Palmer suspiciously. 'What is it you want, buddy?'

'Want?'

'Yeah. Why'd you come over to help two complete strangers being scammed by a hooker?'

Palmer pointed at Quinn's shirt. 'I used to be in the same business as you guys. I used to work for Greenline too.'

Brad nodded. 'Yeah, I know who you are, almost didn't recognise you at first. You didn't have a beard before.'

Palmer nodded. 'That's right. Do I know you?'

Brad took a drink. 'I joined the team around the same time

that you left. I think our paths may have crossed. You were the lead in Delta Team.'

'I was. Delta was a great team. There were some good guys in the company back then.'

Brad looked at Quinn and they bumped fists. 'There still are.' They clinked their bottle necks together and toasted each other. 'The best.'

Palmer pretended to toast them. These two were full of it, but he had to stay on their good side, for now. 'So, what are you doing here?'

Quinn took over as spokesman. 'We're doing some anti-piracy operations in the Strait of Malacca. What about you, man? I heard you were good. Where'd you go?'

'I took a little time off, which turned into a long time off. Just doing some travelling now. A little bored of it if I'm truthful.'

'You should come back to work, man. The anti-piracy stuff is money for old rope, and there's some extra work that pays real money.'

Brad kicked Quinn's foot. 'Which we don't talk about. Right, Quinn? We respect our client's privacy.'

Quinn looked like a scolded schoolchild. 'Yeah, that's right, forget I said anything.'

Palmer waved over to the bartender and ordered more beers. 'I've thought about getting back in, I could do with the money. This travelling lark isn't cheap...' He leaned forwards. 'Especially when I have to pay off hookers.'

The two Americans laughed and grinned.

The three of them talked and drank into the early hours of the morning. With some sleight of hand, Palmer made sure that, although he looked like he was matching them beer for beer, he had only drunk four bottles. He tried to pump the two men for information as they got more drunk. Quinn would let the odd snippet sneak out, but Brad always jumped in to stop him. It was obvious that, in this outfit, Quinn was the muscle and Brad was the brains.

At 2 am, Palmer decided that he had achieved what he had set out to do. He had planted the idea that he might be coming out of retirement and wasn't against earning a little extra money on the side. He said goodbye to Brad and Quinn and walked back to his hotel.

Back in his room, he used his phone and an anonymous email account to send a coded message to Riley. It was her idea to use this as one of their communication channels. She wasn't happy being unable to contact him in any way. He understood her misgivings and agreed to the emails. It wasn't completely secure, if someone really dug into the messages, they might put two and two together but, if he made the messages sound innocent, it was secure enough.

The message he sent simply said, 'Holiday going well. Bumped into some old friends. Hopefully see them again soon.'

He put his phone on charge, took a quick shower, then tried to get some sleep.

Chapter 11

For three days Palmer acted like the tourist he was supposed to be. He spent his days visiting the sights and tourist spots of Kuala Lumpur. He had been up the Petronas Towers to admire the view, visited a Buddhist temple, and climbed the steps at the Batu Caves. He hadn't climbed that many steps in his life, and he was sure one of the monkeys was following him. Although he did like the way the steps were numbered so that, if you had a heart attack on the way up, at least you would know which one had finished you off.

He spent his nights frequenting the bars, looking for anyone else he could interact with to make him more visible, but he didn't come across anyone. It was beginning to look like his plan wasn't working. Maybe Brad and Quinn had drunk themselves into a stupor and forgotten all about him. He needed to pick a different course. It was almost a week since he had left the UK, and time was running out.

It was the fourth evening when a handwritten note on the back of a Greenline business card was slid under his hotel room door. The note said, 'If you're Interested 10 am'. He turned the card over. The name on the front was Travis Vaughn, Operations Manager, South East Asia. It was a name Palmer knew. He and Vaughn had been on more than a few operations together.

Vaughn was once a captain in the British Army. His family background dictated his route through life. Eton, Oxford, and The Guards leading to an honourable discharge and a lucrative position in the city or maybe even parliament. But Vaughn wasn't an honourable man. His conduct was always in question but, with contacts like his, problems were hushed up and his punishments minor. Until the suicide.

After several incidents, Vaughn was put in command of recruits fresh out of basic training. It was a non-combat role where, it was thought, he could do less damage. The assumption couldn't have been more wrong. It was when the accusations of bullying surfaced, and the investigation into the deaths of two young soldiers began, that the years of tolerating him came to an end.

His high-ranking contacts were unwilling to cover up his incompetence anymore. Even his family remained silent, they had their reputation to uphold. When the investigation found Vaughn culpable, he was given a simple choice; resign his commission and leave the army or face a dishonourable discharge. The families of the dead recruits weren't so lucky. They had been given the life sentence that comes with the untimely death of a loved one. Vaughn didn't care. He saw himself as the victim of a witch hunt and threatened to drag his contacts down with him. When the effect on his ability to ever work again was explained to him, he did the only thing he could. He packed up and walked away.

As always with people like Vaughn, he landed on his feet. The office that Palmer now stood in front of was a thirty-story glass palace that sparkled in the afternoon sun. High above the pavement, a window cleaning cradle crept along the front of the building while the occupants washed and polished the mirrored glass and chrome exterior. Palmer imagined that keeping this block clean was one of those jobs that seemed never ending, like painting the Forth Rail Bridge, or trying to keep his ex-wife in shoes. Palmer put the business card back into his wallet and climbed the stone steps that led to the front of the building. As he approached, the automatic revolving door kicked into life, and he walked through into the vast, air-conditioned entrance hall.

Greenline Solutions didn't own the building or even fill it. This was one of the many office blocks in the city that provided fully serviced, rented space for various companies, Greenline only occupied one floor. Palmer stepped into the lift and pressed the button for ten.

When Palmer walked out of the lift he was hit by the fresh wood and new carpet smell that showed that this office had only recently been set up. In front of him was a reception desk where two women tapped at keyboards and answered the phone. On his left was a glass wall with a door leading to a large open plan space that was mainly empty. No more than twenty desks had been installed with workstations and headsets. To the right were, what appeared to be, meeting rooms and offices.

One of the women at reception smiled at him. 'Can I help you, sir?'

Palmer returned the smile. 'Good morning, my name's Logan Palmer, I'm here to see Travis Vaughn.'

'Please have a seat, I'll let him know you're here.'

'Thank You.' Palmer walked over to a group of soft chairs that were arranged in an L shape opposite reception. He picked the chair closest to the lift and sat down.

After a few minutes, Palmer noticed that someone was watching him through the blinds of one of the rooms to his right. He didn't acknowledge it and wasn't worried by it, but it was obvious that someone was interested enough to check him out.

At that moment, Vaughn appeared from one of the other rooms. 'Logan, it's good to see you again.'

Palmer stood up. 'Hello, Travis, how've you been?'

They shook hands but there was no real warmth in it, at least on Palmer's part. Palmer was well aware of Vaughn's past and didn't like him, but he had to hide those feelings. For now, he had to act like they were old buddies getting back together at a regimental reunion.

Vaughn showed Palmer through to his office and closed the door. 'Have a seat, mate.' He opened the door of a small fridge, pulled out two bottles of water, and handed one to Palmer. 'Here you go, got to keep hydrated here, the humidity is crippling.'

'Thanks.' Palmer took the bottle and twisted off the top, taking a long drink.

Vaughn sat at his desk and leaned back in his chair. 'So, I've heard a rumour that you might be thinking of coming out of retirement.'

'Wow, word spreads fast around here. I take it you've spoken to the two guys I bumped into the other night. What were their names again?'

'Brad and Quinn. We always advise our people to report anything unusual, anything that might present us with a business opportunity. Quinn thought bumping into you was unusual enough to mention. To be honest, I'm glad he did.'

'And why would that be, Travis?'

Vaughn sat up and pulled his chair forward, leaning both elbows on the desk. 'I'm sure you've noticed that this is a brand-new office. We've never really covered this part of the world before, but, for some reason, the boss has got a real hardon for the place.'

Palmer finished his bottle of water and replaced the lid. 'It would explain your meteoric rise up the ranks.'

Vaughn laughed. 'If someone wants to pay me an obscene amount of money to sit behind this desk, I'm not going to point out that I might not be the best man for the job.'

Palmer nodded. 'The old boys' network is alive and well. So, what is it you want from me?'

'This whole operation was set up quickly, we didn't have the right resources in place.' Vaughn struggled for the right words. 'Don't get me wrong, the people I have are all good men and women. They're well trained and they follow orders, but they have no real experience in maritime ops.' He pointed at Palmer. 'You, Logan are a natural leader, people follow you. I need you to come out of retirement and work for me.'

Palmer didn't respond. He had hoped that his actions in the bar would pique some interest, but Vaughn was begging him to come back. He had to play it cool, he didn't want to jump in and appear too keen.

Vaughn broke the silence. 'I can pay you a lot more than you were on before. Come on, Logan. I'm a man down and you don't need training up. Just a short contract to begin with. Help me out here.'

Palmer steepled his fingers. 'I'm not interested in leading anyone. I'm only looking at a short contract to see how I feel, top up my pension a bit.'

'Okay, okay, whatever you want. Are you in?'

Palmer paused. 'What about the rest of the team? What will they think of an outsider being dropped in amongst them?'

'It'll be a surprise, but they'll be okay, they're professionals. The team lead is Brad, the guy you met in the bar the other night. Come on, when can you start?'

Palmer shrugged. 'When do you want me?'

Vaughn stood and pushed his chair back. 'Excellent. I'll get the paperwork done, you do the tourist bit for a few more days.' He held his hand out. 'Welcome back.'

Chapter 12

Anna Riley stepped off the third bus she had taken from her flat. Doubling back twice and taking a diverse route to the meeting, she was certain she wasn't being followed. She knew it was important to maintain secrecy, but who would be interested in her? No one knew about Palmer, and she was still on sick leave after her breakdown. A breakdown that most of her co-workers didn't know the reason for.

When her older sister succumbed to breast cancer six months ago, Riley lost the only blood relative she had left. Their parents were killed in a car crash when the two sisters were still at primary school. Their Grandmother did all she could to bring them up on her own, but she was already in ill health and died before Anna left school. After that, it was just her and her sister.

Riley was hit hard by her sister's death. She followed the usual cliché, her life spiralled downwards into drink and drug abuse as she searched for something to dull the pain. She didn't think she was an alcoholic, but that was a warning sign too. Alcoholics never think they have a problem, they could stop any time, but Riley couldn't stop. She couldn't control her addiction any more than a dog could control its urge to lick its balls.

The final straw came the day she turned up for work still drunk from the night before. Up to that point, she had managed to avoid the random drink and drug tests. The tests always tended to be done on the same day of the week and she had managed to cut down her drink or steer clear of the office on those days. On this day, there was no need for a test. She was unsteady on her feet, her eyes were bloodshot and dilated, and she smelled like she had slept on the floor of the pub. That was day one of her suspension.

Her boss had done what he could for her. He let her go on long-term sick leave rather than sacking her. Riley knew that couldn't last. If she didn't sort her life out, the suspension would become permanent. This job was her only chance to stop it. If she stayed sober, if she avoided messing things up, then maybe they would let her back in.

Riley checked the time; she was five minutes early. She walked through the entrance to the park and made her way to an isolated bench on the far side. The bench wasn't overlooked by any property and couldn't be approached from any direction without the person being seen. It was the perfect place for a clandestine meeting, like an old Cold War movie. Riley sat on the bench and waited.

Riley checked her watch again, the time for the meeting had passed and there was still no sign of Vicky Thomson. Riley hadn't taken her eyes off the stone gateposts and rusting iron gates at the entrance, and no one had come through. She checked the path in both directions but couldn't see anyone. The park looked empty.

'Morning, Anna.'

The voice came from behind and made Riley jump. Thomson

70

had been there all along and Riley hadn't even noticed, she wasn't good at this spy stuff. 'Shit. How long have you been here?'

Thomson stepped onto the path and sat down on the bench. 'I got here about thirty minutes before you. I saw you arrive and made sure you weren't followed.' She gestured over her shoulder. 'I've been standing behind that tree. You need to check behind you occasionally, Anna.'

Riley nodded. 'I will. I'm... I'm really not used to being in the field, I didn't even hear you walking up behind me.'

'It takes time. You'll learn more the longer you do it. So, how are things going?'

Riley wasn't sure she liked the sound of learning more field craft. She preferred to sit in an office. 'He's in. He contacted someone he's worked with in the past and they've recruited him. Once he beds in, he'll start sniffing around.'

'That's quick work, Anna. We can't afford any wasted time on this one. We haven't had any specific threats yet, but there's still talk of a spectacular attack taking place over Christmas. The clock is ticking.'

'I'll make sure he keeps it up.'

Thomson smiled. 'That's good. Now, how are you?'

Riley wasn't expecting a personal question. She was expecting things to be quick, professional, secretive. 'I'm doing okay, thanks. I'm staying off the drink. I'm feeling much better. I can do this.' She felt guilty about the lie but telling Thomson that she had slipped off the wagon already wouldn't help anyone.

'That's good to hear. I think you have potential; Edward sees it too. It would be good if you could keep it up and come to work for us.' She stood up and checked around them. 'Stay

71

in touch, Anna, and If you need to talk, I'm here.'

'Thank you, Vicky.' Riley waited for Thomson to leave the park then walked to the main road and took three buses back to her flat.

Chapter 13

Sergei Chernov used a handkerchief to wipe the sweat from his face. The heat and humidity were stifling, it was a big change from home. He thought of leaving the lab, of going out and just relaxing in the fresh air and a breeze for a little while, but he couldn't afford to waste the time. Wallace never stopped checking up on him. The schedule he had been given was impossible. He had three weeks to complete work that should have taken two months. On top of that, he would normally have an assistant. All he had now was someone who kept his water supply topped up and brought him food. Someone with orders to kill him if he didn't complete his work.

Chernov hung the wet handkerchief on a makeshift washing line he had strung between two shelves and took a dry one. Things could have been worse. At least the lab he was working in was well equipped, although some windows would have been nice. There were a couple of fans that moved the air around but being able to open a window would have been heaven. He cleaned his glasses and put them back on.

The door burst open, and Kane Wallace walked into the lab. 'Sergei, how's my favourite communist?'

'I've told you before, I'm not a communist.'

'Okay, okay, keep your hair on. How's my project coming along then? I did tell you about our tight deadline, didn't I?'

Chernov took off his glasses and rubbed his eyes. 'Yes, Kane, you've explained the time I have left at great length, but there really is too little time to give you everything. Maybe if I had an assistant...'

'You are being paid twenty million dollars and a new identity for this. I think that is a reward that deserves a little effort. Don't you?'

'Of course, I'm grateful, but only three weeks.'

Wallace picked up a scalpel. 'This is a once in a lifetime opportunity, Sergei. If we miss the deadline then my client won't be happy, and we don't get paid. Not getting my money would make me angry.' He held up the scalpel. 'Do I need to remind you what happens when I get angry?'

The reason Chernov no longer had an assistant was his fault. A fire had broken out in the lab, caused by him, caused by exhaustion, he couldn't be sure. When Max, his assistant, tried to put it out his hands were severely burned, and he could no longer work. Wallace said he wasn't supporting someone who couldn't contribute to the project. Instead of treating the wounds, he took a scalpel and slit Max's throat.

Chernov was beginning to wish he'd never left Russia. He didn't have the most comfortable life but at least he wasn't in danger of being killed. Not then anyway. If he went back now it might be a different story. 'No, of course not. I'll get it finished on time.'

'That's what I like to hear, commitment to the cause, fantastic.' Wallace stuck the scalpel into the workbench. 'Stick with it, Sergei, keep me happy.' He smiled at Chernov then turned and left.

Chernov, once again, wiped the sweat from his face and put his glasses back on. The nuclear device in front of him still needed so much work before it was finished. Perhaps if he made it simpler, took some shortcuts, he might be in with a chance of meeting the deadline. Wallace wouldn't get everything he had asked for, but it might be enough to keep him mostly happy. Maybe that would be enough to save Chernov's life. He picked up a screwdriver and got back to work.

Chapter 14

P almer stood at the edge of the helicopter pad twenty floors above the GLS office. He watched the lights of Kuala Lumpur begin to turn on as dawn approached and the city came to life. Behind him, the helicopter pilot carried out final checks in preparation for their flight while Vaughn placed a call to the ship. This was the real beginning of the mission. From this point on, Palmer had to assume his undercover character and stay in it twenty-four hours a day. It was easy to let something slip. The only thing in his favour was that he was playing himself, only his reason for being there was a lie. That didn't make it any less dangerous. Palmer knew that if he were caught, they would kill him.

Vaughn finished his call and approached Palmer. 'Okay, Logan. I've arranged the RV with the ship and given the coordinates to the pilot. The rest of the team is already onboard, you'll report to Brad who'll sort you out and introduce you to the others.'

Palmer nodded. 'Right, thanks. Is there any extra work being done on these trips or is it just anti-piracy?''

'What makes you ask?'

Palmer didn't want to push it. 'Well, I don't want to get anyone into trouble here, but Quinn said there was a chance of earning some extra cash.'

Vaughn checked that the pilot was busy in the cockpit. 'Is that something that would interest you?'

'You know me, Travis, I'm always interested in some extra money. I don't mind breaking a law here and there, we're mercs not angels, right?'

Vaughn laughed. 'I'll speak to Brad. Let's see how this first trip goes and, if you still want the work, we can think about bringing you in.'

'Okay, I'm good with that.'

The pilot started the helicopter's engine and beckoned Palmer to climb onboard. Palmer picked up his bag and shook Vaughn's hand. 'See you soon.'

'Good to have you back, mate. Have a good trip.'

Palmer got into the back of the helicopter and strapped himself in. The pilot turned up the power and the rotor blades bit into the air, lifting them off the roof. Palmer gave a thumbs up to Vaughn as the chopper's nose dipped and they set off across the city.

The flight was uneventful, they were flying over the sea so there was nothing to look at. Palmer passed the time reading a book and watching the sun rise, as the pilot navigated towards the rendezvous. It always amazed Palmer that these pilots could find a small grey ship in the middle of these vast areas of water.

The pilot's voice crackled in Palmer's headset. 'There she is.'

Palmer looked out of the window at the front of the chopper. In the distance, sailing away from them, was their landing pad.

The GLS Capricorn was one of three ex-military vessels that

Greenline Solutions had bought to operate in South East Asia and Somalia. It had been stripped of its weapons systems but was still equipped with a flight deck and small hangar, for helicopter operations.

The pilot approached the Capricorn from the rear. Fortunately, the sea was calm, so they didn't have to deal with a ship that was rolling and pitching wildly. A member of the crew stood on the flight deck and gave hand signals to the pilot, telling him when the chopper was lined up and safe to land. Within a few minutes of spotting the ship, the pilot was touching the helicopter's wheels down on the flight deck.

Palmer breathed out. He always hated being in a dangerous situation that he couldn't control. Landing a helicopter on the flight deck of a ship was one of those situations. He would have been happier jumping out of the chopper and swimming to the ship. He patted the pilot on the shoulder, picked up his bag, and climbed out.

The pilot turned the power up and the helicopter rose into the air again. It made a ninety degree turn to the left and flew back out over the water. Palmer waved to the pilot as it went, happy to have his feet on something a little more solid.

Palmer quickly scanned the upper decks. There was nothing out of the ordinary. It looked just like all the other naval ships he had served on over the years. Along with the flight deck and hangar, the Capricorn was equipped with two davits to lower rigid inflatable boats into the sea. The inflatables were of a type used by naval boarding parties worldwide. They were fast, rugged, and could, if needed, be rigged with a belt-fed machine gun.

Various rules of international shipping meant that armed guards onboard cargo ships were frowned upon by many governments. Providing smaller, faster craft to cut off any pirate attack was the best way to provide security and, at the same time, not infringe on the cargo ship's right to innocent passage. The arming of guards onboard escort vessels was a grey area. Some coastal nations could see the Capricorn itself as a pirate ship, simply because it carried weapons. The legalities involved were a minefield and Palmer was happy he didn't have to sort it all out.

The number of attacks in this area had dropped in the last ten years, but the recent resurgence of pirate activity meant that this kind of work was becoming more lucrative, and people like Palmer more valuable. It was probably why Greenline had opened an office in the region.

Brad appeared out of a door in the side of the hangar and beckoned Palmer over. 'Through here, I'll show you where your cabin is, and you can drop your kit off. You've got one hour before the briefing.'

Chapter 15

Palmer leaned on the steel guard rail and looked down at the water as the Capricorn cut through the waves of the Malacca Straight. He turned his face into the sea breeze that blew across the deck as they picked up speed. He enjoyed the feeling of the saltwater spray that hit his face and dripped onto his t-shirt, leaving dark spots in the grey material. He had always loved being on the water. He took off his sunglasses and ran his fingers through his hair and beard. He was still getting used to his newly trimmed appearance, but it was more practical. He looked a little more civilised than he had of late, and it was a lot cooler.

He turned around and checked out the rest of the ship. Some of the crew had found shaded corners to chill out in and a couple of the other guards were working out in the relative cool of the hangar. There was a lot of time to kill until they needed to be kitted out and ready to earn their money.

Today, they had been hired to provide security to a container ship that was on its way to Kuala Lumpur's Port Klang. They would rendezvous with the ship in international waters then escort it through the straight.

As always at times like this, the money men only looked at the bottom line and didn't necessarily worry about quality.

An operation like this would, in the past, have used a team of British Special Boat Service or US Navy Seals to carry out the work. These were special forces soldiers who were used to being on the water, trained to recover hijacked ships and provide maritime security. The men Greenline had quickly recruited to fill the role in this instance, had none of that experience. Two of the team members were Brad and Quinn from the bar in KL. How had Quinn described their anti-piracy work? 'Money for old rope.' Palmer dreaded to think what would happen if it were anything more. They didn't strike him as particularly reliable.

When Quinn had spoken of opportunities to earn extra money, Brad had stopped him. The fact that Brad didn't want Palmer to know about it interested him. It was an indication that, whatever the extra work was, it was illegal. These "opportunities" could involve Chernov and the warhead. Wallace couldn't carry out that kind of operation on his own. He needed a small army to provide security and do the dirty work. They already knew that two guards, the ones who baby sat Chernov, were involved, but Palmer hadn't come across them yet. There had to be another location that Wallace was using. Something out of the way, more hidden. Palmer needed to dig around and find out where that other location was.

Palmer looked at his watch, it was time for the team briefing. This was a chance to weigh up the others. He needed to figure out which of them could be involved in illegal activities and if any of them would be a problem for him, and he had to do it quickly. He climbed down the ladder to where the crew dining hall had been turned into a briefing room and opened the door.

Inside the room, six of the team members sat on red, plastic chairs arranged in a rough semi-circle around a whiteboard.

The two that had been working out in the hangar used towels to soak up the sweat that still dripped from their bodies. Brad stood in front of the group flicking through the pages of a small, yellow notebook. Palmer walked over and sat in the only empty chair, next to Quinn. The big American greeted him with a smile and patted him on the back as he did.

Brad paused for dramatic effect then put down his notebook and cleared his throat. 'Okay, Gents.' He checked himself, pointed at the female member of the team, and winked. 'And lady.'

The woman looked down at her feet, shaking her head. Palmer got the impression that Brad's patronising was a regular occurrence. That created an atmosphere between them, a conflict. It was something Palmer might be able to use to pick up information.

Brad turned and pointed at a photograph that was stuck to the whiteboard. 'This is the container ship, MV Saint Helena.'

One of the others commented. 'Isn't that the same photo you used for the last job?'

There was a ripple of sniggering before Brad, a little annoyed, carried on. 'Okay, I know they all look the same, but this is our current client. It'll be a routine job the same as all the others. We'll get started after dark, as usual, you all know your jobs, get some rest.

Palmer wasn't impressed. He raised his hand.

Brad sighed. 'Yes. What is it?'

'Wouldn't it be better to pick up the Saint Helena in daylight? We can brief the crew and check for any likely breach points before we start the transit.'

Brad smiled and gestured towards Palmer. 'Everyone, I'd like you all to meet our new team member, Logan Palmer. I'm sure some of you have heard his name before but, in case you haven't, he used to be the lead operator in Delta team.'

Palmer knew when he was being set up. Brad's emphasis on the phrase 'used to be' made his intentions clear. He was trying to put Palmer in his place, to make him look small in front of the others. He felt threatened by Palmer and had to muddy his reputation. He had to stop any chance of Palmer taking over as leader.

Under normal circumstances, Palmer would have thrown back his own comment and shot Brad down in flames. He couldn't do that here. This was an operation he needed to get on with. If Brad thought he had got the upper hand, he would be less likely to see Palmer as a threat, less likely to keep a close eye on him. Palmer nodded slowly and waited for Brad's follow up.

Brad smirked. 'I believe your last operation didn't go strictly to plan.'

Palmer's mind flashed back to Geneva, the back of the Limo, the blood. It was seared into his memory, something he would never, could never, forget. He kept eye contact with Brad but said nothing.

'Don't worry, Palmer. We've done this a few times now without your help and we know what does and doesn't work for us. You just try and keep up. Okay?'

There was a collective laugh. Everyone was watching Palmer. All except the female guard, she had gone back to staring at her feet. As the others stood up and dispersed, she stayed in her seat, waiting for everyone to leave. It was a positive sign for Palmer, this woman was being treated as an outsider just like he was. If he could work out why, he could get her on his side, she was a potential ally. Palmer would have to be careful.

If he blew his cover, she could see exposing him to Brad as a way to impress the rest of the team. It could compromise the mission. Even worse, she might be part of the Chernov operation. In that case, it could cost him his life.

Chapter 16

P almer spent the rest of the day exploring the ship. He wasn't looking for information about the warhead, he doubted there was any to find here anyway. He was familiarising himself with the layout of the passageways, the location of ladders and hatches. If something happened, he needed to know what was behind every door. He had to be able to find his way around in the dark. It wasn't a suspicious thing to be doing, it was common practice for the crew of a ship to know where everything was. It was a matter of safety. Somehow, he didn't think all of Brad's team had been so conscientious.

As expected, he didn't find anything unusual. Cabins and bunk spaces, radio shack, navigation room, food stores. Everything that any other ship would have. The crew were mainly Asian and didn't associate with the guards. All they wanted to do was sail the ship and get paid. One thing Palmer did notice was how quickly conversations between the guards stopped whenever he walked past. It was obvious that they didn't trust him yet.

An hour before sunset, Palmer made his way onto the upper deck. He knew from his own time at sea that many sailors often finished their day on the upper deck, smoking, chatting, and watching the sun go down. To many, sundowners was a way of destressing. The naval equivalent of sitting around a campfire.

In the distance, The MV Saint Helena was just visible on the horizon and on target to make their rendezvous. The female guard Palmer had noticed earlier was sitting alone on a bollard by the guardrail smoking a cigarette. She appeared to be in her late twenties or early thirties, around five feet seven with long dark hair tied up in a ponytail. Palmer could now see that a ragged scar ran across her face from the bridge of her nose, under her eye to her left ear lobe. More than likely a wound picked up while serving in some fly-blown shithole.

Palmer approached her and leaned with his elbows on the guardrail. 'You seem about as popular as me around here.'

She looked up at him. 'We're outsiders, we don't fit into their gang. They don't like that.'

Palmer held out his hand. 'I'm Logan Palmer.'

'Yeah, I know. They said at the briefing. I'm Ruby, Ruby Finn.'

'Good to meet you, Ruby. Mind if I join you?'

She gestured in front of her. 'Pull up a bollard.'

Palmer sat down. 'You didn't look like you were enjoying yourself earlier, in the briefing.'

Finn let out a cough of laughter and shook her head. 'Brad, he's such a dick. Thinks he's in with a chance with me, figures I must be desperate, they all do.'

'And you're not tempted? I'm shocked.'

Finn smiled. 'They aren't my type.'

'You aren't attracted to arseholes.'

She flicked her cigarette into the water. 'I'm not attracted to men. Brad thinks he can cure me. Thinks that one night with him and I'll never look back.'

'Well, you don't have to worry about me, I'm under no illusions. My ex-wife says I was never that good anyway.'

Finn chuckled. 'What are you doing here, you're nothing like them.'

'I'm just in it for the money. Make some quick bucks then give it up. What about you?'

'I'm the same. Left the army and needed something that paid well.' She waved her hand in front of her face. 'Modelling wasn't really an option.'

'I don't know. You could model gloves. Shoes, maybe.'

It would sound cruel to a casual observer, but it was typical military humour, a way for Palmer to get Finn on his side.

Finn laughed loudly. 'Nah, my feet are too big.'

They chatted until it was dark. Palmer didn't make up a back story, there was no point. Brad already knew his history and he was sure Vaughn had checked out his more recent past before he offered him a job. Finn didn't disclose much about herself. She was an ex-army medic, trained up by Greenline at their facility in South Africa and dropped into this team two months earlier. Palmer could tell she wasn't happy but couldn't tell if it was the work in general or just this team that was pissing her off.

Brad's voice crackled over the broadcast system. 'All guards muster on the flight deck in twenty minutes.'

Palmer stood up. 'Well, time to earn our money.'

Finn stood and checked around them. She took a step towards Palmer. 'I'm not sure how much you know, but just watch yourself.'

'Is there something I should know?'

'It's obvious that Brad doesn't like you. I don't know why or

87

what your history is, but some of what happens tonight might not be strictly legit.'

Palmer raised his eyebrows. He was surprised that Finn seemed to be confiding in him after such a short time. 'I promise I'll watch my back.'

Finn walked across the deck and disappeared into one of the doors.

Palmer headed back to his cabin to collect his kit. The cabin he had been assigned was designed for two people. He imagined they were all the same, the reduced number of people that the ship now carried meant there were enough cabins for one each. Palmer had always preferred a top bunk and had folded the bottom one into a seat which he now sat on.

Palmer held the satellite phone he had bought in Kuala Lumpur. There was no need to hide it, lots of guards used them to keep in touch with family while they were away. He switched it on and checked it for messages, there were none. He had agreed with Riley that she would only send one in an emergency. If his cover was blown, he needed to know. He switched it off, collected his kit, and headed for the hangar.

When Palmer arrived, Brad was already barking orders at the team. God, he loved the sound of his own voice. Palmer winked at Finn, and she returned a grin.

Brad looked across the flight deck. 'Palmer. Your job is on the bridge. Pick up a radio and let us know if there are any other craft approaching.'

Palmer nodded. 'Will do.'

As he left the hangar and walked towards the bridge, he noticed that the others were readying the assault weapons they had been issued with. Some of the crew were busy lowering one of the rigid inflatables into the water. Palmer thought it was overkill. There were no specific threats in the area and pirate attacks were still rare, there were no other ships in sight. Quinn's words echoed in Palmer's head. 'Money for old rope.' What was going on? What were they expecting?

When Palmer reached the bridge, he checked in over the radio and grabbed a pair of night vision binoculars. The green tinged image didn't show great detail, but he could see that the rigid inflatable had reached the container ship. Palmer watched as six of the team climbed up to the deck while one stayed in the boat. It was hard to identify individuals but, based on size, it looked like Brad and Quinn were heading for the bridge. Nothing unusual so far.

The rest of the team stood around, smoking and chatting with the crew of the container ship. They had obviously met before and looked to be on friendly terms. That wasn't surprising either. Many of these ships plied the same route time and again for months on end. If Brad's team had been doing this for any length of time, they would have come across the same ships and the same crews more than once. What did catch Palmer's eye was the fact that it was Finn that was left in the boat.

From their conversation earlier, Palmer knew that Finn wasn't an expert at handling boats. As an army medic, she would be more used to crawling up dry riverbeds or hacking her way through the jungle to administer first aid than being on the water. So, why leave her there? Unless she was being kept away from what was actually going on. Maybe her treatment as an outsider had more to it than just her gender. He made a mental note to run Finn's name past Riley to check her out. It was looking more and more like Finn was caught up in whatever this was, but not involved. He wanted to make sure the authorities were aware of that when it all went pear shaped.

After a few minutes, Brad and Quinn reappeared out of the bridge. The man that accompanied them, probably the skipper, gesticulated and shouted at his crew. They immediately stopped their friendly chat and threw away their cigarettes. Two of them scuttled back into the bowels of the ship while one climbed into the cab of a small crane mounted on the deck.

Brad's voice came over the radio. 'This is Alpha One, clear for approach.'

Jesus, only Brad would pick Alpha One as his call sign, what a prick. Palmer responded. 'Roger Alpha One. On our way.'

Palmer held on as the engines kicked into life and the helmsman steered the ship towards the Saint Helena. An approach was unusual. Why would the Capricorn need to approach the Saint Helena? The inflatable was there to transfer the guards so why the need to get in close? The only reason Palmer could think of was to transfer cargo. They were planning to smuggle something.

Pulling alongside the massive container ship went much smoother than Palmer expected. It was obviously something that both crews had done many times before, and they were soon tied up as if they were back in port. The small crane's boom swung over to a collection of pallets, which had been pulled out of a container, while another crew member waved signals to guide the crane operator in.

The pallets were twice the size of the ones you might see stacked with compost outside a garden centre. Each one had various sizes of crate piled high and held together with nylon straps. The crew dismantled each pallet and placed the crates onto a large cargo net. The contents of four pallets was stacked up before the cargo net was attached to the Crane's hook and lifted over to the Capricorn's flight deck. The cargo net was quickly detached from the crane's hook and the crates ferried into the hangar.

Palmer counted five nets full of crates in all, transferred and being securely stowed in the hangar. The crane on the Saint Helena was shut down and the rigid inflatable full of guards recovered from the sea. The last person off the container ship was Brad. He shook hands with the captain then climbed down the rope ladder and jumped onto the flight deck. The Capricorn slipped its mooring ropes and pulled away, the captain issuing orders. 'Set a course for Port Klang, fifteen knots.'

'Aye, Sir.' The helmsman turned the wheel and the ship leaned over as it turned south.

Palmer left the bridge and headed for the flight deck. The crew were transferring the last of the crates into the hangar and closing the roller door. The guards were stowing away their weapons and appeared to be in high spirits. Obviously, they had just earned some extra money.

Palmer walked over to Finn. 'What's with all the cargo that was transferred over? I thought this was just an escort job.'

'It's something you shouldn't ask about.'

Brad appeared around the corner of the hangar. 'It's something you don't need to know about, Palmer, so keep your nose out.'

Palmer held his hands up. 'Okay, I was just curious, that's all. If you're making extra cash somehow, I'm not going to do anything to get in the way. Would be nice to be in on it though.'

Brad was on his guard. He didn't trust Palmer at all. 'Just stay out of the way and keep your mouth shut. If you can manage that, maybe we'll include you in the next deal.'

'Thanks, that's all I'm asking, just want to earn as much as I can.'

Brad looked at Palmer and Finn. He didn't like the idea of two outsiders becoming friendly, it was dangerous. He paused for a moment then turned and walked away.

Chapter 17

Four hundred kilometres south of Port Klang, in the South China Sea, the Capricorn weaved its way between the islands that made up Indonesia's Riau Archipelago. It was a busy shipping area, so half of the crew was on watch. There was nothing to guard against and no crates to load so the rest of the crew, and the guards, were asleep. It was time for Palmer to find out what was in the hangar.

Palmer locked the door of his cabin and crept along the passageway. His route was illuminated only by the red lights that were kept on to preserve the crew's night vision. He made his way silently past the other cabins to the dining hall then, pausing to check for any movement, climbed the ladder to the hangar door.

Palmer turned the handwheel that secured the door, wincing at the mechanical clunk. He pulled open the heavy metal door a few inches and listened for any noises that would alert him to someone else being inside, he heard nothing. He stepped through the opening and closed the door behind him.

The inside of the hangar was bathed in the same red light as the rest of the ship. To the right of the door hung several sets of overalls and hard hats used by the crew. To the left, the fitness equipment and weights he had seen some of the team using were stowed in a metal cage to stop them rolling across the deck. On the other side of the hangar were multiple toolboxes and racks of equipment labelled: *Helo Spares. DO NOT TOUCH.*

The crates they had transferred from the Saint Helena were stacked and tied down in the middle of the deck, secured against any movement the ship might make. He now under-stood why the helicopter he arrived in hadn't stayed, they couldn't fit it in the hangar with all this cargo.

Palmer edged his way across the hangar to the pile of crates, always checking for any sound or movement that would give away someone else's presence. If he were caught now, it wouldn't be impossible to explain, but it would be difficult. Brad and the rest of the team were more likely to do him some serious damage and dispose of what was left just in case. Even if they did believe him.

When Palmer reached the crates, he walked around the pile looking for the easiest way to open them up. He unfastened two of the nylon straps and eased them to the side, freeing up one side of the stack. Although the red light in the hangar preserved night vision, it also made everything look the same colour. Palmer pulled a torch out of his pocket and switched it on.

The colour of the crates and the way they were marked up rang alarm bells for Palmer, they obviously contained military hardware. If he had to stake his reputation on it, he would say they were full of weapons. He played the torches white light across the whole pile; the crates were all different sizes and shapes, some long and thin, others small and square, but they were all marked the same. The serial numbers stencilled

94

onto each one showed that they had all been part of the same shipment.

Palmer opened one of the smaller boxes and shone the torch on its contents. Inside it were M67s. US issue fragmentation grenades. Another box contained Claymore anti-personnel mines, another held M4 assault rifles. There were two dozen boxes of 5.56mm ammunition. He unfastened the catches on the largest of the containers and peered inside. 'Holy shit!'

The container held a stinger missile system. There was no way any private security needed this kind of equipment. Some of it couldn't be bought legally on the open market. There was no longer a chance that this was an innocent operation that he had misunderstood, these were military-grade weapons being smuggled out of the middle east.

Wallace had set up an organisation, a whole infrastructure to divert arms shipments from the US, via Iraq, to his own facilities. If he was selling this amount and type of weapon to terrorists, the ramifications didn't bear thinking about. Just one of the stingers could bring down an airliner, there was no way to guard against it at a civilian airport. How many did he have? Another, even more frightening thought entered Palmer's head. With this kind of hardware and a nuclear warhead, Wallace could launch a coup. He could set up his own government somewhere and wage war to order. A well-armed, professional army under the protection of a rogue state, with nuclear capability.

Palmer spun around at the sound of a footstep behind him. Finn shielded her eyes as the torchlight hit her face.

'What are you trying to do, blind me?'

Palmer switched off the torch. He held it ready to use as a weapon if it were needed. 'Sorry. I didn't hear you come in, how long have you been there?'

'Long enough to see you snooping about. I don't think you're supposed to be doing that.'

Palmer looked over at the door he had come through, it was still shut. If Finn made a run for it, he could chase her down before she got it open and raised the alarm. Palmer didn't think she was going to do that. 'What are you doing in here?'

Finn lit a cigarette, the flame creating moving shadows across her face. 'I come up here quite often when I can't sleep. It's a little cooler than my cabin, less claustrophobic. The question is, what are you up to?'

Palmer gripped his torch, forming a plan in his mind. He could drop her right here then throw her body into the sea. No one would know. He doubted Brad would care. He started to close the boxes and fasten the straps. 'I'm just being nosey, couldn't sleep and wondered what was in the boxes.'

'Yeah, okay. Look, I don't care what you're up to. I don't know what's in the boxes and I don't want to. All I do know is that I get paid extra every time this happens. Mind you, I imagine they get paid more than I do.'

'What makes you think that?'

Finn gave a wry smile. 'I've heard the muppets talking about how they'll spend their fortune.'

If Brad's team were expecting to be paid a lot of money sometime soon, they must be involved in something big. Chances were, they were involved in whatever was happening to Chernov.

Palmer made sure he had closed all the crates. 'So, where are we taking these?'

'Some island south of here. Cantik Island it's called. We usually go in, unload and stay overnight.'

'Does that happen often?'

Finn nodded. 'Sometimes we're picking stuff up and other times we're dropping off. Tops up my wages quite well. Why do you want to know?'

'I'm just not comfortable being involved with what looks like an arms smuggling operation.'

Finn stubbed her cigarette out. 'If you don't like it, don't stay. I'm only in this for a short time. If I keep my mouth shut, I'll get enough cash to walk away from these idiots.'

'So, how do we play this? Do I have to worry about you telling the others about me?'

'As I said, I'm not interested in what you're doing. What's your next move, hit me with the torch and throw me in the sea?'

Palmer eased his grip on the torch. 'I'd never think of doing that to someone. I'm just going to leave, go and get my head down.'

'Sounds like a plan.'

They left the hangar together and descended the ladder back down to the dining hall. As they walked along the passageway, Brad stepped out of one of the doors. 'Good evening, and where have you two lovebirds been? A little night-time exercise?'

Finn pushed past him and carried on along the passageway.

Brad moved closer to Palmer and whispered, 'I wouldn't waste your time, mate, I think she bats for the other team.' He wandered off, chuckling at his own joke.

Palmer watched Finn open the door to her cabin. She looked back along the passageway at him then stepped inside. If Palmer hadn't been beaten up, or worse, by tomorrow, he had just found an ally. He opened his own cabin door and went in.

97

Chapter 18

I t was just after daybreak when the Capricorn sailed into the small harbour at Cantik Island and moored alongside the port's only jetty. The crew were now busy unloading the crates from the hangar onto a flatbed truck that was parked at the bottom of the gangway while a tanker pumped diesel into the ship's fuel tanks.

Palmer leaned against the guardrail on the roof of the hangar and tried to look disinterested and nonchalant. He had removed his t-shirt and looked to everyone like he was trying to top up his non-existent tan. What he was doing was scanning the docks and the surrounding landscape of the island.

Could the warhead have been smuggled here? Yes, definitely. The crates of weapons that were being unloaded proved that this was a highly effective smuggling operation. Could Chernov have been brought here? No reason why not. Smuggling him here wouldn't have been any more difficult. Was there a facility that looked like it could be used to build a nuclear device? There were a couple of buildings that looked like possibilities, but it was hard to tell. He would have to try and get a closer look. London would need confirmation that the warhead was here before they ordered a strike of any kind. This was a foreign country. They couldn't simply bomb the island without causing a major diplomatic incident. There was also the possibility that, if the warhead wasn't here, they would just tip off whoever had it and make it even harder to track down in time. Palmer expected he would be coming back with enough equipment to carry out a proper search and recover the warhead.

The rest of the team were milling around on the flight deck. Two of them were putting a barbecue together under an awning that was attached to the hangar. A dozen cases of bottled beer had been brought on board and were being loaded into boxes of ice. From the looks of it, no one was planning to leave the ship.

Palmer returned to scanning the shoreside facilities. Some of the low-level buildings were built with corrugated steel and had large shutter doors that were open. They didn't appear to have any security and from the creates that were being wheeled out and onto the ship, Palmer surmised that these buildings were food stores. Another, newer looking building also had a large shutter door but this one was closed. Armed guards patrolled the exterior and controlled access. This was probably the building that the weapons from the ship were about to be moved into.

At the back of the facility was a smaller, modern building that looked much sturdier. This building was constructed of steel girders and breeze blocks. It had no shutter door and only one access point which was manned by two armed guards. If Wallace was using Chernov to build a nuclear device, that building was the most likely candidate.

Palmer looked down at the flight deck, Brad was marshalling the layout of some deckchairs, he'd finally found something he was good at. After a quick check for anyone keeping watch, Palmer descended the ladder that ran down the side of the hangar and walked towards the gangway.

Members of the crew were ferrying boxes of fresh fruit and vegetables up the gangway and onto the ship. Palmer waited for a gap, then walked down the gangway to the jetty. No one was interested in what he was doing, most assumed he had a right to be there and just ignored him. He walked around the fuel truck and headed towards the food store. He thought that would be a good way to test any security.

'Palmer!'

The shout echoed off the corrugated steel sides of the buildings. Palmer stopped and turned round.

'Where the fuck d'ya think you're going?' Brad had left the ship and was running along the jetty towards him.

Palmer did his best to look innocent. 'Just taking the chance to stretch my legs on dry land. Thought I might go for a run.'

Brad caught up to him. 'No one, except me, leaves the ship. No one. That includes you. Got it?'

Palmer looked innocent. 'Okay, okay, keep your hair on. I wasn't told it was a problem.'

Brad pointed back along the jetty with his thumb. 'Get your ass back on board. There's nothing for you out here.'

Palmer kept eye contact with Brad as he walked past him. At some point, he envisaged giving Brad a severe talking to, but not yet. Palmer grabbed a box of oranges and walked back up the gangway to the flight deck.

Finn was sitting on the deck just inside the hangar. Palmer put down the box of oranges and joined her. She pointed at the jetty. 'You get a telling off from our glorious leader?'

Palmer laughed. 'Yeah, got my legs slapped. I'm a very

naughty boy, apparently.'

'I should probably have told you; we're not allowed ashore.'

'It's okay, I'm a big boy now, I can look after myself. So, what do we do for entertainment around here?'

Finn gestured at the flight deck. 'Well, Brad and the boys will be eating burned hot dogs and getting pissed, as usual.'

'And you?'

'I'll be having a couple of beers and going to bed early. Before anything gets out of control.'

The tone of Finn's voice told Palmer that she was speaking from previous experience. Something had obviously happened during one of these trips that she was determined not to repeat.

Palmer watched the others getting ready for their party. They all looked happy, living the dream. They all had a common purpose. Finn wasn't part of that. Palmer looked at her. 'Why do you stay in this job? You don't look happy.'

Finn paused for a moment. 'I've been in a lot of situations where I wasn't happy. I can put up with it if it's in my interests. I need money to live, this work gets me it quickly. When I've got a nice bankroll behind me, I'm gone.'

'A woman after my own heart.'

Finn leaned towards Palmer. 'I should probably tell you that at least one of them stays sober. Keeps an eye on things at night.'

'Why would that interest me?'

'Oh, I don't know, I thought you might be going for another jog down the jetty.'

Palmer smiled.

Chapter 19

The party had lasted right through the afternoon and into the night. By eleven o'clock, the members of the team were passed out on the flight deck or already back in their bunks. Palmer locked the door to his cabin and made his way towards the upper deck.

At the top of the ladder, he unclipped the metal door and opened it a few inches. There was no one else moving around the ship. There was no real need for any security on board and the crew were taking time to themselves while not being at sea. Palmer stepped out of the door and quietly closed it behind him.

Using the gangway was a risky option, but it was the quickest route. Palmer didn't have time for anything else. If anything went wrong, he wouldn't be coming back to the ship anyway. He crept along the deck and peered around the corner of the hangar.

Quinn and one of the others were flat out in the middle of the flight deck surrounded by empty beer bottles. Palmer stepped out of the shadows, there was no one else in sight. He moved silently across the flight deck and slipped down the gangway to the jetty.

At the bottom of the gangway, Palmer crouched behind

a large crate. Unlike most major ports, the facility wasn't brightly lit during the night. The only lights were coming from the ship and the sentry post outside the building Palmer was interested in. He used the night vision binoculars that he had when they picked up the container ship and scanned the area. There were no CCTV cameras he could see and no obvious security patrols. He put the binoculars back in their pouch and ran across the jetty.

The building, although sturdy and guarded, didn't have a fence. On one side, it was bounded by empty wooden crates and reels of rope and cable. On the other side, trees and dense vegetation reached to within ten metres. The far end of the building seemed to be a car park for various vehicles with the sentry position situated at the end closest to the jetty.

Palmer watched the sentries through his binoculars. Every thirty minutes, one of them made a circuit of the outside of the building while the other stayed at the entrance. They were as regular as clockwork. If he was going to see what was inside, Palmer needed to get on the roof. There was a faint glow rising from the building which pointed to the existence of skylights. Most buildings he had seen that had skylights had some sort of ladder to allow access to the roof to clean them. He was hoping this building would be no different. He made his way between the empty crates around to the far end of the building.

Palmer crawled underneath an old US military truck and waited for the sentry to make his rounds. His hunch about skylights and ladders was correct. In the middle of the far wall, six feet off the ground, was a galvanized steel ladder that led to the roof. It was surrounded by a safety cage with a locked hatch to prevent any access. It seemed that, even in the world of nuclear weapon smuggling, health and safety was king. Palmer lay still and waited.

Exactly on time, the sentry appeared around the corner. He stopped directly under the ladder and lit a cigarette. Palmer had spent enough time on sentry duty himself to know how mind numbing it was. Even stopping for a smoke helped to relieve the boredom. The sentry breathed in a lung full of smoke and exhaled a billowing cloud that drifted towards Palmer. Judging by the smell that wafted into his nostrils, the sentry wasn't smoking regular tobacco. That was something that Palmer might be able to use to his advantage. If the sentries weren't as alert as they should be, his job got easier. The man took several more draws on his cigarette then dropped it to the floor and stubbed it out with his foot before carrying on with his rounds.

Palmer waited two minutes to make sure the sentry wasn't going to come back around to this side of the building. He set the timer on his watch to twenty-five minutes and rolled out from under the truck. After a brief check for any movement, he sprinted the fifteen meters to the wall and jumped up to the ladder.

The safety cage was designed to make sure anyone who fell, landed at the bottom of the ladder. The locked hatch was to prevent a casual passer-by from accessing the roof. What neither of them was designed to stop was someone climbing up the outside of the cage. Palmer climbed the ten feet to the parapet in a few seconds and ducked down behind it, out of sight.

Just as Palmer thought, the faint glow was coming out of a long row of windows that ran along the side of the building that was closest to the trees. It meant Palmer was less likely to be observed from outside than he would have been if the windows faced the jetty. Keeping below the level of the parapet, he dragged himself around the edge of the roof and looked in.

The inside of the building was mainly empty. There were no racks or shelving along the walls, and the smooth concrete floor had no workbenches or machinery fastened to it. Palmer began to think his hunch about the building was wrong. He crawled further along the roof to look inside from a different angle, but it didn't make any difference. The only things inside were two smaller, wooden structures a few feet from the door.

Each of the smaller structures was a single story with a solid door at one end and two windows. They looked like the kind of thing used as an office on a building site, not somewhere that would be used to build a nuclear weapon. In front of the two cabins was a rectangular hole in the floor with a guardrail around three sides. The fourth side was open and led to a concrete staircase. Why would that be there and where did it go? There must be a bunker of some sort, or a lower level under the building.

A light came on inside one of the cabins. The door opened and a large man wearing combat fatigues came out and walked towards the concrete steps. Palmer thought he recognised him. His size, his hair colour, the way he walked. Palmer pulled out his binoculars, switched off the night vision, and zoomed in. He was right. The man he was looking at was Pete Nelson. One of the mercenaries sent to babysit Chernov on the flight from Tehran. One of the men photographed in the hotel in Kuala Lumpur. Chernov and the warhead had to be here. Nelson descended the concrete steps and disappeared.

Palmer made a mental note of the layout of the inside of the building. Somehow, he would have to get in there and down those steps. But that wasn't a job for tonight. He didn't have the time or the tools to attempt it. He checked his watch, he had ten minutes to get off the roof without clashing with the next sentry's rounds. He pushed himself backwards along the edge of the window until he reached the far end of the building. He checked his watch, he had five minutes.

He looked over the edge of the building, it was all clear. He swung his legs over the parapet and slowly climbed back down the ladder cage, just as the sentry appeared around the corner. Palmer froze. The man was early. He stopped directly under the ladder, just as the other one had done. Palmer couldn't hang on while this guy lit up a spliff, but this guy wasn't having a smoke. The sentry put down his weapon and unzipped his trousers.

Palmer had two options. He could drop the last few feet and ambush the sentry, catch him unawares. That would cause Palmer a big problem. With a sentry missing, he would be the prime suspect. Brad would be unlikely to believe he had had nothing to do with it. It was possible that Brad would kill him just to be on the safe side. He wouldn't make it off the island. Palmer's only other option was simply to wait. How likely was it that this man, emptying his bladder as a break from his mundane, mind numbing duties, would look up? Palmer decided to take option two.

Time slowed down. The sentry was taking an age. How much had this guy had to drink? Palmer's muscles tightened; his fingers cramped up, maybe option one wouldn't have been such a bad choice after all. After what seemed like the longest piss in human history, with Palmer on the verge of dropping off the ladder, the sentry finally zipped back up and went on his way.

Palmer clung on long enough for the sentry to get around

the corner, then dropped from the ladder. He sprinted to the old army truck and rolled back underneath. The muscles in his fingers and arms were screaming, he could barely move them. He lay on his back and slowly flexed each hand and arm, massaging the joints to bring them back to life. He was going to be stiff in the morning.

It was after midnight. Palmer had to get back to the ship before someone missed him, he had done everything he could tonight. There was no sense risking discovery by staying out longer. He checked in every direction for anyone who might be out for a night-time stroll, it was all clear. There was no noise and no sign of either of the sentries. Palmer crawled out from under the truck and backed away from the building.

Brad stood on the flight deck and looked out to sea. He wasn't happy that it had been his turn to stay sober and look after things, but someone had to do it. He had kicked Quinn and his mate back to their bunks and swept up most of the empty bottles. He had done a complete check of the ship, and everything was in order. Nothing was happening and there was no one moving about on the jetty. It was time for him to turn in.

Palmer crouched at the end of the gangway, watching. He couldn't risk being seen now. He stood up as much as he dared and looked across to the hangar's shutter door. It had been closed most of the way down but there was still a gap of about two feet. If he could get under the door, he was safe. He could sneak back to his cabin from there.

Brad looked to his right and walked off towards the bridge. Palmer took his chance, he kept low and went as fast as he could without making any noise. Just as he reached the hangar, he saw a shadow fall across the deck. Brad was on his way back. Palmer dived and rolled. His momentum carried him under the shutter door, and he scrambled into the shadows, breathing heavily.

Brad walked across the flight deck then stopped and turned back to the door. Palmer held his breath. Brad pressed the green button that operated the shutter and lowered it all the way. Palmer let out a sigh. He had got away with it. After waiting for a while to let Brad get back to his bunk, Palmer crept across the hangar and through the door.

He was back in his cabin moments later. He wrote down some notes about the building and composed a message to Riley on his satellite phone. He would send it once he was back on the upper deck in the morning. After a quick shower, he climbed onto his bunk and switched off the light.

Chapter 20

P almer was awake early. The stiffness in his arms had eased and he was able to move them freely. One of the joints on his left hand looked a little swollen but there was no sharp pain. He had probably twisted it a little. He climbed off his bunk and checked his face in the mirror. There were no bruises or scratches that could have been a giveaway that he had been up to something. The only visible mark he had was a scrape on his elbow from when he had rolled into the hangar. It was nothing serious and could be explained away quite easily. From the looks of it, he was in the clear. All he had to do now was keep up the act and wait for Riley to get back to him.

Palmer got dressed and was on the upper deck as soon as it was light. He liked being outside as the sun came up, it was quite cool, and he enjoyed the solitude. Most of the others were still sleeping off hangovers. As soon as he was outside, he pressed the send button on his satellite phone. The pencil pushers in London needed to decide what they wanted him to do on the island. He hadn't gathered enough intel to confirm anything one way or the other. Someone at a much higher pay grade than him would have to decide if it warranted blowing up the facility up. In the meantime, Palmer would make his own plans.

'You're up early.'

Palmer spun round. Brad had managed to walk right up behind him without him noticing. He slipped his phone into his pocket. 'Couldn't sleep, just getting some fresh air. Starting to get hot already. I'm used to wind and rain.'

'I noticed you weren't at our party. Something wrong with drinking with us, Logan?'

Palmer tried to look uninterested in what Brad was saying, he was just fishing. He might suspect something, but he didn't know. 'I figured the guys deserved to relax without an outsider spoiling their fun.'

Brad shook his head. 'That's the best you can come up with?'

'You're a tight team. It'll take me some time to become part of that.'

Brad looked into Palmer's eyes. 'And you expect me to believe that?'

Palmer shrugged. 'I can't do anything to change what you believe, Brad, and I'm not really interested in trying.'

'Come on, Palmer. I know that's all bullshit. What's the truth, why are you really here?

Palmer stepped towards Brad. 'Okay, fuck it. The truth is, I don't like you, Brad, you're an arsehole. Your boss asked me to work with you for now, but I don't have to drink with you. Who knows, maybe they're planning to get rid of you and put me in charge. If you've got a problem, take it up with Vaughn.'

Brad smirked. 'The thing is, Logan, when I was doing my rounds at midnight, I knocked on your cabin door. Just to make sure you were okay. There was no reply.'

Palmer began to wonder if Brad had found something out. Maybe Palmer had left evidence of his night-time ramble.

'What can I say, I didn't hear you knocking. I'm a heavy sleeper.'

'Maybe you are, but what you don't know is that I have a key to every cabin. Guess what, Logan? When I opened your cabin, you weren't in. Did you go for another snoop along the jetty, even after I told you not to?'

This was a dangerous situation. Palmer had been caught in a lie. He couldn't explain why he wasn't in his cabin. Brad had done a complete check of the ship and knew he wasn't on board.

'He was with me.' Finn had been listening from just inside the door.

Brad turned. 'What?'

'He was with me. We couldn't let you guys have all the fun. We decided to have some of our own.'

'So, you're telling me he was in your bed all night.'

Finn nodded. 'From about ten until a couple of hours ago.'

'You're sure about that?'

'Absolutely, it was quite a night. Not one I'll forget in a hurry. If you know what I mean.'

Brad looked between Palmer and Finn. 'I must admit, Ruby, I'm really surprised. I thought you didn't like men.'

Finn shook her head. 'It's not men I don't like, Brad. It's you. You turn my stomach, you prick.'

Brad took a step towards Finn, fists clenched. Palmer was ready to throw Brad over the side to cool him down. Finn stood her ground, grinning.

Palmer could see the indecision in Brad's eyes. There was no way to disprove what they were saying.

Brad looked at Finn. 'You are definitely doing the right things to get onto my shit list.'

111

'You mean you haven't got the hots for me anymore, Brad? My luck's changing for the better every day.'

Brad snorted and stormed off.

Palmer watched him go. 'What did you just do?'

Finn looked puzzled. 'What do you mean?'

'You don't really know me. I could have been doing anything last night. Showing yourself as willing to lie for me, that's quite a risk. Why would you do that?'

'I've got my reasons, and he pisses me off. I'd back anyone against him.'

'Well, I'm glad you did, I just hope it doesn't ruin your reputation as the ice maiden.'

Finn laughed. 'Don't get any ideas, Logan. Your still not my type.'

Chapter 21

Anna Riley sat on another bus as she, once again, zig zagged her way across London towards another meeting. This one was different to the last. Palmer's update about the island had really stoked up the fire under Edward Lancaster. Why else would he have asked to see her? A decision must have been made that hopefully meant they could get Palmer away from that ship before he got hurt, or worse.

Riley had received her instructions by text message from an unknown number, she was sure, was untraceable and had already been disposed of. She was starting to get used to the secrecy that had become an everyday part of her life since she met Vicky and Edward. If she was honest, she was starting to enjoy the sneaking around and the subterfuge. She could see herself doing this full time.

When the bus reached her stop, Riley left her seat and stepped out of the door. The area she was now in was definitely more upmarket than she could afford. Tree lined streets flanked by large, mock Tudor houses that had been built in the nineteen thirties. Expensive cars parked on driveways bigger than her flat and sturdy gates fitted with security cameras. She would love to live in a place like this, she would love to have the money to live in a place like this. That would be a start.

She walked along the street to the number she had been given in the text message. The house she stood in front of wasn't the biggest on the street, but it wasn't the smallest either. It looked like it was well maintained, and the garden was full of colourful flowers and shaped hedges. Someone must live here.

Attached to the fence that ran along the front of the garden was a small metal box with a button and a speaker. As she reached out to press the silver button on the intercom, there was a buzz. With an electric hum and a metallic rattle, the wrought iron gates swung open, and she passed through onto the paved driveway.

The front door was fashioned from dark oak with black cast iron adornments. A large round doorknob, ornate scrolled hinges and a knocker that looked like a lion, but no letterbox. Letters were delivered to the black box that was mounted on the wall. Riley noticed the addition of a modern security camera in the top corner above the door. Someone would be watching her, there was no need to knock. She did wonder if she was at the correct door though. Maybe she should be round the back at the tradesmen's entrance.

When the door opened, Riley walked through to the hallway of the house without even checking to see who had opened it. The inside was as nineteen thirties as the outside. Lots of dark oak panelling and extravagant light fittings. The tiled floor was spectacular. Not just black and white, as she had expected, but multiple colours in a geometric pattern that was matched by the stained-glass window above the staircase.

An elderly woman closed the front door and gestured towards the double doors on the right-hand side of the hallway.

'If you would like to go through to the study, I'll let you out once you've finished.'

Riley opened one of the panelled oak doors and went in. Although the décor of the study was every bit as ornate as the hallway, the furniture was plain and functional. It looked more like an office than a house on an expensive street in the suburbs. A handful of wooden chairs were arranged around, what looked like, a large solid kitchen table. There was a flat-screen television on a wheeled stand, a computer with a printer attached, and two phones. In one corner, a small kitchen had been set up with a microwave oven and a kettle.

Vicky Thomson was making them all a coffee in three chipped white mugs that had seen better days. 'Milk and sugar, Anna?'

'Just milk please, thanks.'

Lancaster was sitting at the table shuffling through paper-work. 'Hello, Anna.' He looked past Riley to the door. 'Thanks, Mary.'

Riley looked behind her just as the elderly woman closed the door. 'What is this place?'

Lancaster bundled the paperwork together and put it all into a briefcase. 'The house was left to us in the will of an officer we lost during the Second World War. He had no family to leave it to. We use it for debriefings of assets, that kind of thing. Mary lives here full-time with her husband. The neighbours think I'm their son and Vicky is my wife. It works well.'

'It's a nice house.'

Lancaster looked around the room. 'Yes, it is. We do like to keep it original. So, how are you getting on, Anna? I mean in yourself, not with the job.'

It always surprised Riley that Lancaster wanted to know that she was okay before he moved on to work. He always seemed genuinely interested in her welfare. 'I'm doing okay, thank you.'

'That's good to hear. Now...'

Thomson placed three mugs on the table and sat in the chair opposite Riley. 'There you go.'

Lancaster blew the steam off his coffee and took a sip. 'Lovely. Vicky really does make the best cuppa.'

Thomson smiled at Riley. 'Apparently, that's why he never makes it.'

Lancaster sideways glanced at Thomson while he took another sip then put his mug down. 'Where was I? Oh yes, the update from Logan.' He paused, looking at Riley. 'What do you think we should do next?'

Riley pointed at herself. 'Me? Well...I don't really...I mean...'

'Come on, Anna, you must have thought about it. Don't worry, no one's going to laugh. There are no stupid ideas here.'

Riley tapped her fingers on her mug. Was this a test? 'I think we need to pull Logan out. He needs to concentrate on the island, go back and find the warhead. I think his undercover work has got us as far as it's going to.'

'Excellent, I agree. What do you think, Vicky?'

Thomson nodded. 'He's not going to get much more while he's under scrutiny on the ship. He needs to be on that island when the others aren't there.'

'It's unanimous then. Anna, you get a message to Logan, unleash him. Anything it takes. I'll arrange some extra funds for him, he might have to bribe someone. We need this done quickly.'

Riley could sense the urgency in Lancaster's voice. 'Has

something happened?'

Lancaster looked at Thomson then back to Riley. 'We've had more intelligence. Special forces picked up a target in Syria. You don't need to know all the details, but it turns out that this man was working as a fundraiser for ISIS. Almost as their banker. Seems like they've managed to amass a massive amount of money with the help of some sympathetic supporters in the Gulf states. There was a lot of oil money diverted their way.'

'Who's controlling the money now?'

'We think it's a rogue element within the Iranian establishment. One person in particular.' He handed Riley a photograph. 'This man is Zahir Karimi. He acts as an advisor to the Iranian leadership, very influential.'

Riley studied the photo. The man was middle-aged and had the complexion of someone who had spent their whole life living in harsh environments. 'Why would he be involved? What does he want?'

'In twenty fifteen, his entire family were killed in a drone strike in Syria. Parents, wife, kids, sister, everyone, they were all at a wedding. Although the drone was being piloted from a base in Nevada, it was being flown by an RAF pilot. Karimi wants revenge, pure and simple. No political goals or ideological warfare, no demands, or negotiations, just retribution. He has the finances, and he wants to cause as much damage as possible.'

Riley sat forwards. 'Do you know the target?'

'All this guy could tell us was that a payment of one billion dollars had been made to fund an attack in Europe.'

Riley was shocked. 'A billion? It has to be the warhead, what else would be worth that? He wants to strike back at us and the US. If it's Europe, it must be London.'

'You understand the urgency. We don't know where the money is or how it'll be paid. This is the only tip we have. Logan Palmer is all we've got.'

The colour drained from Riley's face. 'We've only got a few weeks. I'll get the message to him now.' She stood up and headed for the door.'

'Anna.' Lancaster was on his feet. 'He has a deadline. If he doesn't succeed by then, we'll have to hit the island, no matter what the diplomatic fallout is. It's the only info we have and, if the warhead is there, we can't afford to lose it.'

'I understand, Sir.' Riley left the house and walked back to the bus stop. She could feel her hands shaking. What if she messed this up? Hundreds of thousands could die. She needed a drink, but she had work to do.

Back at her flat, Riley sat in front of her laptop, her eyes fixed on the screen. She had to find a way for Palmer to get back on the island unseen. So far, she'd found plenty of background, the sort of information anyone could find online. Cantik Island meant Beautiful Island, which didn't help. It was in Indonesia and used to be a Dutch colony. Taken over by japan during the war then by the US for a short time, which didn't help her either. It has no room for an airstrip and can only be accessed by sea, she knew that already. The coast was too rugged to land any boats anywhere other than the harbour. Come on, there must be something.

She brought up a detailed satellite photo and zoomed in. The harbour and facility were the only patch of the island that wasn't covered in dense jungle and there were no beaches, it was like it had been designed specifically to be difficult to get to. Maybe the only option was parachute, but then how would Palmer get back off the island afterwards? She studied the image in detail, scrolling along every inch of the island. With the clock ticking and no options in sight, she had one last look around the coast. There was nothing but water, rocks, and jungle. Sometimes it was just water and rocks. But then she saw it. That was it, that was the way in. She opened her email, typed a message to Palmer, and closed her laptop. There was nothing more she could do.

Chapter 22

Palmer and Finn sat in a café close to the KL Central train station. The Capricorn had docked early that morning and they didn't hang around to find out what the other guards were planning for their down time. They had one week to themselves, away from Brad.

Palmer looked at his watch. He had thirty minutes to catch his train to Singapore and then onto a ferry.

Finn wrote her contact details down on a slip of paper. 'I've enjoyed our chats, Logan, be good to keep in touch.'

Palmer took the note. 'What are your plans?'

'I have to do one more trip. That's the end of my contract. I'm finished after that, go and live a decent life.' She looked closely at Palmer. 'You're not coming back, are you?'

Palmer idly stirred his coffee. 'I've got a job that I need to do. It's going to be risky, but it's important. I'll look you up when I'm done.'

'Does this job have anything to do with Greenline? They're up to something, aren't they?'

Palmer didn't want Finn caught up in the aftermath of whatever happened. 'Look, Ruby, you don't need to go back. Fuck the contract, just walk away. It won't make any difference.'

Finn pointed behind her with her thumb. 'I'm booked into a swanky hotel for a week. I'm going to live the high life. Pamper myself. I'll see how I feel after that. Maybe I'll just go home.'

Palmer was relieved. 'That would be a good idea. Trust me. You have to look after yourself.'

'What about you?'

Palmer checked his watch again, he had to go. 'I've got to do this for my boy, to make sure he's okay, then I'm out. Right now, I have to go and see an old friend of mine.' He stood up and picked up his bag. 'Take care, Ruby, I'll see you again, soon.'

Finn smiled. 'I'll look forward to it.'

Chapter 23

When Palmer received Riley's message, he knew that getting onto the island was going to be difficult. In truth, he thought it might even be impossible. What he knew for sure was that he couldn't do it without help.

In the years that Logan Palmer served as a Royal Marine, and later as a private military contractor, he became part of a brotherhood. The men that stood beside him in Iraq and Afghanistan were as close to him as family. They worked, lived, and, in too many cases, died as a team. Always together, always watching each other's backs. Even among this tight knit community though, as in all families, some brothers were closer than others. Some were closer than family. Palmer and Jerry Scarlett had that kind of relationship.

They had joined the Royal Marines on the same day. Two eighteen year olds eager to get out and see the world, to serve their country, to dive headlong into danger and adventure. They were both naturals for the job, mentally and physically. They coped with the gruelling training better than most of the other recruits. That put them in competition with each other, both keen to be number one, but it also forged a relationship as strong as any other in Palmer's life. When Palmer left the

Royal Marines, Scarlett followed suit, but he didn't join the world of private security as Palmer had done. Instead, he moved east. He wanted to set up his own business and combine it with his other great passion in life, scuba diving.

As tourists poured out of the Sekupang Ferry Terminal on Bantam Island, Palmer looked for a shady spot away from the hustle and bustle. Some of the tourists he had shared the fifty-minute ferry ride from Singapore with, stood in queues for the taxis that would take them to their hotels and resorts. Those who were heading for dive spots manhandled their bags of equipment into the luggage holds of buses then climbed aboard for a hot sweaty trip to their accommodation.

Palmer stood away from them all and waited for the minibus that he knew would pick him up. He wiped his face and neck with a small, thin, towelling facecloth he had taken from the hotel in Kuala Lumpur. He had two of them. They were the size of handkerchiefs, and he didn't go anywhere without them; they had become his most valuable possessions. He often thought he would have been better off with a couple of beach towels, but these would have to do. He unscrewed the top off a bottle of water and drank half of it, the rest of the water went over his head then he dried himself off. He put the cloth back in his pocket and put on his sunglasses just as the minibus pulled into the car park.

The minibus was a nineteen seventies campervan that had been converted to carry five people plus luggage and dive gear. It was brightly painted in a random pattern and wouldn't have looked out of place at a hippy music festival. Something that could also have been said for the driver. He watched as it rattled its way around the car park and squeezed past the taxis and buses, sounding a horn that sounded like a clown's car as it went.

The vehicle stopped in front of Palmer and the driver jumped out. He was wearing a baggy, tie-dye t-shirt and knee length Bermuda shorts. His sun-bleached hair hung halfway down his back and was tied in a ponytail, as was his beard. His sandals had seen better days and he wore Buddhist beads around his wrist and neck. The only things that didn't look like he'd slept in them were his Ray-Bans.

The driver took off his sunglasses and held his arms out wide. 'Logan.'

Palmer couldn't believe it. He hadn't recognised Scarlett at all. 'What the fuck have you come as?'

'You know me, I always said, when I left, I'd grow a beard and have hair down to my arse.'

Palmer grabbed Scarlett in a bear hug and picked him up. 'God it's good to see you, Brother.'

'You too, man. Now, put me down before I kick your arse.'

'Ha-ha, you'll try.' Palmer let go of Scarlett and put him back on his feet. 'Nice van.'

'Hey, don't take the piss, it does the job. Grab your bag and jump in.'

Palmer picked up his holdall and got in the front passenger seat. Scarlett jumped in behind the wheel and started up the engine.

They headed south, along the narrow main road and across the bridges that linked Bantam to the neighbouring islands. It took them an hour, although it didn't seem that long. They chatted about days gone by, the friends they had, the friends they had lost. They caught up with each other's lives and promised they wouldn't leave it so long next time. In common with veterans around the world, they could go for years without seeing each other but, once they were back together, it was like they had never been apart.

Shortly after they crossed the bridge onto Galang-baru Island, Scarlett turned the van off the main road and, after a few minutes negotiating a rough track through the trees, pulled up outside a small, single story building. Although it was made to look like a beach front banyan hut, the building was made of concrete and looked quite new. Behind it, a gravel footpath wound its way through the thick wall of trees towards the beach and the warm tropical water of the South China Sea.

They got out of the van and Scarlett gestured towards the hut. 'What do you think? We added it as the main reception for guests a few months back. I think it looks cool.'

Palmer looked around at the scenery. 'This is nice, mate.'

'Come in. Meet my wife.'

Palmer followed Scarlett into reception. The inside looked just as much like a beach hut as the outside. A wooden three bladed fan hung from the ceiling and turned slowly, causing the leaflets that were stuck to a cork noticeboard to flutter. Behind the wooden counter, a woman was busy typing on a laptop keyboard. When the two men walked in, she looked up and smiled.

Scarlett held out his hand. 'Logan, this is my wife, Subha.'

Subha walked out from behind the counter. It was only then that Palmer realised she was heavily pregnant. She kissed Palmer on the cheek. 'It's good to finally meet you, Logan. Jerry has spoken about you often.'

Scarlett placed his hand on Subha's bump. 'Who'd have imagined it? I'm going to be a dad.'

Palmer could see how happy Scarlett was. 'When you told me you were getting married, you didn't tell me how much you were punching above your weight.'

Subha looked puzzled. 'Above his weight?'

Scarlett punched Palmer on the shoulder. 'It means you're far too beautiful to be with me.'

Subha took hold of Scarlett's hand. 'He's not punching above his weight, I'm a lucky woman.'

Scarlett kissed her. 'Before I get any more embarrassed, I'm going to show Logan around.'

Subha smiled and went back behind the counter.

The two men left reception and followed the path down to the beach. Palmer got out one of his facecloths and wiped away the sweat again. Even with the heat, this was a place he could enjoy, he could put his feet up and relax. Being next to the sea meant it wasn't as humid and the scenery was breathtaking. Along the edge of the trees was a row of cottages in the same design as the reception building. Each one with its own porch and stretch of decking. A few feet in front of the cottages was a concrete platform with a fire pit built in. A place for communal get togethers at the end of the day.

Palmer was amazed how beautiful it looked. 'This is paradise, man. You've done well for yourself. Maybe I should've come with you.'

'There's always a job here for you, Logan. We're not as big as the resorts on some of the other islands, but we're usually busy during the season.'

'What would I do? I don't know anything about running a business.'

Scarlett smiled. 'Neither do I, mate. It's Subha who runs everything. I just do the diving. If it wasn't for her, I'd have gone bust by now.'

Palmer looked back at reception. 'I'm sorry I didn't make

your wedding, mate. I was in a bad place. Not someone who was good to be around.'

'Don't worry about it. I heard what happened in Geneva, it would have knocked anyone down. I'm glad to see you back on your feet.'

Palmer stepped forward and hugged Scarlett. He hadn't realised how much he had missed him. 'Cheers, mate.'

Scarlett pointed at the cottage closest to reception. 'Come on, let's get you settled in. That one's ours, you can crash out next door. We aren't picking up the next lot of tourists for two days, so we can chill out and have a chat.'

'Sounds good. Lots to catch up on.'

Chapter 24

After a shower and a change of clothes, Palmer sat on the cane chair on his porch and let the view soak in. It was beautiful. He closed his eyes. The sound of the birds in the trees and the waves lapping on the beach was hypnotic. He could feel himself relaxing. Within a few minutes, he was asleep.

He could hear Nathan's voice, shouting, pleading. He sounded like he was in trouble. But Palmer didn't understand, what was Nathan doing here? He saw his face, but he was much younger, maybe five or six. He was holding his arms out. He wanted Palmer to pick him up, to hug him, but Palmer couldn't move. Someone grabbed Nathan and dragged him away.

'Logan. Logan.'

Palmer sat up and screamed.

Scarlett stepped back and held his hand up. 'It's okay, mate. It's me.'

Palmer's heart was racing. The events in his dream were too real for his body to understand the difference. He sat back in the chair, trembling. 'Holy shit.'

'Are you alright, Logan?' Subha was standing next to him with a look of real concern on her face.

Palmer nodded. 'It's just one of my many recurring night-mares. Pops into my head now and then. I'm okay.'

Scarlett put his hand on Palmer's shoulder. 'I know how you feel, I've got a few night demons of my own. I get them less since I moved here though.'

'Well, maybe that's the answer.'

Subha placed a reassuring hand on Palmer's forearm. 'You need to rest. Give your mind time to process everything that's happened in the last couple of years. If you don't, you're heading for a breakdown. I saw it in Jerry.'

'Yeah, I know. I keep telling myself I'll go somewhere and just chill. Perhaps it's time.'

'You're always welcome here. Now, I've made dinner. I'm sure you're hungry.'

Palmer got out of his chair. 'Starving. Lead on.'

The three of them went next door to the Scarlett's cottage and the meal that Subha had prepared, it was incredible. She was an amazing cook and had put on a full spread of dishes, some of which Palmer had never tasted before. As they ate, Palmer regaled Subha with tales of Scarlett's adventures as a young marine. The stupid, and embarrassing, things they had both got up to and the trouble they had ended up in because of it. These were funny stories that could be told at parties. Things that neither of them regretted. Their successes and their epic failures had turned them into the men they were. What neither of them spoke about were the bad times. The memories that came to them at night and woke them up sweating. They kept those stories to themselves, but it was those shared experiences that made them so close.

Palmer sat back in his chair and rubbed his stomach. 'Wow. That was incredible.'

Scarlett finished his last spoon full. 'We don't eat like that every day. I'd be twenty stone in no time. I've gotta keep my boyish physique for the diving.'

Subha finished her bowl. 'I'm glad you liked it, Logan. Maybe you two can cook the next meal.'

Palmer laughed. 'Not a problem. I do a mean corned beef hash or, the vegetarian option, cheese on toast.'

Subha looked puzzled. 'I've no idea what those are.'

The three of them laughed as Palmer tried to explain his signature dishes and where he had picked them up. They talked about the business and about the wedding, about families and baby names. They laughed, chatted, and enjoyed each other's company until, before any of them realised it, hours had passed, and it was dark.

After they had cleared away the plates, Subha brought out a couple of beers then excused herself. 'I'll leave you two to talk. I'm going for a lie down. My back aches a little.'

Scarlett watched her go. He waited for the bedroom door to close then held up his bottle of beer. 'To the boys we lost in Afghan.'

Palmer clinked his bottle against Scarlett's. 'Royals.'

They both took a drink in salute to fallen friends.

Scarlett put his bottle on the table. 'So, Logan, you said in your message that you were looking for some help.'

Palmer checked behind him. 'I don't want to drag you into anything, not now. I'll find another way.'

'Look, we're brothers. If you need me, I'm there. Who are you working for, is it legal?'

'I'm working with the UK authorities, but not working for them. If you know what I mean.'

'Spooks?'

Palmer nodded. 'Something like that. I need to get over to an island called Cantik Island. Quietly, at night, you pick me up after it's over.'

'That doesn't sound too risky. Won't be a problem.'

'I mean it, Jerry. If it hits the fan, you run. You've got too much here to lose.'

Scarlett finished his beer. 'Is it likely to go pear shaped?'

'I've got a weird feeling on this one. Something's not right.'

'Don't worry about me, Logan. I'll make sure I look after myself.'

Palmer drained his bottle. 'Make sure you do. Now, how about another bottle?'

Chapter 25

Nathan Palmer stood at his bedroom window and watched as the two men climbed out of their car and walked towards the front door. The money that had been transferred into his bank account was now sitting on the bed in a canvas bag. One hundred thousand to pay off Harris's debts and keep his mum safe. Even though he was expecting it, the loud knock on the door still made him jump. He waited for the men to enter the house then grabbed the bag and went down the stairs.

Both men looked hardened, uncompromising. They were used to dealing with situations that called for intimidation and violence. That was the reason their boss used them to collect money. No one was going to argue with these two.

One of them, a squat, bald man with a neck like a bull, stood with his back to the front door. He kept his eyes on Nathan as he walked past the door and into the living room. The second man, taller, slimmer, but with scars on his face that gave away his violent past, stood at the fireplace. Nathan's hands were trembling, he had never had to deal with anything like this before. He wished his dad were here. He paused for a moment to steady his nerves then walked into the room.

'Here he is, my son, the money man.' Harris was sitting in a wing-backed chair by the front window. He fidgeted nervously, chewing at his fingernails.

Nathan stared at him. 'I'm not you're son.'

The tall man laughed. 'Looks like you aren't popular with anyone, Connor.'

Nathan threw the canvas bag onto the floor. 'There's a hundred grand in there, take it and leave me and my mum alone.'

'This kid's got more balls than you ever had, Connor.' The tall man picked up the bag and opened it. 'Looks about right. It's not enough though.'

Harris's face visibly paled. 'What? But it was a hundred grand. That's what I was paid. That's what I'm paying back.' He tried to stand up.

The tall man pushed Harris back into his seat. 'I told you to sit down and keep your hands where I can see them.'

Debbie Harris was sitting on the two-seater settee that was up against the wall facing the window. 'You can't expect us to pay more, that's everything we have.'

Tall man shouted to his colleague. 'Smudge, get in here.'

The bald man came into the room and took off his jacket. He looked like he was ready to inflict whatever pain was required to get the job done.

Harris had had enough beatings to know what came next if he didn't play ball. 'We've already paid more than I owed you. What do you want from us?'

Tall man removed a semi-automatic pistol from his jacket and started to screw on a suppressor. 'You were paid to go into Iran and pick up an asset. You decided not to do that, and it caused us lots of problems. We had to pay someone else to do it. The boss reckons that you owe him for the inconvenience and then, of course, there's the interest you've accrued.'

Harris panicked. If he ran, he might make it out of the door. He would be on the run, but at least he would still be alive. He jumped up from his seat and charged for the door. Smudge was ready for it; he took a step to his left and shoulder charged Harris into a sideboard full of glasses and bottles of spirits.

Tall man pointed his pistol at Harris. 'There's the Connor we all know. Trying to save his own skin. Not worried about his family.'

Harris wiped blood from his forehead. 'I can get more money, just give me some time.'

'You've had all the time you're going to get. To be honest, Connor, Wallace wants to use you as an example. Wants to show what'll happen to anyone who thinks of fuckin' him over like you did.'

Debbie stood up. 'Just let my son go.'

Tall man fired twice. Both bullets hit Debbie in the centre of her chest and knocked her back onto the settee. Nathan screamed and ran to her. 'Mum!'

Debbie looked straight at Nathan and tried to lift her hand to his face, but she was losing blood fast. Nathan placed his hands over the wounds and tried to stop the blood, but it was already too late. Debbie's pupils dilated, a trickle of blood ran from her mouth and her breathing stopped.

Nathan held her hand to his mouth and kissed it. His own hands still trembling, tears forming. 'Why? Why did you do that?'

'Just following orders, son.' Tall man aimed at the back of Nathan's head.

Harris held out his hand, palm outwards. 'Wait! I've got something else. I've got information, valuable information.'

Tall man stepped back and lowered his weapon. 'What information would you have that could possibly make a difference?'

'It's Palmer, Logan Palmer.' He pointed at Nathan. 'He told me that he was going away on a job. He gave us the hundred grand. Someone is paying him a lot of money.'

Tall man raised his weapon again. 'Why should I care about that?'

Smudge looked down at Harris. 'Is that the guy you had a fight with, in the car park?'

Harris nodded. 'Yeah, that's him. He told Nathan that he had the hundred grand and there would be more when he came back.'

Smudge stepped over to the tall man. 'I've heard that name before. One of my mates is doing anti-piracy work in Malaysia. Said that a guy called Palmer had joined them, asked if I knew him.'

Tall man fished out his phone. 'Watch them.' He dialled a number and walked out into the hallway.

Harris strained to hear what was being said. This was far from over; he could still be dead within minutes. He looked over at the settee. Nathan was still holding Debbie's hand, talking to her. Nathan turned his head and stared at Harris, tears flowing freely down his face.

Tall man came back into the room. 'It seems you might have some use after all, but don't get any ideas. One step out of line, and you're both dead. Understand?'

Harris nodded.

'Good. Get in the car.'

Chapter 26

Palmer and Scarlett sat at the small table in the cabin of the dive boat. Scarlett used it to take some of his more able scuba tourists a little further afield. It was more comfortable than an inflatable for longer trips and could be used overnight. Six people could be squeezed onto its bunks and kept fed from the well-equipped galley.

Palmer rolled a map out on the table and placed his mug on it to stop it rolling back up. He took out a pencil and pointed at Cantik Island. 'This is our target. The harbour is on this side of the island and it's where the Capricorn docks to unload its weapons deliveries. The newer building at this end of the jetty is the most secure and it's where I reckon they've got Chernov and the warhead.'

'But you don't actually know if they are there at all.'

Palmer tapped the pencil on the table. 'Yeah, that's what London said. They can't do much unless they've got some evidence. It's down to me.'

'What's the plan?'

'It's a volcanic island. It has a coastline of plunging cliffs and sharp rocks. That and the currents in the area make it almost impossible to land anywhere other than the harbour.'

Scarlett looked at a satellite photo of the docks. 'And there's no way to sneak in that way?'

'None. I checked it out when I was there. The harbour mouth is too narrow. They'd see us coming.'

'It doesn't look good, mate. You'd be better off dropping out of a Hercules.'

Palmer slid another satellite photo across the table. 'How would I get out again? Anyway, in the absence of RAF air support and a couple of parachutes, I thought I'd try this.'

Scarlett picked up the picture. It showed the opposite side of the island to the harbour. In an area of thick undergrowth, barely visible from the air, someone had built a jetty jutting out of the rocks. 'You have any intel on this? Is it one of theirs? There could be guards there.'

Riley had already provided Palmer with all the information that she could dig out. It appeared that the jetty had been built during the US occupation of the island. The marines that were based there wanted somewhere they could go and get away from everything for a couple of days. They had cleared an area of trees and built a wooden holiday shack. The jetty allowed them to sail around the coast and not have to tramp across the island. They spent their time there sitting around a campfire, drinking, or fishing from the jetty. It was ideal rest and recuperation.

Scarlett was uneasy about building a mission on the back of incomplete intel. 'It's been there a long time. How do you know it's still useable?'

'The picture shows that there is at least some of the structure left. As long as it's enough to get my feet on, it'll do. Besides, you know what the US Marines are like, they probably built it out of solid steel.'

Scarlett threw the photo back on the table. 'You're gonna

need some weapons.'

'I don't need much. I'm not looking to get involved in any big firefights. Sneak in, do what I can, sneak out. With any luck, I can call in an air strike as I'm leaving.'

Subha shouted up to the boat from the dive schools dock, 'I've made us some lunch.'

Scarlett stood up and stuck his head out of the cabin window. 'Okay, Love, we're on our way.' He sat back down. 'I know a guy a few miles away, an American. Ex-US Marine funnily enough. He has access to some small arms, don't ask how. He sells them on the black market to ex-pats living on the surrounding islands, for security. I'll contact him.'

'Can we trust him?'

Scarlett nodded. 'He's a bit of an eccentric old guy, but he's okay, he's one of us. Rumour has it he's paid by the CIA. Anyway, we won't be telling him what our plan is, and we'll leave as soon as we've got the weapons. We need a day to get in place.'

Chapter 27

Scarlett drove the van away from the coast and along a track that looked like no one had been along it in decades. It was overgrown and full of potholes that Scarlett managed to zig zag his way around. Their progress was slow, but it was better than walking. Palmer didn't know what kind of animals lived in this part of the world, but he was fairly sure some of them were poisonous, or worse.

After forty-five minutes, they pulled up outside a house that looked as abandoned and unused as the road. It had more in common with a garden shed than a house. The paint on its wooden walls was faded and peeling, and the corrugated roof was rusty and had holes here and there. The only indication that anyone lived there was the smoke curling out of its metal chimney and the smell of cooking.

They got out of the van and Scarlett approached the front door. 'Joe, you there?'

Palmer joined Scarlett. 'You sure he's okay?'

'Yeah, he's fine. I spoke to him on the phone. He's got what we need.'

Palmer lowered his voice. 'If he starts playing the banjo, I'm leaving.'

Scarlett started to laugh.

'Who's the joker?' Joe's booming voice came from behind them.

They both spun around, surprised at the sudden appearance of the American. Scarlett held out his hand. 'Joe, this is my mate, Logan. He's an ex-marine too.'

Palmer held out his hand

Joe grunted and looked Palmer up and down. 'Can he be trusted?'

'I'd trust him with my life.'

The American took Palmer's hand. 'Good to meet you, brother.'

'It's good to meet you too, Joe.'

Joe walked towards the house. 'Follow me.'

The part of the house that Joe lived in, unlike the outside, was clean and secure. There was a well-equipped kitchen and a living room with a recliner and a small TV. The bedroom and bathroom were along a short corridor that also led to the cellar. Joe opened the door and took them down the steps.

The cellar had been dug into the volcanic rock under the building and was surprisingly cool. The walls had been painted white and a single naked light bulb hung from the ceiling. The floor was cement and the walls were lined with shelves that were stacked with tinned food and supplies.

Joe moved a pile of tinned beans to one side and slid his hand to the back of the rack. There was a metallic clunk and Joe pulled the whole shelving unit forwards to reveal a door. Behind it was a room no more than six feet square. There wasn't even room for the three of them to fit inside. Joe switched on the light and squeezed in.

Palmer looked over Scarlett's shoulder into the hidden room. There was a gun rack along one wall and a pile of ammunition boxes. The other wall had more shelves, but these ones were stacked with aluminium cases which, Palmer assumed, contained more hi-tech equipment.

Joe picked up a large black holdall and carried it through to the main cellar. 'Everything you asked for is in here. I won't ask what you're going to do with it.'

Scarlett unzipped the bag and checked the contents. 'That's great, Joe. I won't ask where you got it. How much do we owe you?'

Joe closed the door and slid the shelving unit back in place. 'You know that I supply some of this to black ops? If I don't get a good price, they'll want to know where it's gone.'

Palmer pulled a brown envelope out of his back pocket. 'I reckon twenty grand just about covers the kit and your time.'

Joe took the envelope. 'You read my mind.'

The three of them walked back up to the van and put the bag in the back. They shook hands and Scarlett jumped in and started the engine.

Palmer opened his door. 'It was good to meet you, Joe.'

'You too, Logan. Whatever you're doing with that kit, watch your back. You don't want to end up in the middle of a cluster-fuck.'

'I'll do my best, Joe.' He climbed into the van, and they drove away.

Chapter 28

Chernov put down his screwdriver and took off his glasses. He wiped his face with his handkerchief and sat down, relieved.

The door to the lab opened and Wallace walked in. He was happy, buoyant. 'Sergei. My men tell me that you are about to make my day.'

Chernov stood back up. 'Yes, Kane, it is finished, on time I think.'

Wallace stood at the workbench and looked at the device. It was the size of a large suitcase. The black, ruggedized box was made from carbon fibre with aluminium reinforcement along the edges and corners. The open lid exposed a flat steel sheet held in with screws, around its edge, every few centimetres. Built into the surface of the sheet were two lockable switches, an air vent, and a timer. On the left-hand side was, what looked like, a large, hexagonal nut held in with four screws. It measured ten centimetres across and had a D-shaped handle attached to its top. This was the plutonium core, the heart of the device.

'Finished with a day to spare. Well done, Sergei. Very well done.'

'I can instruct you, or one of the men, on the operation of

the device.'

Wallace was running his hand around the outside of the case. 'You're going to be an extraordinarily rich man, once we've planted this.'

'Once we've planted it?'

'Yes, Sergei. You're coming with us. Just in case anything goes wrong.'

Chernov began to think he would never get out of this alive. It would have been better for everyone if he had just refused to build the bomb. They would have killed him, but at least they wouldn't be able to kill thousands. 'Of course, Kane.'

Wallace patted him on the shoulder. 'Don't worry, Sergei. We'll be miles away before the bomb goes off. We can watch it on TV.'

Chapter 29

E dward Lancaster had been summoned to brief a high-level meeting in Whitehall. In attendance were the UK Defence Secretary, the Chief of the Defence Staff, the First Sea Lord, and the Director of Special Forces. On the phone were the Prime Minister, the US Secretary of State, and the Director of the CIA. Each of the attendees sat at the table but, unusually, there were no briefing folders in front of them and no one was taking notes.

Lancaster got to his feet and walked to the large screen to give the briefing. 'Ladies and Gentlemen, thank you for supporting this meeting. This information is of the highest secrecy and cannot be divulged to anyone without express permission. We have done everything possible to keep this operation off the books and have used unofficial assets to get to this position.'

The attendees looked around at each other. They were at a high enough level that they were regularly briefed on the highest security operations. To have an operation that had been going on for weeks without them being aware of it was unusual, almost unheard of.

Lancaster paused for what he had said to sink in then took them through the whole story. The faces around the table were aghast as they realised what the implications were. A viable nuclear device was potentially being built by a rogue actor possibly in the pay of a terrorist organisation. When Lancaster finished, there was a stunned silence.

The Prime Minister's voice crackled over the phone speaker. 'I would like to assure everyone that this isn't a case of MI6 operating on their own. I have been aware of the threat but trusted Edward to keep the details to himself, to ensure security. We are now at a stage where a decision has to be made on how we close this down.'

The Secretary of State's voice was next. 'The US will back you in whatever you decide to do, but you can't just bomb Indonesia. It isn't the Middle east.'

The military officers remained silent. This was the political negotiation that had to be completed before anything else. The Prime Minister spoke again. 'Fully agreed Madam Secretary. We have approached Indonesia, without giving away the full details, to find out their thoughts. They have said that they would be willing to allow a strike on the island but only if there is no other option. Their military must be the first onto the scene and they want full credit for the operation.'

'Of course, and I'm assuming we'll also owe them, big time. That might come back to haunt us but, nevertheless, needs must. We're happy to leave it to you, Prime Minister. Keep us posted.' The Americans left the call.

'I'll leave you to discuss this with the officers in the room, Edward. You have my backing; I will contact the leader of the opposition and give them the full brief.'

'Thank you, Prime Minister.' The call ended and Lancaster looked around the table. 'I'm sure you appreciate why this was kept from you all and why it must retain the utmost secrecy. I will be the link between you and our people on the ground. We need a plan in place to launch a strike if necessary.'

The First Sea Lord raised his hand. 'We could hit the island with Tomahawk cruise missiles fired from one of our attack subs. What's the timeframe on this?'

'Day after tomorrow.'

There was an audible gasp from everyone around the table. The First Sea Lord shook his head. 'A tactical strike on a sovereign country with two days' notice?'

'Sorry to drop it on you like that, Admiral. Is there anything we can do?'

The First Sea Lord opened a folder that he had brought with him to the briefing. 'We have a Trafalgar Class SSN that we can divert towards the South China Sea. It could be within five hundred miles by then. Well within range of a Tomahawk.'

'Does anyone have anything to add or is this the option we are all happy with?'

Everyone around the table nodded their agreement.

'Good. The next time we meet will be as the operation commences. Hopefully, we can get an outcome without the need for a strike. Thank you, everyone.' Lancaster picked up his briefcase and left the room to the sound of low murmurs from the other attendees.

Outside, Victoria Thomson was waiting for Lancaster in the building's reception. 'How did it go?'

'It's a go. We need to get a message to Palmer and give him the details.'

'Okay, I'll get in touch with Anna and arrange it.' She left the building and hailed a cab.

Lancaster made a phone call to his driver then stood at the door. If things went well, this could all be over by the end of the week. *If* things went well.

Chapter 30

Scarlett dropped the anchor of the dive boat over the side and tied it off. He had turned off the navigation lights and moved in as close as he could to the far side of Cantik Island without risking running aground. They were far enough away from any sea lanes and, being such a small craft, the boat didn't have much of a radar footprint. Unless someone was specifically looking for them, it was unlikely that they would be seen.

Palmer loaded their equipment into an inflatable boat and lowered it into the water. Although the inflatable had a small outboard engine, they didn't start it up. There was a danger that the noise could give them away, so they would only use it if things went wrong and they had to leave in a hurry. They pushed themselves away from the side of the dive boat and headed for the island.

After twenty minutes of paddling against the current, the old jetty came into sight. As Palmer had predicted, some of it had indeed been built with steel. Pylons had been hammered into the seabed and connected to the shore by steel support beams. Although the metal had corroded, it was still strong enough to climb onto. Most of the wooden deck of the jetty had rotted but, here and there, some of it still hung on to the metal structure.

Scarlett threw a rope that successfully lassoed one of the metal posts. The two of them pulled the inflatable as close as they could, without risking a puncture, and tied it off. Palmer climbed out of the boat and onto the metal deck support. He tested it for stability then signalled to Scarlett. 'Feels strong enough. Throw me my pack.'

Scarlett picked up the bag and tossed it to Palmer. 'I'll move the dive boat round to the other side of the island and tuck in behind the harbour wall. I'll pick up your radio easily from there. I'll be ready for a fast getaway.'

Palmer opened the bag and took out a 9mm pistol, a press check confirmed there was a round in the chamber. He placed it back into its holster and fastened it around his waist. He slung the small backpack onto his shoulders and fastened the catch across his chest. 'The sun rises at about five thirty, so, if I'm not back by five, you need to get out.'

Scarlett slotted a magazine into an M4 and threw it to Palmer. 'That gives us about eight hours to get this done. Once you get there, leave your radio switched on, I want to know what's going on.'

Palmer applied cam cream to his face then threw the stick to Scarlett. 'I'll be fine. It's just recon. I'm just gathering evidence. I'll check in at midnight.' He turned and clambered the last few feet along the jetty and onto the shore.

Scarlett lost sight of Palmer in a matter of seconds. The undergrowth was thick, and, with a new moon, there was little ambient light. The yomp across the island was going to be hard and Palmer had his work cut out, but Scarlett knew he could handle it.

Palmer made slow progress to begin with. There was a

rudimentary path that led from the jetty but, unused for years, it had mainly been reclaimed by vegetation. The training he had had in the jungles of Belize stood him in good stead though. He knew what to expect of terrain like this, but it didn't make it any easier.

It took two hours of hard, muscle sapping slog to reach the high point of the island. Palmer sat with his back against a rock and emptied one of his water bottles. His clothes were soaked with sweat and his muscles ached, he hadn't done anything that intense for a long time. After a few minutes, he put the empty bottle back in his bag and stood up. At least it was downhill from here.

The forest on this side of the island wasn't as thick as on the way up and he made good time down the slope. It was a few minutes before midnight when he reached the outskirts of the harbour facilities. He picked out his radio and put on the throat mic and earpiece. 'Alpha this is Bravo, radio check, over.'

'Roger, loud and clear, over.'

Palmer was relieved that nothing unforeseen had happened to Scarlett. At least he knew that the dive boat was waiting for him outside the harbour. 'Bravo, in position one, going in, over.'

'Roger, out.'

Palmer tucked the radio into the inside of his jacket and left it switched on. With the throat mic and earpiece in position, he could give Scarlett a running commentary and make sure the boat was where he needed it to be. He could also give him the order to pull out.

There was nothing moving on the docks, the image from his night vision binoculars showed the whole area as an eerie green landscape. The roller doors on the food stores were closed all the way down and the buildings were dark. With no ship in the harbour, there was no need for any provisions to be moved about. The weapons store was equally still, no guards, no movement. Palmer swung his binoculars over to the secure building that he was interested in, there was only one armed sentry stationed outside the door. Palmer assumed the other was taking his turn to carry out the rounds of the perimeter. It didn't look like they had changed their procedure.

Palmer press checked his pistol again, you can never be too careful, and pulled back the charging handle on his M4. He waited for the second sentry to make his way back to the front of the building then, after one last check of the whole area, crawled to the edge of the trees.

Inside the building, Wallace closed the lid on the bomb and fastened the latches. 'We'll be leaving first thing in the morning, Sergei. You'd better get some sleep.'

Chernov didn't feel like sleeping, he felt sick. The enormity of what he had done, what he had built, ran around his head, haunting his dreams. He saw the explosion, the devastation and, worst of all, the corpses. Men, women, children, all dead because of him. How would he be remembered by history? 'Can I go and get some air, Kane?'

'Of course you can, I think you've earned it.' Wallace gestured to two men he had summoned to the lab. 'Take the case and stow it, ready for tomorrow.'

The two men took a handle each, lifted the device off the bench and carried it out of the lab. Chernov knew he had lost his last chance to stop it, Wallace wouldn't risk leaving him alone with the bomb after tonight, there was nothing Chernov could do. He trudged out of the lab and up the concrete steps towards fresh air.

The building was in darkness. The only light came from the cabins Chernov and his bodyguards had been living in for the past few weeks. He carefully made his way across to the main door and left the building.

Chapter 31

P almer saw the door open. He stepped back into the cover of the trees and got his binoculars out. Chernov was talking to the two sentries, asking one of them for a cigarette. Although the image Palmer was watching wasn't sharp, and even with the green glow thrown out by the binoculars, he recognised the Russian. This was the first piece of definitive evidence Palmer had. If Chernov was here, the warhead had to be.

Chernov smoked and chatted with the sentries for fifteen minutes before he went back inside the building. Palmer watched, he had to get inside and find out where the warhead was. There was no way he was going to achieve that without taking out a sentry. Whatever else happened tonight, he was about to become visible.

Palmer waited for one of the sentries to set off on his rounds of the building then crawled out of the trees. He screwed a suppressor onto the barrel of his assault rifle and took aim. Contrary to the portrayal of suppressors in popular films and TV, fitting one doesn't silence the weapon. It reduces the sound of a shot being fired but there is still an audible crack. When Palmer pulled the trigger, the second sentry hurried back to the front to investigate. It was the last thing he would ever do.

Palmer rushed to the front of the building and dragged the bodies of the two sentries out of sight. There was no point spending too much time hiding them, as soon as someone noticed they were not at their post, it would hit the fan anyway.

The door to the building had a keypad lock but, probably because they were at the end of this part of the operation, the guards had become sloppy. The door had been wedged open to allow air to circulate around the inside. Palmer slung his rifle over his shoulder, pulled his nine-mill out of its holster and crept in.

Moving quickly across the floor, Palmer checked for any sign of movement from the two cabins. The one on the left, which he had seen a guard coming out of on his previous visit, was silent and in darkness. These guards were obviously off watch and relying on the security of the building to protect them. The other cabin had a dim light shining through the window. Palmer assumed that that was where Chernov was sleeping. Keeping an eye on the two cabins, Palmer crept over to the hole in the floor and descended the concrete steps.

The passageway at the bottom of the steps was in total darkness. Palmer switched on his small torch and shone it around. The passageway was short and there were only two doors, one on the left and one at the end. He gripped the handle of the door on his left and quietly opened it an inch. That room too was in complete darkness. Palmer pushed open the door and stepped in.

The room he now stood in was the lab. He played the light from his torch around the walls and checked for any sign of Chernov's work. Various tools were stacked up on a row of shelves that ran the full length of the back wall. The workbench in the centre of the room was empty apart from the detritus of something being built. Off cuts of metal, carbon fibre, and instrument wire littered the area. Palmer shone his torch under the bench. There was a large canvas tarpaulin that he pulled to one side. Beneath it were two empty halves of a warhead. At least, what Palmer imagined the warhead would look like. The colour and the markings on the metal casing were typical of military ordnance and, in Palmer's experience, militaries all over the world tended to use similar markings. This, and the presence of Chernov, in Palmer's mind, proved that they had built a device of some kind. But was it a dirty bomb or a full nuclear bomb? There was no way of knowing. All Palmer needed to do was find it.

He left the lab and walked down to the second door at the end of the passageway. It didn't look like a normal, internal door, it looked more like something that would be used on a ship. It had curved corners and a handwheel in the middle that allowed it to be opened. Palmer put his torch in his mouth and gripped the wheel. As he started to turn it, a noise from above stopped him.

Palmer switched off his torch and moved back to the bottom of the steps. He could hear someone moving around inside the building. If they had come in through the main door, they would have noticed the absence of the sentries and raised the alarm. It must be someone who was already inside. If they went out and noticed the sentries weren't there, he was done. He climbed three steps, until his eyes were level with the top, and looked towards the cabins. Chernov was pacing back and forth murmuring to himself. He was in danger of waking up the guards.

Palmer waited until Chernov had passed his position then

quickly climbed the rest of the steps and caught up with him. He grabbed the Russian and clamped his hand over his mouth. Chernov tried to turn around and cry out, but Palmer had hold of him too tight. Palmer waited for him to stop struggling. 'I'm here to stop this. I'm here to help. Do you understand?'

Chernov nodded slowly.

'We are going to walk over to your cabin and go inside. Okay?'

Again, Chernov nodded.

Palmer took his hand away from Chernov's mouth and released him. Chernov made his way back to his quarters with Palmer close behind him. As they reached the first cabin, Palmer paused and listened at the window, but there was no sound, the guards were asleep. The two men tip toed up the two steps outside Chernov's door and went in.

Palmer held his finger up to his mouth. He had to keep Chernov quiet and find out where the device was. He kept his voice low. 'Where is the bomb?'

'I don't know, Wallace had it taken away. He said it was to have it packaged up for the journey.'

'It could be anywhere. Is it still on the island?'

Chernov nodded. 'Until tomorrow. Capricorn is docking in the morning. They must be using the ship to transport it.'

'Do you know what the target is?'

Chernov shrugged. 'I have heard Kane talking, but he has not said. All I know is, it is in Europe.'

Palmer had to get this information back to London. If the target was in Europe, then London was most likely to be it. They had to stop the Capricorn from taking the device away from the island. At least if it were here, they could do something about it. Once it left, it could go anywhere.

Palmer checked through the window of the cabin. There was still no sign of any guards or of the alarm being raised. They were pushing their luck. 'Okay, I'm going to get you away and let the authorities know. If they bomb the island, will the device go off?'

Chernov shook his head. 'The nuclear reaction won't happen unless it is primed first.'

Palmer was relieved. Recovering the bomb was the ideal option but blowing it up suited him just fine. He spoke to Scarlett over the radio link. 'Alpha, this is Bravo. Exfil now. Say again, exfil now. Calling in air support.'

'Roger Bravo. Going silent.'

Palmer removed his throat mic and switched off the radio. If this was about to go wrong, he didn't want anyone tracing the radio back to Scarlett. He coiled the cables around the handset and tucked it under Chernov's mattress.

Chernov put his hand on Palmer's arm. 'If anything happens to me, you must remove the core.'

'What?' Palmer tried to leave.

Chernov gripped his arm tighter. 'Please, it is important. You must unscrew the plutonium core. Without it, only the primary will explode. There will be no nuclear reaction.'

Palmer nodded. 'Okay, okay, I hear you, but we need to get out of here, now. Follow me.'

Palmer opened the cabin door and stepped out. He checked through the window of the other cabin and saw that the two guards were asleep. He signalled to Chernov. 'Okay, follow me. Stay low, stay quiet.'

Chernov put his hand on Palmer's shoulder and followed him. Palmer unholstered his nine-mill and led the way back to the entrance. As they approached the door, he realised it

157

was closed. It was wedged open when he came in, he clearly remembered that. Did he close it on the way in? Had Chernov closed it? Shit. He turned his head. 'Did you close the door?'

Chernov shook his head. 'No, it was open to let air in.'

Palmer stood at the door, listening. All he could hear was his own heart beating. They couldn't stay there, they had to get out. He braced his shoulder against the door, turned the latch and pushed until there was a two-inch gap he could see through. There was no one there. No movement and no noise. 'Stay close.'

Chernov nodded.

Palmer pushed the door open and stepped out.

The fifty thousand volts from the taser that ran through Palmer's body dropped him to the floor, disabling him. He lay on his back shaking violently, his eyes screwed shut, his teeth clenched. Every muscle in his body was contracting and cramping up. Through the pain, he heard a voice. A voice he recognised. 'Hello, Logan. Good to see you again.' Brad raised his boot and kicked Palmer in the face.

Chapter 32

Anna Riley sat in the corner of the room away from the table where the meeting was being held. Even though this wasn't a full COBRA meeting, she had never been in a room with this many heads of departments and organisations before. She didn't even know what she was supposed to do. Did they expect her to stand up and say something? She checked her secure phone, there still hadn't been a message from Palmer.

Vicky Thomson was in a huddle with three other people. Riley knew that one of them was the Director General of MI5, but she didn't know the other two. Thomson turned and smiled, she excused herself from the huddle and walked over to Riley. 'You okay, Anna?'

'I'm fine, I'm just not sure what I'm doing here. I'm a bit out of my depth.'

'You're our link to Palmer. When he sends you a message, we don't want to waste any time.' She patted Riley's arm. 'Don't worry. No one's expecting anything from you. Just relax.'

Riley smiled. 'Thanks, Vicky.'

Edward Lancaster stood at the head of the table, next to a huge monitor. 'Okay, everyone, let's get started.'

Everyone sat in their chairs, filled glasses with water, and shuffled bundles of paper. Lancaster waited for the noise to die down. 'You've all had the briefing and you know what's at stake here. The decision we need to make is, do we go ahead with a strike on the island even though we've had no contact with the operatives on the ground?'

A round faced, grey haired man in his sixties raised his hand. 'What was the last contact we had, and when did we get it?'

Lancaster looked over at Riley. 'Anna's our handler. She received a message that confirmed the asset's intention to enter the facility and gather evidence of Chernov and the warhead at midnight local time.' He checked his watch. 'That was two hours ago. We've had no contact since.'

'And how much time do we have?'

Lancaster pointed at the monitor behind him. 'This is the GLS Capricorn. This is the mode of transport we expect Wallace to use to get the device off the island. It was heading directly south and estimated to arrive at the island's harbour at 06:00 local time. Ninety minutes ago, it did a U-turn and headed north.'

'So, something has changed. Maybe they ferried the device out to the Capricorn, so it didn't need to go into the harbour. Where is it now?'

'The Indonesian Marines assaulted it half an hour ago. There's nothing on board.'

A woman in her fifties looked up from the doodle she had been drawing on her folder. 'We still don't have any evidence that there is a nuclear device on that island.'

'That's correct, but the balance of probabilities points strongly towards it. One thing the Indonesians did tell us is that the team of mercenaries that would normally be on the ship weren't there. The crew said that they were dropped off at the island two days ago.'

'So, they've beefed up their security for some reason. They're preparing for something.'

Lancaster brought up the information that Palmer had provided them with. 'At the very least, we have an organisation that is using this island as a staging post for a worldwide weapons smuggling operation. The increase in security points to something big happening, soon. There's a particularly good chance that that something involves a nuclear device.'

The round faced man butted in. 'I don't see that we have any option here. We use the smuggling operation as a cover and take them out. Link them to as many terrorist organisations as we can, and don't mention the nuke.'

The other attendees nodded.

Lancaster switched off the monitor. 'Okay, those of us who are attending the full COBRA meeting have twenty minutes to get there. Everyone else, thank you for your time.'

The room began to empty. Riley walked over to Lancaster. 'Excuse me, Sir.'

'Hello, Anna. Really good work on this, we need to talk later, but now I need to go.'

Riley stepped in front of him. 'But what about Logan? What happens to him when they hit the island?'

Lancaster's head dropped. 'Hopefully, he knows what's coming and he gets clear, but we can't risk mission security to warn him. You must understand that, Anna. It's important.' He sighed. 'Sometimes bad things happen, and good people get hurt. It's the business we're in. I have to go. We'll talk soon.'

Lancaster left. Vicky Thomson gestured to Riley. 'I'll call you.'

Riley nodded and smiled. She was the only person left in the room. She put her phone in her pocket and walked out.

Chapter 33

Palmer's eyes flickered open, he couldn't see anything. It took him a minute to realise that he had a black canvas bag on his head. He was sitting on, what felt like, a wooden chair, but couldn't move. His arms were tied behind his back and his ankles were fastened to the legs of the chair. He slowly moved as much as he could to check for injuries, he couldn't feel any spots of sharp pain, no broken bones, or dislocated joints. He moved his head, his jaw ached, and he could taste blood. He ran his tongue around his teeth, one of them felt like it was cracked. Whatever they had done to him so far, it hadn't done any real damage, yet. He expected that to change.

He stayed still, listening. He could sense people moving around him, but no one was saying anything. If they intended to torture him, this would be the first step, psychological torture. They wanted him to feel isolated, it heightened the fear. This wasn't Brad's style though. Palmer imagined him standing off to one side polishing his pliers or sharpening a knife.

The canvas bag was roughly ripped from Palmer's head and a bright light shone in his face. He squinted, unable to open his eyes. He tried to turn away from the light, but it was all around him. His mouth was dry, and his heart pounded.

'Who are you working for?'

Palmer couldn't work out what direction the voice was coming from. A punch crashed into his solar plexus followed by one to his jaw. He doubled over but someone grabbed his hair and pulled him back up.

'Who are you working for?'

Palmer's senses were all working in overdrive, trying to get some information to explain the assault his body was going through. More punches landed, more questions. Then, it stopped.

Palmer gasped for breath and blinked his eyes. The floodlights that surrounded him were switched off and moved away. He could now see Wallace standing in front of him. 'That's enough of that. Logan's a big tough guy. He's not going to tell us what we need to know because we beat him up.'

Palmer wasn't too sure. Much more of that treatment and he might have broken.

Wallace bent over. His mouth close to Palmer. 'We don't want to hurt you, Logan. Just tell us who you're working for, and we'll let you go.'

Palmer doubted that too. He was quite sure Brad wanted to hurt him.

Wallace shouted to one of the men. 'Get him a drink.'

One of the guards handed Wallace a plastic bottle. He unscrewed the top and held it to Palmer's lips. 'There we go, Logan. See, we aren't all bad. You were one of us after all.'

Palmer took a mouthful. Here we go, we've had bad cop, this must be good cop. 'How about untying me.' Palmer didn't think there was any chance of that, but it was worth a try.

'Oh, I don't think so. Not just yet. Now, Logan, who are you working for?'

Palmer cleared his throat and whispered. Wallace moved his ear closer to Palmer. 'What was that.'

Palmer shouted, 'I said go fuck yourself!'

Wallace punched him in the side of the head. 'Right, tip him back.'

Two men grabbed Palmer's shoulders and tipped him backwards. A third covered his face with a towel. The water that was poured over him filled his nose and mouth. He couldn't breathe. The water ran down his throat and his lungs screamed for air. He had never been waterboarded before, but they were right about how effective it was.

The towel was pulled off his face and he was pushed upright again. 'Who are you working for?'

'Fuck you.'

Palmer was tipped back over. The waterboarding carried on. Another three rounds of simulated drowning followed by more questions. He was pushed back up again, coughing and spluttering. He vomited water and gasped for breath.

Two of the men were laughing. 'I told you it wouldn't work. You owe me a beer.'

Palmer was close to breaking, but he got the sense that that wasn't what they wanted. He felt like they already knew the answer, this was just their idea of fun. It was at that point that he knew for certain he was going to die.

Brad stepped forward. He pulled a large combat knife from a sheath that was attached to his leg. 'Let me have a go. I'll break him. I could cut his fingers off one at a time, or his balls.'

There was a ripple of laughter around Palmer. Wallace bent over and looked into Palmer's eyes. 'I don't think that will work, Brad. I don't think Logan gives a shit what happens to him. I think he's realised that we're going to kill him.'

Brad ran the edge of the knife along the scar on Palmer's arm. 'This the one you picked up in Geneva, Logan? Maybe if I'd aimed a little bit further left, I could have saved us all this trouble.'

'What the fuck are you talking about?'

Brad grinned. 'Oh yeah, that's right, you don't know. Do you? It was me that killed your girlfriend in Geneva. Kind of a job interview, to prove I was up to it. Went quite well I think.'

Palmer tried to headbutt Brad. 'Bastard!'

'Oh, I think we've hit a bit of a raw nerve their boys. Maybe he thinks more of other people than he does of himself.' He waved over to Quinn. 'Bring her in.'

Quinn walked around in the shadows dragging something behind him. Palmer couldn't quite make out what it was. Then, as Quinn reached the light, Palmer realised what he was looking at.

Finn was in a terrible state. Her clothes were ripped and bloodied, her face bruised and one eye swollen. Blood ran from her nose and one corner of her mouth. Quinn dumped her in front of Palmer.

'Ruby, Ruby! Jesus, what the fuck have you done to her.'

Brad looked down at Finn. 'Plenty, and there's more to come. She's going to die, just a question of when.'

Palmer looked at Wallace. 'Are you happy with these animals you piece of shit?'

Wallace reached down and stroked Finn's hair. 'She took my money, and she turned on us, she'll get exactly what she deserves. People keep dying around you, don't they, Logan?'

'I swear I'm gonna make you pay for this.'

'Yeah, okay. You keep telling yourself that.' Wallace wheeled a trolly in front of Palmer and opened the laptop that sat on top of it. 'Isn't modern technology wonderful? Here we are in the South China Sea, and yet we can see what's happening all the way back in England.'

Palmer looked at the image on the laptop, it showed the feed from a webcam. The image jerked about as someone set it up on a table. As the picture cleared, Palmer could see that it showed the inside of an industrial building. In front of the camera was a man wearing a hood. A rope had been placed around his neck and attached to a chain hoist that hung from a girder in the roof. Next to him was another man who held the electronic controls for the winch. Palmer leaned forward; it was Connor Harris.

Palmer looked at Wallace. 'What's going on?'

Wallace spoke into the laptop's microphone. 'If you'll do the honours, please, Connor.'

Palmer watched in horror as Harris removed the hood from the other man's head. Nathan stared back at the screen, blinking. His face had blood on it and his nose looked broken. 'Dad, Dad, they killed Mum. They...'

As he spoke, Harris pressed the button to raise the hoist. The rope around Nathan's neck tightened and he was lifted off his feet. His body twisted as he kicked air.

'Let him go. I'll tell you what you want. He hasn't done anything.'

Wallace nodded at the screen. Harris lowered the winch and loosened the rope around Nathan's neck.

Palmer sneered at Harris. 'He's your stepson for Christ's sake. I'm gonna fucking kill you. You have my promise on that.'

Nathan was coughing, tears and snot running down his face.

Wallace stood in front of the screen. 'Who are you working for?'

Palmer tried to see around Wallace to the screen but couldn't. He lowered his head. 'MI6. I'm working for MI6.'

'Well, well, MI6, we have gone up in the world. How much do they know?'

'They know that Chernov is alive and that a warhead is missing. They sent me here to find out if they were related. To find out if they were here.'

Wallace stepped away from the screen. 'There, that wasn't difficult. Was it?'

Palmer nodded at the screen. 'You've got what you wanted, Now, let him go.'

'Got what I wanted? You caused me a great deal of trouble, Logan. That's going to cost me a lot of money, and I really don't like that.'

Palmer started to panic. Nathan was staring into the camera, his eyes pleading. Palmer wanted to hold him, to tell him it was going to be alright. 'It's okay Nathan, I'm here.' He looked at Wallace. 'I've got money, you can have it. Let him go.'

Wallace looked at the laptop then back to Palmer. 'Let's not forget the betrayal. I value loyalty, and you just don't have that. There are repercussions for every action.'

Palmer knew that nothing he said was going to make any difference. 'Loyalty? After Geneva? Fuck you.'

Wallace bent over and spoke to the laptop. 'Mr Harris.' He looked at Palmer then back to the screen. 'Do it.'

Harris pressed the green button that activated the hoist then walked away.

Palmer stared at the screen. Tears ran down his face as he watched. Nathan kicked and struggled fighting to stay alive, but the kicks grew weaker, and the struggle slowed until, finally, the inevitable happened, and Nathan stopped moving. Palmer's breathing was deep and harsh, his teeth clenched as he glared at Wallace. His scream, when it came, was full of anger and hate. A scream of anguish from a man who had lost everything. The scream reverberated around the building and echoed off the walls. Palmer was finally broken.

Chapter 34

Anna Riley sat in her flat, a half empty bottle of Vodka on the table in front of her. She couldn't get Palmer's face out of her head. She had sent him into a situation where he was going to die. Lancaster explained to her that it was the business they were in, and she was sure that Palmer accepted the risk as an occupational hazard, but she was finding it hard to deal with.

She looked at her phone screen. Thomson's message told her that the decision to destroy the island had been made, the order sent. Now, it was just a matter of time. She took another drink from her glass. It was no good, she couldn't do it. She couldn't abandon Palmer to his fate, just another soldier sacrificed for the greater good, collateral damage. She typed a message into her phone and added Palmer's number. She knew it was wrong, she knew she was risking the operation, but she couldn't help it. She pressed send and threw her phone onto the table.

At that same moment, seven thousand miles away, silently gliding along below the waves of the Indian Ocean, a Royal Navy Astute Class submarine fired four Tomahawk cruise missiles. The flight time to Cantik Island was a little more than an hour. The destruction of the island was unstoppable.

Chapter 35

The river of tears and snot that ran down Palmer's face had stopped. The blood had dried. He still sat, tied to the chair, head bowed. Physically silent and still, but his mind still screaming, the image of Nathan playing over and over in his head.

Finn lay on the floor in front of him, her wrists tied to her ankles, forcing her into a foetal position. She shuffled round until she was facing Palmer. 'Logan. Logan.'

There was no response from Palmer, no reaction at all. Finn looked over at the guard Wallace had left to watch them. He was standing at the door, smoking, not paying attention. Finn raised her voice as much as she dared. 'Logan. For fuck's sake, Logan. We've got to get out of here. When Wallace and Brad come back, they're going to kill us. I'm bettin' Brad wants to take his time. Logan.'

Palmer raised his head, his eyes bloodshot and vacant. His mouth opened as if to say something, but then silently closed. Without saying anything, his chin dropped to his chest, and he retreated back into his nightmare.

The guard at the door put out his cigarette and rushed back into the room just as Wallace came in with Brad and a handful of the other guards in tow. 'Well, well, well, how are our lovely couple doing, comfortable?'

Finn rolled over to face him. 'Fuck you, Wallace.'

'Now, now, Ruby, we're all old friends here. There's no need for that.' He looked at Palmer. 'What about you, Logan, you're strangely quiet.'

Brad laughed and pointed at his head. 'I don't think his elevator goes all the way to the penthouse anymore.'

The other guards joined in with his joke, one of them shouting to Palmer. 'I thought you were supposed to be a tough guy.'

Wallace raised his hands. 'Come on boys, have a heart. He's had a death in the family.'

Another ripple of laughter spread around the guards. Brad turned to them all with a smile.

Palmer lifted his head and stared at Wallace. It was a threatening, cold, soulless stare that visibly disturbed Wallace. He lowered his gaze, unable to look into Palmer's eyes anymore.

Brad lifted a phone out of his pocket, it was Palmer's. He swiped the screen then walked over to Wallace. 'We need to go.'

'What is it?'

Brad showed Wallace the screen. Riley's message, the warning about the Tomahawk strike, reflected off his eyes. He looked back at Brad and nodded. 'Okay.'

Brad gestured to Quinn and Chernov's two bodyguards then pointed towards the concrete steps. It was obviously something that had been planned already. The three men left the group and headed for the steps without any comment to the others. They knew exactly what they were supposed to do next. Brad threw the phone away and walked over to the cabins.

Finn saw Chernov watching the events from the window of his accommodation. She doubted very much that Wallace had told him anything like this was going to happen. Palmer had told her that Chernov's family were killed in a car crash, that's why he had felt free to defect to the west. He must have known exactly what Palmer was feeling.

Brad kicked open the door and shouted at Chernov. 'Get your stuff, we're leaving.'

Chernov appeared at the door. His face was white, and he was carrying a small bag. He didn't look like he wanted to go anywhere with them, but he did as he was told. At least he was getting out alive, for now anyway. He grabbed his jacket from behind the door and followed Brad down the steps.

Wallace, still seemingly unable to look at Palmer, focused on Finn. 'Well, I'd love to stick around and chat, but I've got more important things to get on with. I'd say, "see you later", but, trust me, this is goodbye.' He looked around at the guards that were staying. 'I want these two taken care of. I want them to suffer. Enjoy yourself, boys.' Wallace turned and headed for the steps.

As soon as he had gone, one of the guards turned to the others. 'I don't know about you lot, but I need a drink first.' He pointed over his shoulder at Palmer and Finn. 'These two aren't goin' anywhere. We can deal with them later.'

Another of the guards stared at Finn, smiling. 'Might as well enjoy ourselves, you heard what Wallace said.'

Five of the guards left and crawled back under whichever stone they normally spent their evenings drinking under. Only one remained, the one that had been watching over them earlier. He went back to his position at the door and lit another cigarette. He didn't look happy.

Finn rolled back over to face Palmer. 'Logan.'

This time Palmer looked straight at her. His eyes were no longer vacant, but there was something in them that hadn't been there before, something dark and menacing. 'Are you okay, Ruby?'

Finn exhaled. 'Don't worry about me. It's just cuts and bruises. I thought you were never going to snap out of it.'

Palmer took a deep breath. 'I just needed to shut down for a while and process what happened to Nathan.'

'I'm sorry, Logan.'

Palmer shook his head slowly. 'Nothing for you to be sorry about.' He nodded towards the guard at the door. 'They'll be sorry, all of them, especially Wallace and Brad. I'll make sure of it.'

Finn tried to free her hands, but it was no use. 'What do we do now?'

'We find a way out of here, then we cut those fuckers up into small pieces.'

Finn was relieved to have Palmer back. Still broken, but back. 'I'm doing Brad.'

'He's all yours.' He looked around them, there was nothing that would help. 'Got any ideas?'

Chapter 36

Scarlett stepped out from behind the door and shot the guard in the forehead. He dived over the crumpled body and through the entrance into the building. As he landed, he rolled and came up onto his knees, sweeping the building, ready to kill anyone in his way.

Palmer looked at Finn. 'Oh good, it's the cavalry.'

Scarlett hurried over to them. 'I didn't have to do this. I should be sitting on a beach with my feet up.'

'No, really, we're impressed. I'm not sure about the dive and roll though. A bit over dramatic for me, but I suppose it worked.'

'Fuck you, Palmer.'

Palmer grinned. A grin that wasn't matched by his eyes, as if his body was just going through the motions. 'Ruby, this is my best friend and sidekick Jerry Scarlett.'

Scarlett nodded to Finn. 'Happy to meet you. Now, let's get the fuck out of here.' He pulled his dive knife, from the sheath strapped to his lower leg, and cut the ropes that secured them both. 'Where are the bad guys, Logan?'

'Half of them left in a hurry, down the steps. There was a message on my phone, panicked them a bit.'

'Air strike?'

'They haven't heard from me in a while, it would make sense.'

Finn stood up and rubbed her legs, encouraging blood flow, getting rid of the numbness that the ropes had caused. 'You bring any other weapons?'

Scarlett unholstered his sidearm and passed it to her. 'Just that. We can take the assault rifle from the mess by the door, but it doesn't give us much.'

Palmer took Scarlett's knife and slid it into his belt. 'It'll have to do. Fast and quiet. No hesitation if we bump into anyone, okay?'

Scarlett and Finn both nodded.

'Let's go.'

They left the building and crouched by the open door, listening for any sign of movement. There was nothing. Palmer crawled to the corner, looked around, then gave the all-clear. 'Where's the boat, Jerry?'

'I've anchored it just on the other side of the harbour wall. If we get across the jetty and into the water, we should be good to go.'

Palmer picked up the guard's weapon and checked it. He had one magazine of ammunition. Not enough if it kicked off. 'I'll go first. If there's any trouble, you two get out another way. Ruby, you next. Jerry, you go last. I want to make sure that we're all clear before you make a run.'

They agreed and checked their weapons.

Palmer crept out onto the jetty. There were several empty crates that he could hide behind as he made his way to the water's edge. He crawled to the first one and looked back. One hundred metres from where Scarlett and Finn were crouching, there was a light on in one of the other buildings. It must be where the guards were spending their nights. He signalled a warning to the other two then made his way to the second crate.

Within ten minutes, Palmer had reached a large cable drum at the edge of the jetty. The ladder down to the water was only a few feet away. He checked the guards' building then waved a signal to the others.

Finn kept low, slithering the thirty feet across to the final crate. After looking up at Palmer for the final go ahead, she crawled the last twenty feet to the cable drum.

Palmer, once again, checked the other building, then waved all clear to Scarlett.

Military operations, no matter how well planned, can be undone by bad luck. This part of the operation was as far away from well planned as it's possible to get, and their luck sucked. When Scarlett reached the halfway point between the last two crates, the door to the other building opened and a guard came out.

Scarlett froze, but the light from the doorway lit up the area. Palmer and Finn held their breath, praying that the guard would turn round and go back to his drinking. Unfortunately for them, this guard was the only one who wasn't drinking. He spotted Scarlett within seconds and took aim at him.

Palmer levelled his assault rifle and fired two aimed shots, knocking the man back through the door. The remaining four guards burst out of the doorway, firing indiscriminately into the shadows. Palmer and Finn returned fire, dropping another two. At that moment, Scarlett stood up and ran. Bullets kicked up dust around him as he closed in on the cable drum. Palmer was out of ammunition and threw his rifle away. Finn killed another guard but now she was out too. The final guard

177

dropped to his knee, took aim, and shot Scarlett in the back.

Palmer let out a scream and ran towards the open doorway. The guard fired off two rounds before he was empty. He franticly checked for another magazine, finding one in his jacket pocket. But, by the time he had it slammed into place and cocked his weapon, Palmer was on him. The dive knife glistened in the light as Palmer brought it up in an arc into the man's solar plexus. The Guard fell backwards as Palmer struck again, burying the eight-inch blade to the hilt. The man started to go limp, but Palmer wasn't done. His anger, his rage, his guilt was overwhelming. He drove the knife in again and again.

Finn pulled open Scarlett's Jacket. The bullet had gone right through him. She took off her t-shirt and tore it into strips, packing the wound. Scarlett's breathing was rasping. Blood bubbled around his nose and mouth as he passed into unconsciousness. Finn looked across to Palmer. 'Logan! Help me!'

Palmer stopped his attack, the guard long since dead. He stood over the body, blood dripping from the blade of the dive knife. He turned and looked at Finn. Framed in the light from the doorway, he looked like something out of a horror film.

Finn shouted again, 'Logan!'

Palmer dropped the knife and sprinted across the jetty. He knelt next to Scarlett. His breathing was shallow, he was in a bad way. Palmer looked at Finn, pleading. 'We have to get him home.'

Finn tied off the makeshift bandage she had applied. 'Help me lift him up. Get him to the boat.'

Palmer grabbed Scarlett under the arms then lifted him onto his shoulders. When he stood up, he could just make out the shape of the boat on the other side of the harbour wall. He patted Scarlett's leg. 'Stick with me, mate. I'll get us out of here.'

The sound of the first Tomahawk's rocket engine was deafening as it flew over their heads and obliterated the building behind them. The ball of flame seemed to engulf the whole island. Finn was blown off her feet and into the water. Palmer landed face down, Scarlett landing on his back. Broken glass and concrete began to fall like rain as Palmer crawled for the edge of the jetty, dragging his friend behind him. When he reached the end of the concrete, he grabbed Scarlett in a bear hug and rolled off the edge, into the water.

Chapter 37

The great and the good of the UK establishment sat in a darkened COBRA meeting room and watched the live footage from the satellite. The glow from the screen lit up their faces as each Tomahawk slammed into the island. One after another, the buildings were destroyed. Each hit blew huge chunks of wreckage out into the harbour and consumed the surrounding trees in fire.

Edward Lancaster sat at the back of the room with Vicky Thomson. He took no pleasure in any of this. He understood the need and, when the inevitable wash-up came, this operation would be classed as a success. That didn't make it any easier to swallow. They had just bombed an island where they knew one of their assets was. Either he was dead already or there was the possibility that they had just killed one of their own. Lancaster knew that Anna Riley was struggling with it. He hadn't been able to contact her since the meeting earlier. That was worrying him.

He leaned across to Thomson. 'First chance you get, check on Anna. Get her any help she needs. She's one of us now.'

Thomson nodded. 'I'll get on it as soon as we're out of this.'

The Chief of the Defence Staff switched off the monitor and turned on the lights. 'That, Ladies and Gentlemen, is what a successful Tomahawk strike looks like.'

The others in the room all agreed, turning to each other, shaking hands, and slapping backs. One of the ministers actually had a smile on his face. 'It's really quite impressive.'

Lancaster was furious. None of these people had ever been on the frontline in a hot war. None of them knew what it was like to watch their friends die. He looked back at Thomson. 'You don't need to stay for this shit.'

Thomson nodded silently, her lips pursed and her eyes moist. She grabbed her bag and left them to their celebrations.

Chapter 38

When Palmer came to, it was daylight, and Finn was navigating their way back to Galang-baru. Her own wounds hadn't slowed her down at all. Her face was no longer as bloody, and she had found some clean clothes to put on, but she must have been in some pain.

Scarlett was stable. It was lucky that the boat had to carry a fully equipped medical kit in case of a shark attack. It even had a fridge of saline and plasma to treat blood loss. He wasn't out of the woods yet, but he was alive. He had Finn to thank for that, she had been unbelievable.

When Palmer and Scarlett had hit the water like two sacks of King Edwards, Finn had kept Scarlett afloat while Palmer recovered. They stayed under the shelter of the Jetty while the rest of the missiles hit their targets and lumps of twisted metal, concrete and wood fell all around them. Once it was clear, Palmer managed to find a large plank of wood that had been blown into the harbour. Between them, they got Scarlett onto it and used it like a raft to get them to the dive boat.

By that point, Palmer was running on adrenaline. The previous twenty-four hours had drained him completely. The physical exertion, the torture, and the emotional trauma of seeing Nathan die caught up with him. The two of them managed to get Scarlett onto the boat before Palmer crashed, but after that, it was all Finn.

Once they were back at Galang-baru, they got Scarlett to the nearest hospital. The injuries were easy to explain, they just passed it off as a pirate attack. All three of them needed some treatment and their story was believable. Finn and Palmer gave fake names and, even if it hadn't, the local police didn't seem interested in looking for any other explanations. Perhaps they didn't want a story about foreign tourists being attacked by pirates hitting the headlines. They just wanted to keep it quiet.

Palmer's body ached all over, even after a week. The bruises on his face and body were now turning a greenish yellow and his swollen eye had opened enough for him to get his vision back. Most of the cuts and scrapes he had suffered were minor but two of the deeper ones had to be stitched. Something else he had to thank Finn for.

Scarlett was still in hospital. The doctors said his injuries were no longer life threatening and wouldn't cause any long-term disability, but he would require plenty of treatment and some physiotherapy. That came as no surprise to Palmer. He had seen lots of gunshot wounds in his time, and he knew just how bad it was.

Subha wasn't happy at all, who could blame her? They went out on an apparent dive trip and Jerry came back with a bullet hole in his back. Subha was staying in a hotel near the hospital while they recovered at the dive school. She made it clear that she blamed Palmer, but he was Scarlett's friend, so he could stay. Palmer had a great deal of apologising to do to try and mend his relationship with her.

Palmer got out of bed and stood under the shower for thirty minutes. There were still clots of dried blood dropping off him every time he washed. He put on some clean shorts and a t-shirt and wandered over to the cottage Finn was using. He climbed the three wooden steps and knocked on the bamboo door.

'Come in, Logan.' Finn was already dressed and had made coffee. She handed him a bowl with freshly cut fruit in it. 'Breakfast.'

She was much more capable than he was. 'Thanks. How do you do it?'

'Do what?'

'After all the shit that happened, you act like it's nothing. If it wasn't for the bruises on your face, everyone would just assume you were a tourist.'

Finn gestured to her face. 'This? It isn't the first time I've been beaten up by a man. My Dad had a mean right hook that he tried out on me and my mum on a weekly basis. Every time he had enough money to get pissed.'

Palmer stirred his bowl of fruit. He wasn't used to all this healthy eating. 'It wasn't just a beating though, was it?'

Finn put her spoon down. 'Whatever happened, happened. There's no changing that. All I can do is push it out of my mind for now. All I want is some time in a room with Brad. Once that's done, there'll be enough time for therapy.'

'I'm going after Wallace, that's all I care about. But I owe you my life, Jerry does too. Whatever help you need, I'll be there.'

'We've got a common goal now, Logan. Wherever they are, you can bet they're together. That little shit can't do anything on his own. Don't forget the bomb.'

184

Palmer was totally focused on tracking down Wallace. If that led them to the bomb, he would do everything necessary to prevent it from going off. The problem was, what would he do if going after the bomb meant losing Wallace? Could he push his own rage and desire for vengeance to one side for the greater good?

He looked at Finn, she had given enough. 'I'm tied up in this because I was paid to get involved, you weren't. Wherever this device is, whatever the target is, you need to be as far away as possible when it goes off. This isn't your fight. Getting Brad can wait.'

'I know you don't see it like this, Logan, but it's all wrapped up together. If we get Wallace, we get Brad. When we get them, we get the bomb. You can't do one without the other. I'm tied up in this no matter what.'

Deep down, Palmer was happy that Finn would be there to help him, but he didn't want to be responsible for her getting hurt. He was already worried about Riley. He hadn't been able to get in touch with her since before the island. She had tried to warn him about the strike. That was a risk she didn't need to take.

Palmer finished his fruit and drained his coffee cup. 'I reckon we've got another week for the bruises to fade enough to not look suspicious, then we can travel. I've got a contact I can use to get you some ID, I've got a fake passport already.'

'Fake passport, dodgy contacts, you're what my grand-mother used to refer to as, "the wrong sort".'

'Always pays to plan ahead, you never know when a fake passport might come in handy.'

Finn pretended to write a note on her hand. 'I'll make a note of that for future reference.'

'You're sure Brad said he was planning to go to London?'

Finn nodded. 'He kept banging on about how much British women like an American accent.'

'Okay, that's where we'll start. Just so you know, this isn't just about the warhead anymore. For me, it's personal. I'll keep tracking them down even if it takes years.'

'That's okay by me. I didn't have much else planned anyway. I appear to be unemployed.'

Chapter 39

Vicky Thomson sat on a bench in the garden of Yardley Manor. It was a private medical facility that the security services used to treat their operatives. The ones who cracked under the pressure or came back from foreign operations mentally and physically scarred. Thomson had spent months here herself, recovering from the trauma of Afghanistan. She owed the people here her sanity. It was the first place she thought of when she found Riley.

When Thomson left the COBRA meeting, she went straight to Riley's flat. She had tried to contact her by phone all the way there but with no success. She stood outside the flat and banged on the door but had no joy. It was when she tried Riley's phone one more time, and could hear it ringing inside the flat, that she kicked in the door.

Riley was lying face down in the middle of the room. An empty bottle of vodka lay in a pool of vomit next to her head, and a myriad of coloured pills were strewn across the table. Thomson phoned the ambulance without hesitation, then turned her over and checked her vitals, she wasn't breathing. Thomson cleared Riley's airway then carried out CPR until the paramedics arrived and took her away.

The first twenty-four hours were touch and go as doctors

tried to figure out how many of which type of pill she had washed down with the vodka. After two days, she was conscious again and out of immediate danger, but Thomson knew that wouldn't be the end of it. She needed help.

It was Lancaster who pulled the strings to get her admitted to Yardley Manor, that was four weeks ago. Physically, she recovered quite quickly. The pills hadn't done any lasting damage and she was back on her feet after a few days. Mentally, she needed much more work. The sessions that she had every day touched on all parts of her life. The loss of her sister, her descent into alcohol abuse, and, just to round things off, her belief that she had killed Palmer. The psychiatrists said she was okay to be discharged for now, but would have to come back for further sessions, probably for years. All Lancaster and Thomson could do was be there for her. Try and keep her busy and make sure she didn't have too much time to dwell on the past. Lancaster was keen to get her back in the game. She had hacking skills that could be extremely useful. Thomson wasn't sure.

The front door of the Manor opened, and Riley came out. She pulled her collar up against the chill wind and tucked her scarf in. She walked down the long flight of stone steps that led from the door to the garden and stepped onto the cinder path.

Thomson stood and walked over to meet her. 'Good morning, Anna.'

Riley threw her arms around Thomson. 'It's great to be out. It feels so good to be going home.'

Thomson still wasn't sure that this was the best option. She had had the flat cleaned up and had even paid for it to be decorated so that Riley would have somewhere fresh to go back to once she felt ready. Thomson didn't think she was ready. 'Are you sure you want to go back to your flat? You can always come and stay with me for a while. I've got plenty of room and would enjoy the company.'

Riley shook her head. 'I've got to face it sooner or later, but thanks anyway. Thank you for everything.'

'I just don't want you slipping back into any old habits.'

'I won't, I know where that path leads now. It isn't somewhere I want to go anymore. I know I'm not better yet, but I'm better than I've been for a long time. Besides, I've got a real friend I can talk to now. It's like having a big sister again.'

Thomson squeezed Riley's hand. She had seen a lot of her younger self in Riley and was glad she had got to the flat in time. 'Any time you need me, you know where I am. Now, I've got a car waiting for you. Go home and relax, get used to being there again. I'll see you on Monday.'

Chapter 40

When Riley left the Manor, she already knew she wouldn't be relaxing over the weekend, she needed to find Palmer. She couldn't accept that he was dead. The thought that, somewhere, he was suffering, inhabited her dreams. She had to help him.

Riley spent a full three days, trawling through information. Some of it she had approved access to, some of it she didn't, but that wasn't going to stop her. Her skills were developed enough for her to gain access to just about anything.

The bank account that Palmer had given her to pay money into was only being used to accept payments. The money was never in there for long. Palmer paid it out again to another account that he used for day-to-day expenses. There was nothing unusual in that, but there were also several wire transfers to the account of a company based in the Cayman Islands. From there, money was paid to hundreds of accounts all over the world. It was a shell company that offered people the ability to disguise the source of their finances. It made it almost impossible to track, well, for anyone else it would have been almost impossible. Riley soon had the details of the accounts that were being paid form the Cayman's account and set to work checking them out.

She had to find out which name Palmer was using to hide his money. A lot of the accounts could be discounted for now as they were corporations or hadn't had any payments for a few years. That gave her a list of names that she was quite sure were all fake. She compared the names against Palmer's family records and, within an hour, had a hit.

One of the names was Harlon James. Riley discovered that he was a cousin of Palmer's who was the same age as him, they had probably played together as kids. Riley also found a death certificate for James. He had died when he was fifteen, run over by a truck outside his school. A bit more digging and Riley had a national security card, driving licence, and passport all issued years after James had died. It was perfect. Palmer had assumed Harlon James's identity as a cover.

Riley knew that Palmer had been involved in black ops and there were parts of his history that were inaccessible even to her. For reasons that only Palmer knew, he had set up a fake identity for himself when he was twenty-four. He obtained all the documentation that a normal person would have and used it to resurrect his cousin. He took a driving test in his name, set himself up as self-employed, and paid taxes as James. He even applied for a passport and regularly used it for travel. Palmer's fake identity had a complete history. He wouldn't have to learn some fake details or back story; he knew it all already. Only someone really looking, like her, would find him.

She followed the money trail and found that, across all of Palmer's bank accounts, there was a little over two hundred thousand pounds in total. That must be the payments she and Lancaster had arranged plus his wages from the anti-piracy work, but that wasn't important. What she was happy to find was that money had been taken out of the James account since the island was bombed. Palmer must be alive. Who else would have access?

Riley's next stop was a trawl of airline records. Palmer wouldn't stay in Indonesia. He would want to follow Wallace. Airlines were the first option, if she had no joy, she would try cruise ships and ferries.

She was looking for a passenger named Harlon James who had flown out of South East Asia in the last month. After a couple of hours, she had it. Harlon James had caught a flight from Singapore to Dubai two weeks ago. He then flew from there to Paris and, finally, jumped on the Eurostar. Palmer wasn't just alive, he was home.

She checked the other passengers on each flight, looking for anomalies. She found one. Someone else, a woman, had made the same journeys on the same days. Either Palmer was being followed, which she thought was unlikely, or he had teamed up with someone.

Riley's next step, arguably the most important, was to find Wallace. That was a much more difficult job. He had the resources to create multiple identities. He could disappear completely and materialise as someone else anywhere in the world. This search took Riley the rest of the weekend, but by the time Monday morning rolled around, she believed she had the answer. She had to tell Lancaster. After making sure she had saved all the information, she closed her laptop and headed for the shower.

It took Riley less than thirty minutes to shower, get dressed, and leave the flat. She had never been one for spending hours putting on make-up and doing her hair. If people didn't like the way she looked, that was their problem. She locked her

CHAPTER 40

door and set off for the bus stop.

Chapter 41

Lancaster was sitting in his office when there was a knock on the door. He checked there was nothing confidential left out on his desk. 'Come in.'

Vicky Thomson opened the door and walked in. 'I've brought a visitor to see you, Edward. Someone I think you'll be pleased to see.'

Lancaster got up from his desk. 'Anna, how are you feeling? It's good to see you looking so well.'

'I'm a lot better than I've been for a long time, thanks to you and Vicky.'

Lancaster held out his arm. 'It's the least we could do after the work you put in. Please, have a seat.' He stood at the door and called to his secretary. 'Justin, could you hold all my calls please? Oh, and shuffle that meeting I've got this morning to another slot. It's only a briefing, it can wait a day. Tell them something earth shatteringly important has come up.'

'Will do, Sir.'

'Thank you.' He closed the door and sat back at his desk.

Thomson was sitting on an easy chair in the corner. 'Anna's been a busy little bee. Even though I told her to rest.' She gave Riley a disapproving glance that wasn't too serious. Like a parent would give to a mischievous child. 'She's got a lot to tell you.'

Lancaster looked at Riley. 'I'm all ears, Anna. What has that big brain of yours been figuring out now?'

Riley pulled some papers and her laptop out of a bag and arranged them on the desk. 'It's Logan Palmer, Sir. I've found him.'

Lancaster flashed a worried look at Thomson. 'I thought you went over this at your sessions at Yardley Manor. Palmer is dead. It wasn't your fault. You have to accept that he's gone.'

Riley opened her laptop. 'No, you don't understand. I've got proof.' She took them through everything that she had found over the weekend. The bank accounts, the fake identity, and the flights. It all made for compelling evidence.

Lancaster took off his glasses. 'It all sounds plausible, Anna, but you don't know that this identity is definitely Palmer.'

Riley brought up James's passport photo. The image showed a man with a shaved head and a goatee beard. He wore thick glasses and had a mole on the side of his face. Riley pointed at the screen. 'That's Logan.'

Lancaster paused, trying to think of the best way to bring Riley down without hurting her. She was still fragile. 'The face is the same shape, but the eyebrows are different. This man has a facial mole and he's a different height.'

'What about the fake documents and the bank accounts?'

'It looks like someone has used Harlon James's identity and whoever this man is he's probably up to no good, but there's no evidence that it's Palmer.

Riley looked back at Thomson. 'But it all makes sense.'

'I think this makes more sense to you because you want it to be true. Who's the woman you think he's travelling with?'

Riley pulled out another sheet of paper. 'Palmer asked me

to check up on someone, so I went through the records of Greenline Solutions. I believe that this, 'she pointed at a CCTV image on the screen. 'Is a woman called Ruby Finn. She's one of Greenline's private military contractors. The scar on her face is a dead giveaway. Surely, we should at least follow this up.'

'Where does Finn fit into the story? Who is she?'

'She was on the Capricorn with Logan. She wasn't on it when the Indonesian Marines boarded the ship.'

Lancaster raised an eyebrow. This was too much of a coincidence, but it still wasn't enough. 'We can't hold this up as proof that Palmer's alive. If he is, I'm sure he'll come back when he's ready. At least you can relax and stop blaming yourself.'

'But we can't relax. If Palmer got off the island, even though all the evidence and satellite images showed that no one did, maybe Wallace is still alive too. Maybe the warhead is still in play. Let's face it, the search of the island wasn't extensive, everyone was too busy congratulating themselves to worry about it.'

Lancaster already had concerns about the lack of physical evidence from the island. They found parts of the warhead casing, but not all of it. There were body parts strewn around the harbour, but nobody carried out autopsies or positively identified any of them. The rest of the island was covered in dense jungle that wasn't searched. 'Have you found anything that makes you think Wallace could be alive?'

Riley moved her chair around to Lancaster's side of the desk. She pointed at her laptop screen as she went through it. 'We said that no ships or aircraft left the island after the strike, but that's not entirely true. She zoomed in on part of an image and circled the corner with her finger. 'If you look here, hidden in the shadow of the harbour wall, is what looks like a boat.'

Lancaster got as close to the screen as he could. 'Okay, you could be right.'

'I've checked, and I think that belongs to Jerry Scarlett, an old friend of Logan's. It left Galang-baru Island the day before and limped home the day after. I found a police report that said it had been attacked by pirates and Scarlett was suffering from a gunshot wound. He had two passengers with him. That's how Palmer escaped.'

'Do you have details of the passengers?'

'No, they gave fake names at the hospital and then left.'

Lancaster looked up at Thomson. 'Okay, that's understandable. What else do you have.'

Riley unfolded a large sheet of paper onto the desk. It was made up of several sheets of A4 that had been stuck together. 'These are the Japanese plans of the island from World War Two. They show a tunnel which leads to a subterranean cave. The Japanese used it to refuel midget submarines.'

Thomson had now joined them at the desk. 'You're not telling us that Wallace had a submarine. Where the hell would he get one from?'

Lancaster thought that Riley was stretching it a bit, but he was willing to give her the benefit of the doubt for now. 'Go on.'

Riley continued. 'In July 2010, the Ecuadorians found a fully functional, completely submersible, diesel-electric submarine in the jungle bordering Columbia. It could carry up to six people and ten tons of cargo. Since then, several more narco-submarines have been found, each more sophisticated than the last. They only cost a few million dollars to make.'

197

Now Thomson was getting as close to the screen as she could. 'You think he built a submarine and used it to escape with the nuclear device?'

Riley tapped the laptop keys. 'I've found lists of things ordered by Greenline from suppliers of submarine equipment. Why would they need those if they weren't building a sub?'

Lancaster picking over the blueprints of the island's facilities. 'Okay, let's say we agree that a sub is possible, far-fetched, but possible. Where would he go? I don't imagine you can just sail into a port in a homemade submarine.'

'Some of these narco-subs are capable of travelling thousands of kilometres, but Wallace wouldn't need to. He has a small fleet of ships that he could have rendezvoused with.'

Lancaster rubbed the bridge of his nose. 'I think I know what the answer to this is going to be, but do you have any information that shows how he might have done that?'

Riley tapped the keyboard again. 'If we assume that this sub was capable of a speed of around ten knots, and we look at the movements of Greenline's other ships, it gives us this.'

The image on the screen was a map of South East Asia with several coloured circles drawn on it.

Lancaster looked at the screen, then at Thomson. 'Okay.'

Riley pointed at one of the circles. 'The course of this ship intersects with the area the sub could have covered.'

'Could have?'

'I am making quite a few assumptions, but we also have to look at the fact that the ship did a U-turn within a few miles of that intersection and sailed to Muscat in Oman. It stayed in Oman for two days then sailed back to Singapore. Why would they do that?'

Lancaster looked at Riley. He wanted to check how certain

she was of her facts. There wasn't time to get someone to go over all of this to confirm it. 'So where is Wallace now?'

'I don't believe that they would risk bringing a nuclear device over land. I think they transferred it to a ship.' She pointed at the coloured line that showed the track of another vessel. 'This is the MV Augustus. It also belongs to Greenline and left Muscat the day after the other ship arrived.'

'And where is it now?'

'It's currently heading for Southampton. Due to dock there tomorrow.'

Lancaster stared at the screen. Riley's evidence was a mixture of assumption and guesswork, but he had launched missions on less defined information. 'I want that ship boarded as soon as it docks. Pass it off as a random customs check or anti-drug smuggling operation. Find me any evidence that what, Anna says is correct. They'll need armed backup if Wallace is on board with his men.'

Thomson grabbed her coat and headed for the door. 'I'm on it.'

Riley closed her laptop. 'What do you want me to do?'

'This is where you leave it to us, Anna.' Lancaster could see that Riley was disappointed, but she wasn't up to being out in the field just yet. 'You can stick with me.'

'What about Logan? I wouldn't want to be anywhere near Wallace when he catches up with him.'

Lancaster could see that Riley was looking for him to agree that Palmer was still alive. She wanted to assuage her guilt. 'Look, Anna. I can see how much this means to you and I understand. Palmer, if he's alive, is out for revenge. We're bound by the law. We can't get involved in anything like that.'

'But he can help us.'

199

Lancaster shook his head. 'I know men like Palmer, they are valuable up to a point. When something like this happens, they become more of a liability. If he turns up, he might get in touch with you. If he does, you must let me know. I must get the police involved and bring him in. We can't have him running amok. Do you understand, Anna?'

'Yes, I understand.'

Lancaster could see from the look on Riley's face that she didn't mean what she said. She looked angry. After everything Palmer had done for them, he didn't blame her. He was angry too.

Chapter 42

Vicky Thomson stood on the dockside of the Port of Southampton's cargo terminal and watched the tugs that manoeuvred the MV Augustus into position. The port was a vast area capable of taking the biggest vessels and offloading their cargo. Whether that be containers full of electrical goods, imported cars, tons of gravel or food, or people. Thomson could see two cruise ships berthed in the distance and two huge ocean-going container ships. Compared to them, MV Augustus was tiny.

Greenline had registered that the MV Augustus was being used to move large consignments of military hardware to and from deployments all over the world. The containers filling the ship's decks were full of the supplies needed to keep a private army operating in the field. Everything from armoured vehicles to tents, portable toilets and showers to kitchens, and, of course, weapons.

The weapons that MV Augustus routinely carried were never offloaded in the UK, firearms restrictions were too tight. They were onward shipped to Greenline's facility in South Africa where they trained most of their assets. Regardless of that fact, they were still liable for inspection by the authorities. Manifestos had to be checked, everything accounted for, and anything that was disembarked had to be searched, including people.

Border Force and Customs Officers backed up by police stood along the dock ready to board as soon as a gangway had been lifted into position. A coastguard boat was following the MV Augustus into the harbour just in case anyone tried to make a run for it, and six police vans were parked along the jetty. Unseen from the outside, the armed officers within readied their weapons. They hadn't been told the exact threat but knew there could be a well-armed paramilitary unit on board. As the gangway was lifted into place, the customs and police officers filed along it to the deck of the MV Augustus.

A bitter wind whipped around the cranes that ran along the jetty and Thomson pulled her coat tighter. There was nothing she could help with, the rummage teams that searched ships knew what they were doing. In the past, they had found drugs, weapons, cigarettes, and people hidden away in some of the most ingenious places imaginable. Containers that were longer on the outside than the inside, false decks and bulkheads, even fan trunkings and water tanks, all had been used to smuggle. Sometimes the giveaway was the body language of the crew or simply that something didn't feel right. Thomson watched as the teams began their search on the upper deck. It was going to be a long day.

It was just before midnight when a knock on Thomson's car window woke her up. The senior officer from the Border Force beckoned her over to a building that ran along the dock, opposite the berth where MV Augustus was docked. Thomson rubbed her eyes, fastened her coat, and got out of the car.

Inside the building was a small office that had been commandeered to hold the impromptu meeting away from curious ears that didn't need to hear what was said. Senior officers from the British Transport Police, Hampshire Constabulary, HM Customs and Excise, and the Border Force stood around a deck plan of the MV Augustus. Each compartment had been crossed off as it had been searched and reported to be clear.

One of the customs officers handed Thomson a cup of tea. 'Sorry, we've drunk all the coffee.'

Thomson held the cup in both hands, warming up her fingers. The wind had stopped but it was still bitterly cold. 'This is great, thanks.' She pointed at the deck plan. 'I assume you didn't find anything.'

The senior Border Force officer spoke first. It was his teams that had carried out most of the search. 'Nothing at all, it's one of the cleanest ships we've ever searched. Normally we would find something, even if it's just the crew with some contraband.'

'But there was nothing on board? How unusual is that?'

'It's very unusual. Normally we would find small items but not take any action. It's a matter of scale. There was one thing though.'

Thomson blew steam from her cup. 'What was that?'

The officer pointed at a compartment on the plan. 'Here, in one of the machinery spaces, some welding had been done recently. One of my rummagers said it actually looked like they'd built a false bulkhead to hide something, but then put it back again.'

'Anything else?'

The customs officer who had handed her the tea stepped in. 'When I was talking to the captain during the day, his body language was a bit off.'

'In what way?'

'It seemed like he was nervous but wasn't worried about us finding anything. If he knew the ship was clean, why be nervous?'

Thomson didn't think that was evidence of any wrongdoing. The captain could have been nervous because of the size and intensity of the search. For all he knew, one of his crew members could have been smuggling something. 'Okay, is that everything?'

The Border Force officer threw his empty cardboard cup into the bin. 'Just one more thing, I don't know how useful it'll be.'

Thomson put her cup on the table. 'Everything helps, no matter how small.'

The officer's facial expression showed he was thinking of the best way to put this information across without seeming stupid. 'Ships, especially older ships like this, tend to have a smell of oil and diesel about them. They smell industrial. The areas that don't are the galley, which obviously smells of food, and the accommodation spaces. The accommodation smells of people. Over the top of the oil and diesel, there is a smell of soap, shampoo and deodorant hanging over an underlying aroma of sweat and old socks.'

Some of the people around the room laughed at his description and nodded in agreement.

Thomson had no experience of life on a ship but couldn't imagine living somewhere that smelt like that. 'Okay, I'll take your word for that. You found something unusual?'

'Compartments that haven't had people living in them for a while soon go back to the industrial smell. We entered a six-berth cabin on three deck that was empty but still smelled of people. When we asked about it, the crew said it wasn't used.'

'How long would the smell linger for?'

'In my experience, a couple of weeks at most. People were living in there when it left Oman.'

Thomson thanked them all and waited for them to file out of the room. Fifteen hours of intensive searching and they had found nothing, except a bulkhead that might have been moved and an empty compartment that smelled of old socks. It wasn't a great day's work to report back on. She checked for anyone standing within hearing distance, picked up her phone, and called Lancaster at his home.

Chapter 43

As the sun rose over the south coast of England, Wallace, Brad and Chernov sat in a white campervan waiting to board the ferry from the Isle of Wight to Portsmouth. The rest of the team were behind them in a black people carrier. When the MV Augustus entered the English Channel, they had climbed into an inflatable boat to complete the final part of their journey. Before dawn, while the MV Augustus was still in the approaches to Southampton harbour, they were landing on a secluded beach on the south coast of the island. There were no customs officials or police officers to stop them and no immigration officers to check their passports. No one was looking for them here and the beach was deserted.

Their first stop was a garage close to the beach. It belonged to a relative of one of the guards. It was small and basic, but it had all the tools they needed. The owner had been paid a substantial amount of money to stay at home for the day and was happy to do it. Business hadn't been great lately and the extra cash would come in handy.

The building itself was large enough to fit three cars in. It had a pit and a lift next to an area for changing tyres. There was a toilet and a separate screened off area where customers could make themselves a cup of coffee and watch their cars being worked on. The two vehicles were backed in through the roller doors and the windows were covered up. Two of the guards got to work with blow torches and welding equipment while Wallace, Brad, and the others helped themselves to coffee.

Over the next few hours, Chernov's device was secured into a compartment that had been created in the bottom of the campervan. It looked like part of the chassis, a support for the bench seat and bed at the back. The top plate had been welded into position and painted. The only way to get the device back out was to cut the compartment open. Anyone carrying out a casual search would be oblivious to it. The same was true of the compartments in the back of the people carrier that were full of weapons. All of them, bar a couple of nine-mill pistols that were under the front seat, had been sealed in.

Once the modifications were complete, they spent the rest of the day prepping for the completion of the job. The plan was fine-tuned and memorised, all the guards had to do was follow the plan and do as they were told. The bumper pay packet they would receive at the end of the operation would make them all rich men. The extra resources they needed had been arranged and would be picked up en route. With preparations complete and a meal inside them, they remained hidden in the garage until they had to leave for their ferry. With everything loaded up, they climbed into the vehicles and set off for the port.

Chernov shuffled about in the front passenger seat. 'Could we get something to drink soon? I could also do with a toilet break.'

Brad sat behind the wheel with his elbow hanging out of the side window. He looked in the rear-view mirror. 'It's like being on holiday with a four-year-old. The only thing he hasn't asked so far is, "are we there yet?" for fuck's sake.'

Wallace was relaxing on the back seat, his head back and legs stretched out. 'Shut up, both of you. You'll get plenty to drink and time for a toilet break when it's safe. Sergei, you don't go anywhere without me, understand?'

Chernov turned round in his seat. 'I understand, Kane. I'm just thirsty.' He pointed at Brad. 'He could at least close the window, it's cold in here.'

Wallace sat up. 'Jesus. Brad, close the window. Sergei, stop complaining. Both of you, shut up.' He lay back down again, shaking his head.

Brad shot a menacing stare at Chernov. 'Just remember, Sergei, you're only valuable to us for a little while longer. After that, watch your back.'

Chapter 44

It was mid-morning before Thomson made it to Lancaster's office. She didn't get back to London until 3 a.m. and was worn out by the drive. Lancaster told her that he would wait for her to arrive before he spoke to Riley about the previous night's events. He wanted someone there who Riley felt close to in case she needed support.

Thomson knocked on the office door and went in. 'Good morning, everyone.'

Riley was making coffee. 'Morning, Vicky. Do you want a cup?'

'Yes please, Anna. I need something to keep me awake.'

Riley poured milk into the three cups and handed them around. 'I didn't sleep much last night. I kept wondering what was happening on the ship, what you found.'

Thomson sat down next to Riley and put her hand on her knee. She knew that this wasn't going to be easy. Riley wouldn't take this well. She spoke softly, reassuringly. 'There's no easy way to say this, Anna, so I'll just explain it how it happened. We didn't find anything.'

Riley sat forwards. 'But that's not possible.'

Thomson put her hand on Riley's. 'We searched for fifteen hours. There was no sign of Wallace or the bomb. There was nothing concrete to show that they had ever been there.'

Riley pulled her hand away and stood up. 'No, I followed the trail. It had to be there, they had to be there.'

'The searchers thought the crew might have been up to something, but it doesn't mean they're linked to Chernov.'

Lancaster walked round the desk to where Riley stood. 'I'm sorry, Anna. There just isn't enough to go on. There's no trail for us to follow.'

'But if I was wrong about that,' her heart began to pound. 'I could be wrong about Logan.' Riley was trembling, tears began to run down her face.

'It doesn't mean that. I'm sure he's alive and well somewhere. We'll see him when he's ready.'

Riley stepped away from Lancaster. 'No.' She was shaking her head. 'No!' she looked at Thomson then ran out the door.

Thomson had seen people lose it before. The extreme pressure of the job, the constant secrecy. Riley was showing all the signs, it was too soon for her. She needed to be back at Yardley Manor, now, for her own wellbeing.

She looked at Lancaster. 'Don't worry, Edward. I'll look after her.' Thomson picked up Riley's backpack and headed out the door.

Chapter 45

Yardley Manor was originally a nineteenth century country house belonging to an industrialist whose family had made their fortune in coal. Eager to show off their newfound wealth, they bought a large plot of land and built a country house. The last occupant, Frederick Yardley, left his entire estate to the crown after the First World War and the subsequent Spanish Flu pandemic robbed him of his heirs. After a spell as a convenient country home for a couple of minor royals, it became a hospital during World War Two. Soldiers returning from the battlefield with disfiguring injuries or with mental scars were treated there. From that point, it never returned to being a family home.

In the last twenty years, it had mainly been used for the treatment of those returning from the wars in Iraq and Afghanistan. The number of soldiers needing treatment meant that Yardley Manor became experts in mental trauma, in the same way that hospitals in Belfast became experts in kneecap injuries during the troubles. It was a matter of need. Although there were a number of NHS facilities to treat physical injuries, hospitals like Yardley Manor were tragically few and far between. The number of beds that they had was nowhere near enough.

The original nineteenth-century part of the house had now

been given over to admin and consultation rooms. Its rabbit warren of corridors and narrow staircases were no longer suitable to house patients. A modern extension at the rear was where the accommodation was now situated. Each of the sixty rooms was a decent size and had its own bathroom. They all had televisions, desks with space for a laptop, and comfortable chairs. The kitchen facilities were shared between each group of six rooms and there was a large communal garden. It reminded most people of a student halls of residence or some of the more modern military accommodation. There had been a concerted effort for it to be a calm, restful place and at the same time avoid anything that made it look and feel like an institution.

Yardley Manor wasn't a secure unit. It existed so that veterans who wanted help could get access to the treatment they needed. No one was forced to stay there, and they could all, technically, leave whenever they wanted. However, they were watched during the day and the building was secured at night. If anyone decided they wanted to leave, the staff wanted it to be controlled. They didn't want to wake up in the morning and find out that someone had disappeared. They didn't want any of their patients putting themselves at risk. Security guards regularly patrolled the grounds and residents were reminded that staying there was for their own good. There was no doubt that staying here was in Riley's best interests.

Thomson caught up with Riley, after the breakdown in Lancaster's office, just as she exited the building. She wasn't in a fit state to be left on her own. Her demons had resurfaced, and she needed help. They went back to Riley's flat where Thomson, in an attempt to ease Riley's anxiety over her failed recovery, explained the full extent of her own mental health history.

After being sent to Afghanistan to convince tribal elders to work with the security services, she had been kidnapped and held for ransom. Government policy meant that that ransom was never going to be paid. Thomson was held for months. Tortured and beaten, she was regularly paraded in front of the cameras and threatened with beheading. Her mind, body, and spirit were all broken.

Eight months after her abduction, she was found, by US marines, malnourished, dehydrated, and chained to the wall in a darkened room. Her captors had been frightened off by the rapidly approaching coalition forces and abandoned her. She had been without food or water for three days and was close to death. In her mind, she had already accepted her fate and was ready to die.

When she got home, she was in pieces. After Lancaster arranged the best medical care, she had slowly recovered her health. Her mind, on the other hand, was a different matter. Psychiatrists did everything they could during the numerous sessions she had. The medication they gave her helped a little, but she was still prone to bouts of anxiety and depression. Her answer was to self-medicate with alcohol. It was never going to be a workable solution and mixing drink with medication just made things worse.

She considered suicide on more than one occasion, but something within her wouldn't allow it. She wanted to live. Some in the service wanted to put her out to pasture, a wounded hero. A whip-round in the office and a "Thanks for your service" card. A pat on the back and an invitation to the yearly reunion. That would have finished her off and Lancaster wouldn't let that happen. He kept her in his team, kept her busy, kept her sane. Yardley Manor had played a big part in her recovery.

Thomson convinced Riley that going back was what she needed. It wasn't unusual for discharged patients to relapse, there was no shame in it. Riley reluctantly agreed and Thomson helped her pack some things. They arrived back at Yardley Manor in the early afternoon. Once Riley was settled back in her room, Thomson made sure she was calm and promised to come back and visit the next day.

Chapter 46

Riley lay on her bed. The rest of the day had passed unnoticed by her. She had been given something to eat and then some medication to keep her calm and help her relax. It knocked her out. Within an hour of taking the pills, she was in her room, unconscious. She turned her head to look at her clock, it was 2 a.m. Her stomach was grumbling at her, she was hungry and wouldn't get back to sleep unless she ate something.

She opened the door to her room and crept along the hallway to the shared kitchen. She knew that it was always kept well stocked with the basics. She could, at least, make some toast and a cup of tea. If she were lucky there would be some chocolate biscuits in there too. To avoid flooding the hallway with light and disturbing the others in her part of the building, she closed the kitchen door before reaching for the light switch, but as she was plunged into darkness, she was grabbed from behind.

Her assailant clamped one hand over her mouth and lifted her off the floor with the other arm. She twisted and kicked, trying to force them to let go, but they were too strong. After a few seconds, which felt like minutes, the light came on and a familiar voice whispered in her ear, 'It's okay, Anna, it's me,

It's Logan.'

Palmer put her down gently and took his hand away from her mouth. Riley jumped into the corner of the room, hands out in front of her, trying to ward off the nightmare that she was convinced she was having. 'No, no, you're not here, you can't be.'

Palmer put his finger up to his lips. 'Shhhh, it's okay.'

Riley looked at Finn and back to Palmer in panic. She tried to find a way out, a way back to her room, but he was standing in front of the door. She screwed her eyes shut and tried to force herself to wake up.

Palmer reached out and took Riley's hand. 'It's me, Anna. I'm really here. You're not imagining it.'

Slowly, cautiously, Riley stepped forward. The man in front of her didn't look like the Palmer she remembered. His hair and beard were growing back, but they were little more than stubble. She reached out her hand and placed it on the side of Palmer's face, he was real. 'Oh my god, it is you.'

Palmer nodded.

Riley's eyes welled with tears, and she buried her face into his chest.

Palmer wrapped his arms around her. 'It's okay, I'm here now.'

They switched off the kitchen light and went back to Riley's room. She and Palmer perched on the edge of the bed while Finn sat in the chair by the desk. Riley wiped her eyes with a tissue and blew her nose. 'I knew you were alive, I kept telling everyone.'

'Let's keep that between us for now. It's better for me if everyone thinks I'm dead, especially Wallace.'

Riley looked at Finn. 'I checked up on her like you asked me

216

to, she's one of them. She works for Greenline, she works for Wallace.'

'This is Ruby, she's on our side. She saved my life.'

Finn nodded to Riley. 'You're welcome.'

'Can we trust her?'

Palmer held Riley's hands up to his chest. 'Do you trust me, Anna?'

Riley nodded.

'Then you can trust, Ruby. She stuck her neck out for me when she had no reason to. Because of that, she has suffered as much as I have and is in as much danger as any of us.'

Riley looked at Finn and smiled. 'I never know who I can trust these days.'

Finn nodded. 'It's Okay, I understand. You've been through a lot. You can trust me, I'm here to help.'

'Thank you.' She looked back at Palmer. 'What do you want me to do?'

'We need to find out where Wallace has gone. We need to know where he's hiding.'

Riley reached for her backpack and took out her laptop. 'I told Edward and Vicky all about it. I showed them how he escaped and where he must have gone to, but I was wrong. They don't believe me.'

Palmer looked at the screen. 'We believe you. How do you think he escaped?'

'I think he got out through a tunnel to an underground cave, then onto a submarine.' She lowered her head. 'Stupid. I know.'

'No, it isn't stupid. We both saw Wallace and his band of ar-seholes leave down a set of stone steps before the Tomahawks hit. I was down there beforehand, there was a door like you find on a ship.'

Riley got out the island blueprints. She put her finger where the tunnel started. 'That's it, that's what it shows on here. When they put up the building, they must have decided to keep access to the tunnel.'

'So, you weren't wrong about it, Anna. You were right. You were right about me, and you were right about the under-ground cave. Where do you think Wallace went?'

Riley was spurred on. 'There's a lot of information.' She shuffled sheets of paper and typed into her keyboard. 'Too much information.'

'Just tell me the basics.'

'Right. He got onto a ship that was heading to Southampton, but when Vicky went to search it, there was nothing there.'

Palmer looked at Finn. 'They must have got off it early. They all have experience with inflatables and boarding large container ships. Getting off one in the channel wouldn't have been a problem.'

Finn was looking at the map Riley now had up on the screen. 'They could have landed anywhere on the south coast, plenty of empty beaches. They could have landed there and picked up some vehicles. Could be anywhere by now.'

'Yeah, but they're likely to be headed for London. Or somewhere to hold up 'till they're ready.' Palmer turned to Riley. 'Who else might know where they've gone? There must be someone, anyone would be a place to start. They can't have arrived here with no hideout or resources in place.'

Riley opened a browser and punched some numbers into the laptop. 'According to the records, the only other person connected to this whole thing is Travis Vaughn.'

'What? Vaughn is here. I thought he would have run for the

hills.'

Riley read from the screen. 'It says here that they are holding him in a safe house. He is going to give evidence in the inquiry into Kane Wallace and Greenline.'

'That sounds more like him. Testifying to cover his own arse. We need to talk to him. I'd bet my house he knows where Wallace's hideout is.'

Riley was writing down the address. 'You don't own your house, Logan. That's not much of a bet.'

Palmer took the paper from Riley. 'You know what I mean. Thank you for this, it should help.'

Riley got up. 'I'll get dressed.'

Palmer held up his hand. 'Wait a minute, you aren't going anywhere. This could turn nasty. In fact, I'm sure it's going to turn nasty. You don't need to be there.'

Riley turned the screen to Palmer. 'I know one of the police officers assigned to guard Vaughn. I've still got my old MI5 ID. You need me to get in.' She smiled at Palmer.

Finn looked at Palmer and shrugged. 'It would make it easier.'

Palmer looked sceptically at Riley, then seemed to realise that it made sense. 'Okay, but it's as far as you go. Once we're in you're done. We leave you there and you tell the police that we abducted you and made you take us there. You don't need any more shit over this.'

'I don't want to get you into trouble either.'

Palmer stood up. 'It's that or nothing, Anna. Besides, by the time this is over, I'm going to be in plenty of trouble. Kidnapping you won't make it any worse.'

Riley sighed. 'Okay, I'll put some clothes on.' She pulled a few things out of a chest of drawers by the door and went into

219

the bathroom.

As she was closing the door, she heard Finn speaking in the other room. 'She seems a bit jittery. Do you think she's up to it? We don't want her getting hurt.'

Palmer spoke quietly. 'All she has to do is smile, flash her badge and say she's come to question Vaughn. That should be enough for the police to open the door. After that, it's down to us.'

Riley locked the door and sat on the edge of the bath with her head in her hands. She wasn't sure if they were ever going to trust her again.

Chapter 47

Kane Wallace stood at the end of the wharf and watched the boats travelling up the Thames towards London. The boatyard behind him was in darkness, all the welders, carpenters and painters had left days earlier. They would be at home now, sitting on their sofas nursing hangovers and swollen stomachs from the overindulgence of Christmas. Their bodies had a few days to recover before the second wave of cheap drink and rich food began. The trees they had planted in the corners of their living rooms still twinkled but now were only surrounded by shed pine needles and tinsel, the presents long since opened and enjoyed.

The security guard who was on duty that night had been paid off. His job was to turn a blind eye and stop anyone from disturbing them. For that, his family would have an incredibly good new year.

Wallace looked upstream towards the glow on the horizon. He imagined the Londoners scuttling about as they prepped for their New Year celebrations, restocking their fridges and cupboards ready for the chimes of Big Ben. None of them had any idea what was coming, none of them would live to see the aftermath.

Brad approached him. 'Boss.'

Wallace turned. 'How's it coming along? Are we still on target?'

'We've finished cutting the weapons out of the people carrier, just about to start on the van.'

Wallace walked back along the wharf towards the shed where the two vehicles were parked. 'That's good. Make sure Chernov is there when the device is cut out, I don't want it damaged. I want him to make sure everything is working. We don't want any slip ups this late in the game.'

Brad walked beside him. 'Will do, Boss. We've had some other information that you need to hear.'

Wallace stopped. 'I hope it's not bad news, Brad. You know how I hate that.'

'Not bad news, just something we might want to tidy up.' He beckoned over a man who was standing a few feet from the end of the wharf. 'This is Owen Gregg, he's one of our local boys, helps us out here and there. He says he knows where they are holding Vaughn.'

Wallace looked at Gregg. He was short and stocky with a shaved head and broken nose. He looked like the archetypal night club bouncer, a man who could handle himself, but wasn't particularly skilled in thinking. 'How do you know?'

'One of our young lads seen him goin' into a house wiv a copper. Said he recognised the copper 'cause he's been lifted by him before. We kept an eye on it. We've seen uvver coppers goin' in, like they was changing shifts. It's a bloody safe house.'

Wallace smiled. 'It's not a particularly good safe house, is it?'

'We always spot strangers and coppers on our patch, they stick out.'

Wallace nodded to Brad. 'Pay him what you've agreed and go and get Harris. I don't want to use any of the guards for this. They're too valuable to the operation.'

Brad pulled a thick roll of twenty-pound notes out of his pocket and handed five hundred pounds to Gregg. 'You stick around. Show Harris where the house is. He might need some muscle to back him up.' He whistled at Harris and waved him over.

Connor Harris wasn't part of this team, not yet anyway. Maybe if he did everything he was told to do, and did it well, they might let him in. He could get back in their good books, earn some real money. He jogged over to the wharf. 'You want me?'

Wallace pointed at Gregg. 'This is Owen, he's going to take you to an address on his patch. You can pick up any extra muscle you need on the way, a couple of his guys should do it. When you get there, you kick the door in and kill the coppers. I want to know what Vaughn has told MI6, then you can kill him too. Understand?' Harris nodded. 'Understand?' Gregg nodded. 'Get on with it.'

The two men walked away and got into Gregg's car.

Brad watched them drive away. 'You think we can trust them not to fuck it up?'

'I wouldn't trust him to take a piss without soaking his shoes. This isn't important to the operation, but if he comes back and hasn't done what I've told him to, kill him.'

Brad and Wallace walked over to the shed. The last part of the van's secret compartment was being cut away and the device was lifted out. Chernov stood off to one side, ready to check that it was still functional.

Wallace gave him a thumbs up. 'Watch yourself, Sergei. I

223

don't want anyone damaging our case of instant sunshine.'

Two guards put the case down in front of Chernov. He unfastened the catches and opened the lid. 'Everything looks like it's still in place, there is no obvious damage to the case or the mechanism.' He put the key into the first lock and turned the switch. The LED lights on the steel panel lit up one after the other and the numbers on the display flashed into life. He pressed the buttons on the timer and looked over at Wallace.

Wallace nodded once.

Chernov inserted the key into the second lock and turned the last switch. He pressed a red button beside the timer and pulled out the key. The last LED started to pulse and the numbers on the display began to count. He closed the lid and threw the key to Wallace.

Chapter 48

In a small one bedroomed flat in a not very fashionable part of London, Travis Vaughn sat on his bed and pressed the buttons on his TV remote, there was nothing he was interested in watching. It was like being in lockdown again but more boring, he couldn't even go out for a walk or nip to the shop. He didn't understand the need for all the security. Kane Wallace and his cohorts were dead, they couldn't do him any harm. They had done enough damage already by leaving him to face the music on his own.

He changed the channel again, more bloody reality television. The least they could have done was arrange for some decent cable or satellite TV. He wasn't feeling much like a star witness. He poured himself a glass of scotch, at least they'd got that bit right. Well, almost. It wasn't particularly good scotch, but it would have to do. Might as well get drunk and fall asleep again, just like every other night. This sucked.

Outside the bedroom, in the combined living room and kitchen, two police officers weren't having a great time of it either. They didn't know what Vaughn had done or seen; they didn't need to know. All they knew was that there could be an attempt on his life. Only authorised personnel from the security services were to be allowed anywhere near him, and he wasn't to leave the flat.

One of the two, DC Bob Allen stood beside the open window, smoking. His colleague, DC Mark Evans wasn't thrilled by that. 'Can't you go outside and do that?'

'You must be joking. It's freezin' out there.'

Evans had his coat on. 'It's freezin' in here with the window open.'

'Oh, stop complainin'. It's not like I'm asking you to smoke one. What happened to peace on earth and goodwill to men?'

Evans picked a day-old newspaper and turned to the half-done crossword. 'Yeah, merry fuckin' Christmas.'

Out in the street, Riley, Palmer, and Finn stood in the shelter of a vandalised bus stop. It was more shadowed than the rest of the street and, if anyone started nosing around and asking questions, they were just waiting for a bus. They had left the car two streets away and walked the rest of the way. At this time of night, there weren't many people around, but they still had to be careful. Few people were there to see them, but that also meant they couldn't blend into a crowd. They had already ignored one bus and if they failed to get on the next one it would look suspicious. If either of the police officers in the flat took the time to watch them, it would be obvious that they were up to something.

The flat was on the other side of the road from the bus stop, diagonally, about fifty metres away. The window that Allen stood next to, smoking, was on the third floor and the only one that didn't have closed curtains. It was also the only one that had no Christmas decorations hanging up.

Palmer and Finn checked their pistols. Riley looked worried.

'Do you think you'll need those?'

Palmer put his back in its holster. 'They're just for show, Anna. Nothing to worry about. As long as we go in hard and fast, they won't know what's hit them.'

Finn lit a cigarette. 'Remember, as soon as the door opens, you step to your right, we'll do the rest. You just follow us in and close the door.'

Riley looked up at the flat. 'When do we do it?'

'As soon as that window closes again, we make a move.'

Allen took his last draw and stubbed out his cigarette on the windowsill. One last plume of smoke from his lips, then he shut the window and closed the curtains. 'There, happy now?'

Evans didn't look any happier. 'I'm going to check on laughing boy.' He stood up and went over to the bedroom door.

Vaughn was fast asleep. Half a bottle of scotch had that effect on him. The TV was still blaring out whatever crap he had decided to watch, and he hadn't managed to get undressed. Evans shook his head. He switched the light off and closed the door. 'This guy is a waste of space. What has he got that makes him so valuable?'

Allen shrugged. 'Fucked if I know. I'll just be glad when our shift finishes tomorrow. Get back to the wife.'

'Me too. I'm grabbing a nap.' Evans sat down on the fold-away camp bed that had been set up behind the flat's two-seater settee. He kicked off his shoes and lay down. 'Keep the noise down.' He pulled his jacket over him and, within minutes, was snoring.

Allen picked up another old newspaper and pondered the clues in the crossword. They had completed all the easy clues, but neither of them was particularly good at puzzles. In the two days they had been there, they still hadn't managed to finish one.

Palmer stood at the bottom of the stairway that led up to the flat. The door had a Yale style lock, which had never been one of his fortes. Kicking it in would risk raising the alarm in the flat above. He waved to the others, who crossed the road and quickly joined him.

Finn stepped past Palmer and pulled a small pouch of lock picking tools out of her pocket. She got to work with two of the picks and, within seconds, she had opened the door and the three of them were in.

Palmer, once again, took the lead and crept up the six short flights of stairs to the landing outside the top flat's door. The steps and the landing were made of concrete, so there was no need to worry about squeaking floorboards, but they still had to make sure that there was nothing on the landing that could be kicked over. Palmer and Finn pulled on balaclavas, not to hide their identity, but to make them appear more menacing to the occupants of the flat.

Riley stepped forward, steadied herself, and knocked on the door.

Allen shouted from inside the room. 'Who is it?'

Riley smiled and held up her MI5 ID card to the peephole. 'It's Anna Riley. We've met before.'

'I thought you were off sick.'

'I got better. Come on, Bob. Open the door. I don't want to be here all night.'

'Okay. Keep your hair on.' There was a clunk and a rattle from the other side of the door then, with a creak, it opened.

Chapter 49

P almer was first in the room. He grabbed a fistful of Allen's shirt and pushed him back towards the window. Palmer's gun was under Allen's chin. 'Don't fuckin' move.'

Allen nodded. He looked terrified.

Finn followed Palmer into the flat. She rushed to the camp bed and straddled Evans, pinning his arms down. 'Don't even think about it.'

Evans now had the barrel of a 9mm in his mouth. His response to the threat from the balaclava-clad figure was pretty much the same as Allen's: he gave a weak nod.

Riley came in last and closed the door. As they had agreed previously, she stood in the corner and did her best to look terrified, like someone who had been kidnapped and was under duress. She didn't really need to act. She had never done anything like this before.

The two police officers were tied to the kitchen chairs that sat next to a fold-up table in what appeared to pass for a dining room. The officers were secured using their own handcuffs – they would never live that down – and gagged with a strip of duct tape. Finn shouted at Riley and dragged her over to the settee. Riley would have been scared if she hadn't been in on the act. It was that convincing.

Finn gently wound duct tape around Riley's wrists and ankles, then winked at her and stood up. Palmer took the duct tape off Finn and went over to the bedroom door.

Vaughn rolled over and sat up when Palmer switched on the light. 'What the fuck do you . . .' His voice faded when he realised who was standing at the foot of his bed.

Palmer placed the duct tape onto the bed. 'Hello, Travis, how've you been?'

'Logan! They told me you were dead, you and Wallace.'

Palmer took a claw hammer out of his jacket and placed it on the bed. 'What can I say? The reports of my death were greatly exaggerated.'

The blood drained out of Vaughn's face. 'It's good to see you, mate.'

Palmer unfolded a four-inch bladed knife and wiped it on his sleeve. 'You know that Wallace killed my boy, don't you?'

'I had nothing to do with that, I swear. If I'd known they had grabbed him, I would have done something. I would have reported it to the police.'

Palmer placed a bottle of lighter fluid, and a Zippo lighter onto the bed. 'I know you weren't involved in that, Travis. That's the only reason you're still alive. If you want to stay that way, you'll tell me everything I need to know.'

'I swear I don't know where he is, Logan.'

'You know where he might be though. I'm betting that you'll know of any properties he's got. Somewhere he might hole up.'

Vaughn swallowed hard. 'If I did, I'd tell you. I've got no reason to lie for him. He hasn't done me any favours.'

Palmer walked around to the side of the bed and picked up

the half-empty bottle of scotch. He unscrewed the lid and poured some of the amber liquid onto the blade of the knife and lit it. 'We don't want you catching an infection. Better safe than sorry.'

Vaughn tried to back away, but he was already against the wall. Palmer's calm, matter of fact tone was truly menacing. 'Really, Logan, I don't know.'

Without waiting for the flame to die out, Palmer plunged the knife into Vaughn's thigh.

Vaughn screamed. His face twisted in agony. He grabbed at the handle, but Palmer twisted the blade and pushed it further into the muscle. Vaughn kicked and rolled, falling off the bed. Palmer pulled out the knife as Vaughn fell and brought it down on his hand, pinning him to the bedside cabinet. 'Where are they, Travis?'

Back in the other room, the two police officers stared at each other with wide eyes. Finn stood at the door listening for anyone coming up the stairs. 'It's okay, boys, you're not on his shit list. Just stay calm and stay quiet, and you'll be fine.' She looked at Riley and raised her eyebrows.

Riley turned her head away. She didn't want to see what Palmer was doing, but she could still hear the awful screams. After what seemed like an age, the screaming stopped. She didn't know if that was a good sign or not. Had Vaughn talked, or had Palmer killed him? She didn't want to look, but she had to.

In the bedroom, the answer was neither. Vaughn was back on the bed. Blood from several wounds to his legs and arms ran onto the sheets. He breathed heavily through gritted teeth, spit and blood running down his chin.

Palmer opened the nozzle on the bottle of lighter fluid and

poured it over Vaughn. He threw the empty bottle onto the floor and picked up the Zippo.

Riley had never seen anyone in so much pain, so much fear. Vaughn had started to cry, and a stain was spreading across the front of his trousers. Riley thought about standing up to try and stop it, but, deep down, she realised it was necessary. She also realised that there was no stopping Palmer.

Vaughn held up his hands. His speech punctuated by sobs. 'Okay, okay. Please don't kill me. Not like that. I'll tell you . . . I'll tell you what I know.'

Palmer shook his head. 'You had your chance to talk, now it's time to die.'

'No, no, no, I'll tell you everything, they've got a farm, it's used as a weapons cache, that's where they'll be, that was always the plan. They're using that as their base, please, no.' Tears were streaming down his face.

Palmer threw a notebook and pencil at him. 'Write down the details.'

Vaughn did as he was told. 'Thank you, Logan.'

'For what?'

Vaughn handed the blood-stained book to Palmer. 'For letting me live.'

Palmer flicked open the cover of the Zippo and lit it. 'I don't remember that being part of the deal.'

Finn walked to the door. 'Logan, let's go, you've got the info.' She looked at the mess on the bed. 'Look at him, he's pathetic. Killing him won't help, it's Wallace you want.'

'It would make me feel better. He has to pay. I can't get the image of Nathan out of my head. It keeps me awake at night. It's eating away at me, and I can't turn it off.'

Finn walked over to Palmer and placed her hand on his arm.

'He didn't kill Nathan. He's unarmed. This isn't who you are, Logan.'

Palmer lowered his head. He closed the lighter, threw it onto the floor, and left the room.

Finn looked at Vaughn. 'If I were you, I'd stay very quiet until we've gone.' She picked up the lighter and held it up. 'This isn't over yet.' She turned and walked out.

Palmer had turned the chairs that the officers were tied to so that they faced away from Riley. He crouched in front of her holding a strip of duct tape and nodded. Riley smiled and nodded back. Palmer placed the tape over her mouth, making sure he left a gap for her to breathe through, and he and Finn left the flat.

After a few minutes, Riley heard the screech of car tyres on the street outside. The noise of the door downstairs being smashed in filled her with relief, then dread. At first, she had assumed that it was the police coming to save them. But she had only heard one vehicle, and whoever was coming up the stairs hadn't identified themselves. The police always did that. She looked across at Allen and could tell that he was thinking the same thing.

Allen managed to rub his face against his shoulder and remove the tape from his mouth. He shouted over to Riley. 'Get the handcuff key, it's on the keyring on the table. You need to get us out.'

Riley stood up, the tape on her hands and face was easy to remove. She grabbed the bunch of keys from the table and tried to free the officers. Her hands were trembling, and she struggled to get the key into the cuffs. Allen tried to calm her down. 'It's okay, just breathe, concentrate.'

Evans struggled to get free, but his hands were cuffed behind

233

his back through the spindles of the wooden chair.

Riley managed to unlock one side of the cuffs and Allen ripped off the duct tape that fastened his ankles to the legs of the chair. He dived across the settee, where Palmer had left their weapons, and frantically tried to reload, but it was all too late. The door of the flat burst inwards, splinters of wood flying from the shattered lock.

Allen cocked his weapon and brought it round to aim but, before he could squeeze the trigger, thug number one shot him. Evans stopped struggling and looked at Riley. His eyes were full of fear. Thug number two raised his weapon and ended Evans's life.

Thug number one carried on through to the bedroom. Vaughn screamed but was soon silenced by two shots. 'All clear.'

Gregg and Harris came through the door of the flat. They weren't armed, they weren't doing the hands-on dirty work this job required, that's what the thugs were for.

Riley stood by the settee, staring at Allen's body, she knew she was going to be next. Why would they leave a witness behind? She closed her eyes and held her breath.

Chapter 50

Edward Lancaster was back in the briefing room in front of the decision makers, his least favourite place to be. He didn't enjoy this part of the job, he never had. He had always been happier working in secret. His background was as a field agent. He wasn't one of the new breed who were elevated to their positions without ever knowing what operations on the ground felt like. He had served his time at the sharp end and knew the reality of what was involved.

Lancaster switched on the monitor. 'It seems that the celebrations after the destruction of the facility in Indonesia were a little premature.'

The faces sitting around the table were ashen. They had already reported the success, each of them letting slip that they were the key to the whole thing. Some of them already looked forward to a promotion or an honour on the back of an operation they, in reality, had little to do with. This could affect the thing they cared about most, their careers.

Lancaster paused for effect, waiting for the enormity of the situation to sink in. 'We are faced with the very real possibility that Wallace is still alive and that the nuclear device is not only still viable, but right here, in London.'

The Chief of the Defence Staff was the first to comment.

He was one of the only people in the room that Lancaster respected, at least he had operational experience. 'Where are we getting this intel from? I thought our asset on the ground had been killed.'

'One of our own people. She was Palmer's handler and attended one of our previous briefings. She analysed the aftermath and came up with a plausible chain of events that showed how we arrived at this point. We should have listened to her.'

One of the civil servants from the Ministry of Defence opened her notebook and checked her notes. 'Would this person be Anna Riley by any chance?'

Lancaster knew what was coming. The arse covering was starting already. 'Yes, it is.'

The civil servant looked back at her notebook. 'She was admitted back into a psychiatric facility after giving you this information. Is that correct?'

Lancaster nodded. 'That is correct, but it has nothing to do with the validity of the analysis she carried out. If the information she had found was incorrect and she was simply unhinged, we wouldn't all be sitting around this table. Would we.'

The Met Police Commissioner raised her hand, as if she was silencing everyone. 'Can I just get this right? We are worried about a successful operation, that we have already closed down, because of analysis from a woman who can't be here because she's looked up in an asylum?'

The Commissioner was one of the people Lancaster didn't respect. By all accounts, her rank and file officers didn't respect her much either.

'Anna Riley is a very capable operative who has suffered

some mental wellbeing issues. It's what happens in the field, Commissioner. But then you wouldn't know that, would you?'

The Commissioner sneered at Lancaster. 'If you've brought me here simply to...'

'Be quiet, Commissioner, you're out of your depth.' Lancaster was sick and tired of placating these people. He had no intention of pandering to their egos anymore. There wasn't the time. 'Anna Riley was abducted from Yardley Manor by Logan Palmer and an, as yet unidentified female.'

The civil servant checked her notes again. 'Logan Palmer was killed during the Tomahawk strike at the same time as Wallace.'

'Precisely my point. Logan Palmer is still alive. Why wouldn't Wallace be alive too?'

The attendees around the table looked at each other, the reality of the situation dawning on them.

The civil servant cleared her throat. Sweat started to form on her forehead, she was one of the people who had used the success of the operation to boost her career. 'Why would he abduct her? Do you know where they are now?'

Lancaster brought up a photo of Vaughn on the screen. 'This is Travis Vaughn. He was the Regional Director for Greenline Solutions in South East Asia. He agreed to give evidence against Wallace and the company in return for an easier ride in his own court case. Last night, he, and the two protection officers who were looking after him, were murdered.'

The Commissioner frowned. 'I haven't been made aware of this.'

'I'm sure the report is on your desk as we speak. Probably one of the things you should have looked at before coming here.'

The Director of MI5 shook her head, she wasn't a fan of political appointees either. 'Why would Palmer kill Vaughn?'

Lancaster brought up a scan of a handwritten witness statement. 'I don't think he did. Riley would have known where Vaughn was, she had access to the files. It's obviously why Palmer took her. But we also have this witness statement that says two people, a man and a woman, were seen leaving the flat before the shooting started. Four men, one of whom we have identified, were seen arriving and breaking down the door to the flats. It was them who killed Vaughn and the officers, not Palmer and the other woman.'

'And the probable reason to kill Vaughn was to keep him quiet. He knew what they were planning. Who's the guy you've identified?'

Lancaster brought up another photo. 'This is Owen Gregg, he's a sometime enforcer for a low-level gangster called Ivan Mason. We found a link between Mason and Wallace. Apparently, Greenline pays Mason's wages.'

The MI5 Director bundled together her notes. 'No time to waste. We need to track down Gregg. Finding him will lead us to Wallace, it'll get us to the bomb.' She stood up and walked to the door. 'I'll set things in motion. Any help you need Edward, just let me know.' She left the room.

The Chief of the Defence Staff and the Royal Navy Captain with him also stood up. 'I can't deploy troops on the streets at this point, Edward, but we do have special forces we can use. They'll be at your disposal, Home Secretary.'

Everyone turned to look at the man who sat at the other end of the table. He hadn't said anything up to this point. He didn't feel qualified to butt into the operational discussions. Now was when his job kicked in. He had to advise the Prime

Minister and the other members of the cabinet of the threat. He had to advise the evacuation of VIPs from London. Looking around the table, he imagined that some of the faces looking at him would be first in the queue for a flight out. 'I'll brief the Prime Minister and deal with any political fallout. Operational authority sits with you, Edward. What do you plan to do about Palmer?'

'He isn't the problem. With any luck, he'll take out Wallace and save us the job. If he gets in the way, we'll deal with it then.'

The Home Secretary nodded and walked to the door. 'Keep me posted.'

Lancaster switched off the monitor. The rest of the attendees of the briefing poured out of the room as if it were on fire.

Thomson picked up her briefcase. 'Do you think Anna is still alive?'

Lancaster tried to look optimistic, but he wasn't sure he was managing it. 'The witness said that three people arrived first but only two left. Once the shooting started, he kept his head down so we don't know what happened after that. What we do know is, if Anna was killed in the flat, where's the body?'

Chapter 51

Palmer turned up the collar of his coat and pulled on a woollen beanie hat. If anyone studied the CCTV closely, he could still be identified, but that didn't matter. By the time that happened, this would all be over one way or another. He knew there was a chance that the police already had his description and were trying to track him down, but they would be looking for the bearded him with a full head of hair. The last thing he needed was an armed response team descending on the building and taking them in because some eagle-eyed operator had spotted him on camera.

Finn zipped up her coat and pulled up her hood. The scarf that she pulled up across her face hid her scar. 'You think they've been to the flat yet?'

'The police would need to check in regularly. Any failure to do that would, at least, mean a car being sent to check up on them.'

'I hope Anna's okay. I like her.'

Lancaster picked up an empty holdall from the boot of the car and threw it to Finn. 'She'll be okay. She just needs to stick to the story that we abducted her. They'll just take her back to Yardley Manor.' He picked up another holdall and closed the boot. 'You ready?'

'Yeah, let's get this done.'

The front door of the storage facility was an old roller door left over from its previous life as a shipping merchants' warehouse. Palmer entered the PIN into the keypad beside the door and, with a noisy rattle and metallic screech, it slowly opened.

The office just inside the door was deserted, the facility had been left to run itself during the holidays. All the customers had numbers to get in and the door closed automatically when the timer ran out. Palmer and Finn kept their faces away from the CCTV camera, walked past the office and straight into the lift.

The third floor of the building had previously been a huge open space. A place where piles of packing crates were stacked ready to be loaded onto ships or trucks for onward delivery. Now, it was filled with a steel framework that divided it into separate storage lockers. Several corridors ran between the lockers to allow access to the numbered doors.

The first lockers they came to were only big enough to fit in a couple of large suitcases. They were similar to the left luggage lockers that used to populate every railway station. Past those was a row where each one was the size of a telephone box. The main part of the room contained three long rows of lockers the size of a small single bedroom and, at the back of the room, was a row where they were much larger. These units were big enough to park a car in.

Palmer counted the numbers on the doors. 'Twenty-eight, twenty-nine, thirty. This is it.' He worked the dial on the combination lock and opened the door.

The roof of the lockers was made of a steel mesh that was secure but allowed a flow of air in and out of each unit. It also meant that the main lights in the building lit up the insides of the lockers and there was no need for separate lights and switches.

Finn looked around at the contents. 'Who did you say owned this?'

'An old colleague of mine, Frank, has some friends who may not be entirely legit.'

Inside the unit were two camp beds, a couple of chairs and a coffee table. A row of shelving racks along one wall held bottled water and various tins and packets of food.

Finn picked up one of the tins. 'This place is better stocked than my last flat.'

Along the length of the other wall were several long fibre glass shipping crates. Palmer opened one of them, it was full of Glock, nine-millimetre, semi-automatics. The second contained four M4 assault rifles. Each box that Palmer opened held the type of equipment you would expect only the army to have.

Finn lifted one of the rifles and worked the action. 'Not entirely legit? Bit of an understatement there, I think.'

Palmer started loading equipment into his holdall. 'Just take as much as you need. I'm going to owe a lot of people favours after all this.'

'If we're still alive.'

Palmer smiled to himself. How did he end up in these situations?

They both packed their holdalls with the kit they needed and had something to eat. Two empty tins of baked beans with sausages in, a favourite of army ration packs, now sat on the table next to an Ordnance Survey map and a photograph of the farm.

Palmer drew a circle on the map. 'This is the farm that Vaughn gave me the details for. There's only one road in and out so we'll have to go cross country, on foot, for a couple of miles.'

Finn drew a line on the map. 'This looks like the best way in. We'd be coming down a slope and we'd be shielded by the hedges.'

Palmer moved his pencil to the photo. 'There's no way of knowing which of these buildings they're in.' He drew a cross on one of the buildings. 'We can assume that they are in the house, but that could be a mistake. We'll need to watch for a while before we make our move.'

'How many do you expect to be there?'

'Wallace, Brad and Quinn, and Chernov definitely. The two bodyguards from the island should be with them. I would expect a handful of Wallace's other men to be there too to boost the numbers. They're probably the ones patrolling the outside. The expendable ones who aren't part of the big operation. Basically, we have no idea how many. We could be up against it on this one.'

Finn took a piece of paper out of her pocket. 'If anything happens to me, and you're still alive, I want my mum to know what really happened. I don't want her thinking that whatever shit the authorities put out about us is the truth. Promise me you'll give her this and tell her.'

Palmer took the note. 'I will. I promise.'

Chapter 52

O wen Gregg was well known on his patch. As an enforcer and leg breaker for Ivan Mason, he was protected from any of the lowlifes who fancied their chances. On top of that, he also had a reputation as a brutal villain in his own right. Anyone who dared to go up against him was risking their life.

He had grown up with an abusive father and an alcoholic mother. His survival depended on no one but him. Not an unusual circumstance in his neck of the woods, it was how he dealt with it that was different. By the age of twelve, he was involved in a minor protection racket. His job was to smash the windows of the shop owners who didn't pay. He did his job well and, by the time he was twenty, he had graduated to breaking the legs of unfortunates who were unable to pay back the extortionate payments on their loans.

Gregg committed his first murder at the age of twenty-one, although he was never caught. Over the next twenty-five years, he fluctuated between breaking legs, disposing of people, and serving short prison sentences. Now he was on the eve of turning fifty, he was the head of Mason's enforcers. The team of thugs who made sure Mason kept his position as number one and dealt with anyone who got in the way. Gregg was fiercely loyal to Mason and particularly good at what he did.

He sat at a corner table in The Golden Lion. It was the table he always sat at and, even when he wasn't there, no one else dared sit there. The Golden Lion was a traditional, working class pub. The only difference between it and an old-fashioned spit and sawdust pub was the lack of sawdust. It hadn't been bought out by one of the large pub chains, they always got warned off, and it hadn't given itself over to the hipster fad. Expensive pubs that served small portions of food on a shovel, or pints of home brewed beer in an old piss pot, didn't fare well here.

Gregg enjoyed drinking in The Lion. The pub was never full and didn't make any money, it was a front. The premises belonged to Ivan Mason. It was somewhere to do business away from prying eyes, somewhere that outsiders stood out. Gregg knew that his position as someone to be feared meant he never paid for any of his drinks. He could sit in peace and study the form of the dogs he bet on. No one was going to come at him in here.

That was why the tinny sound of the voice over the megaphone came as a complete surprise to him. 'Owen Gregg, this is the police, come out slowly and keep your hands visible at all times.'

The bartender went over to the window and rubbed some of the dirt from the inside. 'The street's full of Old Bill, Owen, looks like they've come mob handed.'

Gregg thought about the job at the flat. Two dead coppers tended to bring out the big guns. How had they tracked him down so quickly? 'Someone check out the back.'

A young man who had been sitting at the bar disappeared through a door at the back of the room. After a few seconds, he came running back in. 'The alley's full of 'em too. They're everywhere.'

Gregg stood up and put on his coat. 'Fuck it, I'm gettin' too old to run anyway.'

The bartender still peered through the grime on the window. 'There's a lot of 'em, mate. Tooled up too, what the fuck you done this time?'

'I'm always innocent, you know that.' He smiled at his own joke. 'Call Ivan, let him know what's happened, he'll get me a lawyer.'

The bartender nodded and went to pick up his phone.

'Owen Gregg, this is the police, come out slowly and keep your hands visible at all times. This is your final chance.'

'Alright, alright, keep your 'air on you fuckin' wankers.' He threw open the pub's double door and stepped out into the street.

Chapter 53

Connor Harris pulled up at the farm gate and got out of the car, the gate was locked, as always. He pressed the intercom button that had been installed on the gate post and waited for a response.

After a few minutes, a voice came out of the speaker. 'What?'

Harris bent over and pressed the button again. 'It's Connor.'

'Connor who?'

For fuck's sake, when were they going to start treating him like one of them? Treating him with a little respect? He was putting his neck on the line just as much as they were. 'You know Connor fuckin' who.'

He could hear laughter coming out of the loudspeaker. There was a buzz and the gate unlocked. 'Make sure you shut it.'

Harris opened the gate and drove through, closing it behind him.

Wallace was standing in the farmyard when Harris pulled up. 'Where's Gregg?'

Harris shrugged. 'Not a clue. He said he'd done his bit. Said he had other things to be gettin' on with.'

'I don't like you being on your own. You could have led anyone back here.' Wallace turned to walk away.

Harris walked after him. 'I know what I'm doin'. I wouldn't

get followed. I'm as well trained as any of your monkeys.'

Wallace carried on walking. He didn't seem interested in what Harris was saying.

Harris kept following him. 'I picked something up at the flat. You'll want to see this.'

Wallace stopped and turned back around. 'What do you mean you picked something up?'

Harris was beginning to think this might not have been a great idea. He went round to the boot of the car and opened it, smiling.

Wallace sighed and shook his head. He walked over to where Harris was standing and looked in. Riley was tied up in the boot of the car, a strip of duct tape over her mouth.

Wallace stared at her. 'Who the fuck is this? I said kill everyone.'

'We did. We killed Vaughn and the coppers just like you said.'

'Then who is this?'

Harris could sense trouble coming. 'This is the woman that was with Palmer at the pub, the MI6 one you've been lookin' for.'

'Pick her up, get her inside.'

Quinn stepped forward and lifted Riley out of the boot, he threw her over his shoulder and went inside.

Wallace closed the boot. 'I'll let you off, but I don't want you thinking for yourself anymore. You're not particularly good at it, okay?'

Harris nodded. He had got away with it this time, but he couldn't keep living like this. He thought it was time to get himself some money and disappear.

Riley was lying on the floor in the kitchen of the main house when Wallace walked in. 'Don't just leave her on the floor you animals, get her a seat.'

Quinn picked her up and sat her on a worn, leather chair in the corner. 'Sorry.'

Wallace patted Quinn on the shoulder. 'As loyal as they come this one. Not the sharpest tool in the box though.' He crouched down in front of Riley and ripped off the duct tape. 'Well, MI6 lady, what's your name?'

Riley said nothing.

Wallace pulled a knife out of his pocket and extended the blade. He carefully cut the ropes that were tied around Riley's wrists and ankles and put the knife away. 'Someone get her a drink.'

Brad handed Wallace a bottle of water. He took the top off and gave it to Riley. 'Here you go, have a drink. I'm sure you're parched.'

Riley wasn't sure if they were trying to drug her, but, at this point, she didn't really care. She hadn't drunk anything since the previous evening and her throat was bone dry. She put the bottle to her lips and emptied it.

'Looks like you needed that. Now, I'll ask again, what's your name?'

Riley looked around at the men who surrounded her, she looked scared and humiliated. Harris had kept her locked in the boot for hours and there was a wet patch that spread across the crotch of her jeans. She looked back at Wallace but still said nothing.

Wallace grabbed Riley's wrist. 'Listen to me, I'm only going to give you one shot at this, then I'm going to let Brad ask the questions. You won't like that. Brad has a real passion for inflicting pain on women. You don't want any pain, do you?'

Riley shook her head, unable to take her eyes off Brad.

'I didn't think so. Look, just tell me your name. How can that hurt?'

Riley rubbed her eyes. 'It's Anna. Anna Riley.'

'Anna. That's a nice name. How do you know Logan Palmer, Anna?'

Riley knew she had made a mistake. She had shown them that she was willing to talk. Now they wouldn't stop asking her questions. Her head dropped. 'I'm his handler.'

'Waddaya know, boys, Palmer had a handler. You mean you were his handler, Anna. I'm sorry to tell you this, but Logan Palmer is dead.'

Riley's eyes gave her away.

Wallace stood up. 'He's not dead, is he, Anna...Is he!?'

Riley looked at Brad. She didn't want him asking the questions, she just wanted to go home. Tears ran down her face. 'No. No, he's not dead. He's alive and he's coming after you.'

Wallace was stunned. He hadn't even thought of the possibility that Palmer could be alive. The last time he had seen him he was tied to a chair in a building that was levelled by cruise missiles a few minutes later. How the hell could anyone get out of that? He could feel his pulse quickening. He knew Palmer's reputation for being a loose cannon. The assassination in Geneva had given Palmer enough reason to hate him, but now he had killed his only son too.

He pointed at Quinn. 'You, put her upstairs with Chernov. Everyone else, outside. No one in, no one out.'

Chapter 54

Owen Gregg sat in his cell. He was used to this kind of thing. The number of times he had been arrested in his life was too many to count. He looked around. They hadn't managed to decorate the place since the last time he was in. It was the same shitty green colour and still had that ingrained smell of piss and vomit. He was going to have to throw his clothes away when he got out. He would never get rid of that smell.

The spy hole in the door opened and someone peered through. Gregg gave them his biggest cheesy grin. They couldn't intimidate him. There was a clunk that echoed off the walls as the key turned in the lock. The door swung open, and Edward Lancaster walked in. He put on his glasses and looked at the front of a brown folder he was carrying. 'Owen Gregg?'

'Who are you? Where's my lawyer?'

Lancaster opened the folder. 'You won't be getting your usual lawyer today, Owen. When he turns up, we're going to send him home.'

'You can't do that. I'm entitled – '

'To a lawyer. Yes, I know. We'll provide you with a good lawyer, we do that for all our informants.'

'What? I'm no grass.'

Lancaster pointed to a page in the folder. 'It's not what it says here, Owen. It says here that you gave us vital information about a drug smuggling operation being funded by your boss, Ivan Mason.'

'I 'aven't said anyfin'.'

'It also says that we raided the place, arrested your boss, and confiscated four million pounds worth of cocaine.'

Gregg was confused. If something like that had gone on, he would know. They were trying to bluff him. 'That didn't happen. You're lying.'

'Didn't happen yet, Owen. Didn't happen yet.'

'What? What do you mean?'

Lancaster closed the folder. 'We know all about your boss's drug smuggling operation and we're going to bring it down sooner or later. The only question is, how do you come out of it?' He knocked on the cell door. A young PC opened it. 'Have him taken to an interview room.'

'Yes, Sir.'

Lancaster walked out of the cell.

Gregg tried to follow him. 'I don't understand. What do you mean, how I come out of it?'

The young PC led Gregg into a room that didn't look like any interview room he had ever been in before. There was no camera or tape machine. Four chairs, one table, and nothing else. The PC sat him down on one of the chairs and walked out.

Lancaster and Thomson entered the room and sat at the table opposite Gregg. Thomson took a notebook out of her briefcase and prepared to take notes. Lancaster drummed his fingers on the table. 'You'll have noticed there are no recording devices in here, Owen.'

'Yeah, I noticed.'

'So, whatever happens in here is just between us.'

Even though there was no one else in the room, Gregg still lowered his voice. 'What did you mean about me looking like a grass.'

Lancaster knew he had him. 'What I meant was that if you don't work with us and tell us what we need to know, we'll frame you.'

'You can't do that.'

'Believe me, Owen, I can, and I will. Your life won't be worth living. The price that Mason puts on your head will have every scumbag in London out looking for you. Without his protection, you'll be easy meat.'

Gregg knew what Mason would do to him if it even looked like he was a grass. He'd seen the punishment with his own eyes. He had dealt some of it out himself. 'What is it you want from me?'

'Your boss, Ivan Mason, has been doing some work for a man called Kane Wallace, as have you. We want to know where Wallace is. You tell me that, I'll let you go next door where your real lawyer is waiting for you. You're going down for the murder of the two police officers, Owen, but at least you won't be a grass.'

Gregg considered the mess he was in. 'What about the drugs?'

'As I said, sooner or later we're going to take it down. If I were you, I'd use the time from now till then to make yourself look as loyal to Mason as possible. It'll make your time inside a lot easier.'

'There's a building.'

Lancaster handed the folder to Thomson. 'Carry on. What

building is this and why should I be interested in it?'

'It's an office block in the city. Ivan bought it for Wallace. Got it cheap 'cause it's got asbestos in it. Said Wallace was going to turn it into a new headquarters or somefin'.'

'And.'

'Two days ago, we got told to take a crate over there. We took it up to the top floor, Wallace has got his men guarding it. That has to be important.'

Thomson slid the notepad across the table. 'Write the address down.'

Lancaster nodded. 'Do as she says.'

Gregg picked up the pen and scribbled an address, then passed the book back to Thomson. 'Does this get me off the hook?'

'It gets me off your back. You're still on the hook for the murders so your days of freedom are well and truly over. Although I imagine, in your twisted little world, going down for the murder of two police officers will only add to your reputation. If it were up to me, I'd have already arranged for the nearest crematorium to burn your corpse.'

'Well, at least I ain't no grass. Who are you two anyway?'

Lancaster looked at Thomson. 'We are nobodies. You should forget us. Any mention of this little meeting to anyone and the accusations of grass will be spinning around you like flies round shit.'

Thomson stood and opened the door. 'You can take Mr Gregg to his lawyer now.'

'Yes, Ma'am.' The young PC guided Gregg into the neighbouring interview room and closed the door.

Lancaster looked at the address written on the notebook. 'Find out everything you can about this building. I want records, blueprints, everything. Get a surveillance team over there right away. Put special forces on standby.'

Chapter 55

Wallace sat in the kitchen of the farmhouse and stared at his phone. The map on the screen showed a circle, where the bomb was located, and a timer. He watched as the remaining time clicked round to six hours. Nothing could stop this from happening now. In a few hours, he would have enough money to disappear and live a life of unimaginable luxury.

Brad walked into the room. 'You looking for me?'

Wallace put his phone away. 'Yeah, it's almost time for us to leave. Is everything in place?'

'We've set everything up at Oldmarsh Tower. There's a team there for security, they obviously don't know what's about to happen, and the chopper is on its way.'

Wallace walked to the sink and filled a glass with water, taking a sizeable gulp. 'Go and get Chernov and the woman. We'll deal with them as we planned. I want the team that's coming with us in the chopper ready to go. Everyone else can load up the van and get out in that. We'll meet them as agreed.'

'Right.' Brad left the room.

Everything was in place, the plan was going smoothly, but there was still something preying on Wallace's mind, where was Logan Palmer? All the money in the world was of no use to him if Palmer tracked him down. Palmer wouldn't be concentrating on finding the bomb, and he wasn't interested in why it was being detonated, all he wanted was Wallace dead. That made him extremely dangerous. He couldn't be bargained with or bribed, he couldn't be deflected or drawn away from his single goal. The only way to stop Palmer was to kill him.

Brad reappeared. He had hold of Riley's arm and dragged her into the kitchen. Chernov meekly followed behind and sat at the kitchen table. Brad pushed Riley into the worn leather chair and turned to Wallace. 'I'll go and finish up, get the boys ready.' He turned and walked out.

Wallace filled another glass with water and handed it to Riley. 'I hope Sergei didn't bore you too much while you were locked away with him, Miss Riley.'

Riley took the glass. 'He's more of a gentleman than you'll ever be.'

Wallace laughed and looked at Chernov. 'You hear that, Sergei? You,' he pointed at the Russian. 'Are a gentleman.'

Wallace walked around the room, muttering to himself. He pulled one of the chairs out from the kitchen table and sat opposite Riley. 'What you don't seem to know, Anna, is that Sergei here is in this for the money just like I am. I didn't have to kidnap him, he's here of his own accord. All I had to do was offer him a few million dollars, and he jumped on board with the rest of us. He'll do anything for a comfortable retirement. You still think he's a gentleman?'

Riley took a drink from her glass. 'I just said he was more of a gentleman than you, that wouldn't be difficult, would it?'

'Tell me, Anna. Who is your idea of a real man? Logan Palmer? A man who consistently fails to protect those he cares

257

about.'

'At least he doesn't set out to hurt innocent people. How does it feel knowing he's coming to get you?'

Wallace's face reddened. 'I'm not scared of Palmer, by the time he figures any of this out, I'll be out of his reach.' He took out his phone and showed the screen to Riley. 'You see this? This red dot shows where the bomb has already been planted. There is no time to stop it. You and your boyfriend are too late, when this timer gets to zero, London vaporises and I'm an extraordinarily rich man.'

'You won't get away with it, someone will stop you.'

'Who? Palmer? He can waste as much time as he likes coming after me, the bomb isn't here. If he goes after the bomb, I get away. There's only one person who can disarm the bomb, and that's Sergei.' He pulled out his pistol. 'But I can do something about that.' Wallace aimed at Chernov and squeezed the trigger.

The unsilenced shot echoed off the bare walls. Chernov grabbed his chest, his eyes questioning, staring at Wallace. He looked down, blood seeped between his fingers, and ran into his lap.

Riley ran over to him and looked at the wound. She held her hand to the Russian's chest, vainly attempting to stem the blood flow. Chernov was gasping for breath as his life ebbed away. He looked at Riley and nodded, a half smile on his lips. 'It's okay. I'll be with my family.'

Riley applied more pressure to the wound. 'No.'

The blood flow had slowed, but it wasn't because Riley's first aid was working, it was because Chernov's heart had stopped beating. His eyes still stared at Riley, but there was no life left in them.

Riley glared at Wallace. 'Bastard. You didn't have to kill him. He did everything you asked him to.'

'You're right, Anna. I didn't have to kill him, I wanted to. Now there's one less person who can get in my way, and I don't have to pay him. That's a win, win for me.'

Riley ran at Wallace and slapped his face, but it had little effect. Wallace slapped Riley hard and pushed her back into the leather chair. 'Don't test me, Anna. I don't really need you either. I could just as easily dispose of you.'

Brad came into the kitchen, alerted by the gunshot. He looked at Chernov's lifeless body. 'What the fuck happened?'

'I brought the plan forward a little. Are we ready to go?'

'Yeah, everything's in place. We're ready to leave when you are.'

Wallace grabbed Riley's arm and lifted her back out of the chair. 'We're taking her with us just in case Palmer turns up.'

Brad grabbed Riley and dragged her towards the front door.

Wallace stood in front of Chernov, he reached out and closed the Russian's eyes. 'Thank you, Sergei, we couldn't have done it without you.' He wiped his hand on a handkerchief and walked out of the room.

Chapter 56

The winter sun had long since dropped below the horizon when Palmer pulled into a lay-by on a narrow country road and switched off the engine. He got out and scanned the whole area with a pair of night-vision binoculars. The only movement was the vehicles on the motorway behind them. The farmyard was two miles, as the crow flies, across the neighbouring farm's fields, he could just make out the roof of the barn. They needed to get a lot closer before they could assess the size of their opposition.

Finn sat on the bonnet of the car smoking a cigarette. 'If we stick to the edges of the field, it'll be almost impossible to see us, unless they've got night vision, obviously.'

'Yeah, fingers crossed, they haven't got any and they aren't watching up here for us. We're higher up than them anyway so we should get some shielding from the hedges.'

Finn jumped down and stubbed out her cigarette. She fastened the tactical vest, which held her extra equipment and magazines, and pulled on her gloves. Whatever happened tonight, life was going to be vastly different afterwards. 'Okay, I'm ready, lead on.'

Palmer press checked his Glock and cocked his M4. 'Stay low, surprise is on our side, for now.'

They climbed over the wooden field gate and set off at a slow jog.

Staying out of site for the first mile and a half wasn't a problem. It was after they reached the edge of the slope that led down to the farm that things changed. Palmer lay in the ditch that ran around the edge of the field and watched through his binoculars. The lights at the farm were on and he could see movement in the farmyard. There was something happening, Wallace and his men were getting ready to move.

Finn knelt beside him. 'You see anything?'

'They're loading a van, looks like they're about to bail out. We need to get there quickly.'

'Go.'

Palmer climbed out of the ditch and ran across the middle of the field. If any of the guards looked in his direction, they would see him coming. He got to the first hedge and crawled under it. He still had four hundred metres to go. Finn arrived at the hedge and knelt beside him. She took aim at the farmhouse, if anyone saw Palmer, she would lay down covering fire. Palmer took a long, slow breath and set off again.

With one hundred metres to go, Palmer dropped to his knees. Their luck was holding, but now they were in real danger of being spotted. He checked the farm through the binoculars, the yard was empty. The van and two cars were still there, but the guards were out of sight. They must be inside one of the buildings, maybe getting briefed. This was their chance. He waved to Finn and sprinted the last hundred metres to the edge of the farm.

Finn veered off at an angle and headed for the opposite corner of the farmyard. She ducked down behind a slurry tank and looked across to the barn. It looked like all the guards were in there. She could see Brad out front, giving the briefing. He still loved the sound of his own voice. He had even made himself a little stage to stand on out of packing crates. The van was ten metres in front of Finn, she crawled out from behind the slurry tank on her elbows and approached it, keeping her eyes focused on the barn.

Palmer watched through his binoculars as Finn edged closer to the van. He was beginning to regret his plan. His need to get to Wallace and make him pay for Nathan's death was overriding his situational awareness. There were only two of them and this was a bad idea.

If they didn't manage to kill Wallace and Brad, it was unlikely that they would be able to stop them escaping. If they couldn't track them, then it was over, they would never be able to find them again. Any chance they had of stopping the bomb would be gone, but this was too risky. The GPS devices they had found in the storage lock-up had put the idea into his head. Once again, he was putting someone else at risk to get what he wanted.

Finn reached the van and crouched beside the driver's side door. She took the small GPS device out of her vest and switched it on. There was no light to show it was working, she just had to trust that it hadn't broken since they tested it. She checked that the guards were still busy in the barn then stood up and attached the GPS to the metal roof rack on the van.

Palmer's heart was in his mouth as he watched Finn stand up. He swung his binoculars around the farm, looking for anyone that would see her. He looked back to the van, Finn was crawling back to the slurry tank, job done. Now they could concentrate on the assault.

Palmer's phone rang in his earpiece, he pressed the button to answer. 'Did you get it attached?'

Finn's voice was little more than a whisper. 'It's on. Hopefully, it'll work if we need it. We'll worry about that when it happens.'

'Okay, we wait for confirmation that Wallace is here, then we take out as many as possible before they even know what's hit them. If we get Wallace and Brad, we pull out. It doesn't matter about the others.' He went back to scanning the farmyard through his binoculars.

He watched as Finn made her way back up the hill towards his position. It would give her a higher vantage point to get a better field of fire. As she crawled behind the fence, Brad walked out of the barn.

Finn stopped and unslung her assault rifle, taking aim at Brad.

Palmer spoke into his microphone. 'Not yet, Ruby. We need to know if Wallace is here first. We need to know where the bomb is.'

There was a gunshot and Brad disappeared into the house. 'What the hell was that?'

'Take it easy, the other guards will be on edge after that. Stay out of sight.'

Palmer watched as the guards left the barn and took up various positions in the yard. Two went around behind the house while three of them stood close to the van. The rest spread out. Palmer kept his eyes on the house, anything that was about to happen would happen there.

When Brad came back out of the house, Finn aimed straight at his head.

'Wait, wait, wait.'

Finn lowered her weapon. 'Shit.'

Brad dragged Riley out of the house and threw her in the van. 'We have to wait. We can't risk killing Anna. We need–'

'Logan? Logan?'

Chapter 57

Palmer walked down the slope towards the farmyard with his hands in the air. The guard who followed had his weapon pressed to the back of Palmer's head.

From the corner of his eye, Palmer saw Finn duck back behind the fence. All the guards were ready for a fight now, the element of surprise had gone. There was no way of winning this. They were fucked.

Wallace came out of the house. Finn could have shot him, but the guard with his pistol at Palmer's head would have pulled the trigger. The van was full of guards, but, if she took it out, it would kill Anna. Palmer knew there was only one possible option that might work. He readied himself for action as Finn knelt back up, took aim, and pulled the trigger.

The guard behind Palmer dropped to the floor, dead. Finn's second shot took out another guard. Palmer dived out of the way and rolled behind a stone water trough.

Finn ducked down and crawled up the slope under a shower of wooden splinters from rounds hitting the fence. The noise as each bullet slammed into the wood with a loud crack was deafening.

Palmer reached out from his cover and picked up the dead man's weapon, dropping two more guards. The remaining guards scattered around the yard, taking cover behind various pieces of farm equipment. Palmer kept his aim on the tractor that Wallace and Brad were both behind. It was on the far side of the yard furthest from the van. When they made a break for it, Palmer would have plenty of time to bring at least one of them down.

The helicopter came in from the east and banked over the farmyard. The sudden thudding of the rotor blades biting into the air startled Palmer. Its spotlight played across the field that ran next to the farm, it was looking for somewhere to land. Palmer looked back to the tractor. Wallace wasn't breaking cover. He knew that he had to wait until the helicopter landed before he made a run for it. As soon as he did, Palmer knew that every guard would be firing at him and Finn to keep them down.

Palmer knew that he had to stop the helicopter now. 'Ruby, cover me, I'm going to try and take out the chopper before they get anywhere near it.'

Finn scanned the farmyard, firing shots at each guard's position to keep their heads down.

Palmer stepped out from behind the trough, aimed at the cockpit of the aircraft, and emptied his magazine. The helicopter dipped and yawed as the rounds penetrated the plexiglass windows. It banked to the left then headed straight down, the rotor blades shattered as the aircraft impacted the ground nose-first. Pieces of the blades became missiles. They shot into the air and across the farmyard, slicing through the wooden sides of the barn. One of the guards was hit in the chest by a large chunk and dropped to the ground behind the van.

Palmer was back behind the stone trough, waiting for the

carnage to stop. When he looked up, he saw Wallace climbing into the back of the van. As soon as the side door was closed, the van's wheels spun and fishtailed in the mud as the driver accelerated away.

'Fuck.' Palmer wanted to run after the van, Wallace was getting away and he had Anna with him. In all the scenarios that Palmer had run through his head, none of them had ended like this.

The guards that remained were covering Wallace's escape. Two of them were crouched behind one of the cars, one was inside the barn, and another had taken Wallace's hiding place behind the tractor.

Finn vaulted the fence and dived under an old trailer, bullets pinging off the metal as she did. She was under heavy fire and Palmer had to help her out. He dragged himself up to one of the dead men and found two more magazines. He loaded one of them into his M4 and returned fire.

When the guards ducked down, Finn was able to fire off some shots. She aimed at the barn and fired through the wall next to the door. The man who had picked that badly thought-out position for cover fell to the side and rolled away.

Palmer concentrated on the car that two of them were behind. He couldn't see the men, so he fired through the windows, hoping for a lucky shot.

Finn took careful aim and squeezed the trigger. The guard hiding behind the tractor screamed as the bone in his lower leg shattered. He dropped to one knee then onto his back clutching at his leg. The second bullet hit him in the neck and severed his artery. His lifespan had now been reduced to a handful of minutes.

The two remaining guards ran the few feet to the other car,

jumped in, and started the engine. Palmer and Finn both stood and fired simultaneously. The bullets ripped into the car from both weapons and, as it started to pull away, an explosion tore through the vehicle. The fireball lit up the area and sent sparks flying across the farmyard, setting fire to the barn.

Finn edged over to the tractor. The man behind it had breathed his last and his body lay in a pool of blood that steamed in the frigid air.

Palmer slotted in a fresh magazine and walked out into the open. It wouldn't be long before someone called the police, they had to get away. He shouted over to Finn, 'I'm going to check the house. Be careful, I think there's one we didn't get.' He disappeared through the front door and into the farmhouse.

Connor Harris watched as Finn walked back towards the house. With Wallace gone and the guards dead, he had to get away. If Palmer found him, there would be no discussion or negotiation, all he could expect was a bullet in the head. If he was lucky. He had managed to steal a backpack full of money out of the van and it was time for him to leave. He had to go somewhere that Wallace and Palmer wouldn't find him. A burning beam fell from the roof of the barn and landed behind him. With Palmer in the house, this was his best chance, his only chance to get away. He slung the backpack over his shoulders, re-loaded his semi-automatic, and sprinted out of the door.

Finn caught the flash of movement out of the corner of her eye and turned towards it, but Harris was ready for her. He pumped two rounds into Finn's chest and disappeared into the darkness.

268

Chapter 58

Inside the farmhouse, Palmer heard the shots. He ran to the door and checked left and right for any threat. The barn had now succumbed to the fire completely. The flames lit up the sky and created shadows that danced across the farmyard. Palmer stepped out of the house and saw Finn lying on her back next to the tractor. She was gasping for breath. The impact of the bullets had driven the air from her lungs.

Palmer dropped to his knees next to her. He lifted her arm and felt for the two entrance holes. It looked like they were both high on the right-hand side of her chest. 'Ruby, what happened.'

Finn swallowed, still short of breath. 'Harris, it was Harris. He must have been hiding. He was the one you couldn't account for.'

'I promised I'd kill him, and he manages to get away. Slippery bastard, it's just like him to be hiding in a corner while everyone else is in danger.' He unzipped Finn's vest and slipped it off. He ripped open her shirt and checked the wounds. It was as he had thought, two entrance wounds but not gushing blood. 'I need to get you to hospital.'

'Check my back. Are there exit wounds?'

Palmer rolled her onto her side and lifted her shirt up. 'There's one exit wound, close to your armpit.'

'I think the other one's lodged in my shoulder. I'm not bleeding out. You need to go.'

Palmer shook his head. 'I'm not leaving you. No one else dies because of me, because of something I want. Wallace can wait.'

Finn grabbed the front of Palmer's vest. 'It's not about him anymore. You need to find Anna. You need to find the bomb. That's more important.'

Palmer could hear sirens and see blue lights in the distance as the emergency services approached the farm.

Finn let go of Palmer's vest and put her hand on his. 'I'll be okay once they get here. Take the weapons, get out of here.'

Palmer hesitated, he owed Finn his life, he didn't want to leave her bleeding on the ground, but she was right. He had to find Anna, he had to stop the bomb. Palmer brushed some dirt from Finn's face and squeezed her hand. 'When this is over, I'll find you.' He tucked the spare magazines into his vest, holstered the Glock, and slung the M4 over his shoulder. 'I promise.'

Finn smiled at him.

Palmer stood up and ran across the farmyard, heading back to where they had left the car.

Chapter 59

The room wasn't as full as it should have been for a briefing of this type. Normally, an anti-terrorist operation would include those at the sharp end, the people whose teams would be carrying out the assault on the building, and the decision makers.

MI5, MI6, police, and special forces were all present, but the politicians were conspicuous by their absence. Although most of the politicos didn't believe that Wallace and the nuke were still a threat, they had somehow found New Year's Eve functions outside of London that they just had to attend. They had cheered far too loudly after the destruction of the island to admit they had got it wrong. If they showed they were worried now, it would make their previous failure even more visible. But they also realised that this was big, this size of operation could make or break careers. They had to be seen to be involved. The spider phone in the middle of the desk had at least ten people dialled into it.

Lancaster sat at the back of the room with Thomson. He was leaving this briefing up to the Police Commissioner. Once she had finished, the politicians would hang up, happy that they had done their job and the real work could begin. Some of the people in the room, either too low down the food chain to have prior knowledge of the threat, or too stupid to run away, were already checking their watches or swiping their phone screens. They were eager to get off to whatever New Year's Eve celebration they had managed to blag. If they had any sense, they would be running for the hills.

Sitting next to Lancaster was Mick Butler. An SAS Sergeant with a decade of experience carrying out assaults like this. They had worked together on operations in the past and knew they could trust each other. His team would be on standby, waiting for an update and the green light.

Butler tapped his watch. Lancaster gave a slight, almost imperceptible nod, they had to get on with it. The time for committees and discussions was over. They needed a final decision and the go ahead from the top. However this operation ended, there would be an inquiry and the inevitable recriminations, but they couldn't let worries over that delay them any longer. After a few more minutes of slides and questions, the Commissioner finally stopped talking and sat down.

The discussion that the decision makers had was, thankfully, short. The Home Secretary was fully aware of the time pressure and overruled everyone who had dialled in. He gave the operation the green light and, at that point, excused everyone who wasn't directly involved in the assault and handed over operational responsibility.

Mick Butler stepped forward and unrolled a plan of Old-marsh Tower out on the table. 'This building was put up in the late sixties. It's mainly constructed from prefab concrete slabs and then lined with asbestos. There are three stairwells,' he pointed at the features on the plan as he spoke. 'One at either end, for fire evacuation, and one in the middle that looks like the main access. We know there are two lift shafts, although we don't know how useable they are. Our biggest problem is we don't have up to date plans of the internal structure. We might come up against walls and doors that aren't shown here.'

Lancaster put on his glasses and studied the plan. 'How big a problem is it?'

'If we were rescuing hostages, it could jeopardise the operation. We would have to clear every room without knowing where the hostages were. That would cause delay and potentially put lives at risk.'

Lancaster took off his glasses. 'What about in this situation, without hostages? How risky is it now?'

'We're fairly safe to assume that everyone in the building is a bad guy so don't have to worry about any collateral damage to innocent bystanders, that's a plus. However, we know that all the targets in the building are ex-military, some might be ex-special forces, they'll know what to expect. Either way, it's a risky operation, but, considering what's at stake, what other options do we have?'

The Director of MI5 opened a folder and spread its contents on the table. 'Our intelligence shows that the occupants of the building are based on the third floor. They appear to be using the main stairs in the middle of the building for entrance and exit.'

Butler marked the stairwell with a cross. 'We have to assume that the other entrances are mined, maybe Claymores, it's what I would do.'

The Director nodded. 'It would make sense. You'll have to use their entrance, but that's where their sentries will be.'

Butler used his pencil to point to the plan. 'We can put a team on the roof. They'll descend the outside of the building

273

and blow the windows. That will be the trigger for the second team to hit them on the stairs. We go in hard and fast. We know there aren't many of them in there, we'll get it done. Bomb disposal will follow us up.'

The Police Commissioner looked at the plan. 'Excellent. It sounds like it won't be too much of a problem.'

Butler threw his pencil on the table and walked over to the Commissioner. He looked her up and down, his disdain for the woman was obvious. 'Be under no illusions, ma'am, this is a high-risk assault that will likely result in casualties within my team, that's almost inevitable. There is another risk though, perhaps the biggest, which you don't seem to have considered.'

The Commissioner stepped back. 'And what would that be?'

'The risk that the last man standing detonates the bomb.'

Chapter 60

When Palmer got back to the car, he dug out another pair of binoculars from the boot and checked the farm. He could see the glow from the remnants of the barn fire mixed with the flashing blue lights of the emergency services vehicles. There didn't seem to be anyone heading in his direction, perhaps they decided that the carnage at the farm was enough for them to be getting on with.

Palmer watched as a helicopter arrived and landed in the field close to the wreckage of the other one. Hopefully, it was an air ambulance to get Finn to the hospital, but he couldn't make out the markings. There was no time to wait and see what happened, he had to get after Wallace and the bomb. He had to rescue Anna. He threw the binoculars onto the passenger seat and got in the car.

The app on his phone showed the location of the van, it was heading for London. He brought up his own location and hit the other icon to bring up directions. All he had to do was follow the voice on the satnav and it would take him right to Wallace. He started the engine and pulled away.

Chapter 61

Brad turned the van into the access road and pulled up in front of the chain link gate to the boatyard. Wallace was in the front passenger seat while Riley was crammed in the back with Quinn and three other guards.

Brad pulled on the handbrake and sounded the horn. 'Tell me again why we drove into London when we know that a massive explosion is about to level it. Why not put our foot down and head south? We would have been far away from the blast and the fallout. We could have been on the coast in a couple of hours.'

Wallace was becoming irritated by Brad. If he didn't need him to control the others and do the dirty work, he would have shot him already. 'How do we get out of the country? By then, they'll know it's us. We'll have every law enforcement and security services organisation in the country actively trying to track us down. I would say that that puts a blocker on us just turning up at the airport and trying to book a holiday flight.'

'We could've gone to Southampton or back to the Isle of White, picked up the Augustus again.'

'Except the Augustus isn't there, is it, Brad? It's already on its way around to the Baltic to pick up a consignment in St Petersburg. Where do you think the chopper was coming from?

It's only a minor detour to pick us up from here instead. We can arrange a chopper to take us wherever we want to go from there.' He shook his head. 'It's a good job I do the thinking.'

Brad flicked his cigarette out of the window. 'Yeah, well, Palmer has already taken out one chopper. If we don't get away from here by midnight, we're dead.'

'Relax, Brad. We'll get picked up in plenty of time, we can watch what happens on TV.'

Brad sounded the horn again. 'I hope you're right.'

Inside the boatyard's fence, a door opened in the security hut and light flooded out. The security guard appeared, pulling on his high viz coat. He looked like he had just woken up. He had a stretch, fastened his coat, and headed towards the gate.

Brad opened the door and climbed out of the van. 'Keep your eyes open. Can't be too careful.'

The security guard stood at the gate and shone his torch at the van. 'Sorry, mate, we're closed. You'll have to come back after the holidays.'

Brad was hoping that it would be the same guard they had paid off last time, but no such luck. He took a tourist map out of his pocket. 'We're a little lost, buddy. We've just flown in from the States and we're supposed to be meeting up with some old college friends for the fireworks.'

'Just go back the way you came and turn right at the end of the road. Follow the signs, for central London and the tourist spots, there are plenty of them.'

Brad took another step towards the gate. 'Look, we couldn't use your phone, could we? Ours are all American. Cost a fortune to use over here. Just one quick call, please?'

The security guard paused then shook his head. 'I'm not allowed to let anyone through the gate, sorry.'

Brad glanced back at the van. 'Come on, Buddy. We're meeting a couple of girls there. It could be a good night. Chance to rekindle some old relationships if you know what I mean.'

The guard sighed. 'Okay, but just you, the van stays here.'

'No problem, Buddy, that's great, thanks.'

The security guard pulled his keys out of his pocket, opened the padlock that secured the gate, and slid open the bolt.

Brad took his pistol out of his jacket and shot the security guard in the head. The man dropped to his knees then slumped forward against the gate.

'Shit.' Brad turned around and signalled to the van. The side door opened and two of the men got out. 'Get the gate open and get rid of the body.' Brad got back in the van and shut the door.

With the gate open and the body dragged away and thrown into a skip, the van pulled into the boatyard. One of the men closed the gate and snapped the padlock shut.

Wallace got out. 'Get the van under cover, put one of the men in the security hut and stay alert.'

Brad issued orders then turned back to Wallace. 'Nobody knows where we are. All we need to do is stay out of sight until our transport arrives, if it arrives.'

Wallace kept his voice low. 'I don't like the way Palmer turned up at the farm. He's determined to catch up with us, we shouldn't underestimate him.'

'Look, he obviously got information from Vaughn about the farm. It was just bad luck that we used it as a hideout. Anywhere else and Palmer wouldn't have found us. He doesn't know about this place because Vaughn didn't know we were coming here.'

'I'd be happier if I knew Palmer was dead. How can we enjoy our money if we know he's still out there?'

Brad lit another cigarette. 'With the amount of money we're about to be paid, we can hire the world's best bodyguards to deal with him.'

'Just make sure the woman is tied up, we don't want her raising the alarm before we're gone.'

Brad nodded and went inside the workshop.

The rear doors of the van were open. Riley had been tied hand and foot and put in the back. Brad rolled some bottles of water towards her. 'There ya go, don't want people saying we didn't look after ya. Who knows, maybe, if you keep your mouth shut, you'll live through all this.'

'Fuck you. You're about to murder thousands of people and you're worried what they might think of you?'

Wallace appeared at the open door, he dialled a number on his phone and listened, but there didn't appear to be anyone answering. 'Shit.'

Brad didn't need more drama. 'What is it?'

'There's no answer from the farm.' Wallace dialled again.

'It doesn't matter about the farm. No one there knew about this place either. Even if Palmer managed to take them all out, he isn't coming after us.'

Wallace lowered his phone and pressed the red button. 'Shit.' He looked at it for a few seconds then threw it into the back of the van.

'There ya go. Stop thinkin' about it and chill out. Just make sure our transport is coming on time.'

Wallace picked up another handset. This one was a bright yellow satellite phone. He stepped out of the workshop and made a call. Wallace nodded as he spoke, like the person on the other end could see him. After a couple of minutes, he put the handset away and gestured to Brad.

'The transport is being prepped; it'll be on its way soon. I want a man on the wharf watching out for it.' He sat on the edge of the van and checked his watch.

Brad grabbed an assault rifle. 'I'll sort it out.' He called one of the men over and they went outside.

Chapter 62

Palmer was watching the map on his screen. The van had disappeared twenty minutes earlier. Either they had found the GPS tracker and destroyed it, or the van was now under cover. He had made a note of where the signal had been lost. It had vanished from the screen inside the boatyard that he was now watching from a building site opposite.

He could see a security guard inside the hut at the gate. He was sitting with his feet up on the desk and watching a small television screen. Every now and then, he lifted a bottle of whiskey up to his lips and took a drink. If Wallace was in there, that had to be one of his men, but there was no sign of the van.

Behind the hut was an old brick building with several large, shutter doors along its length. Palmer assumed that these were workshops of some kind. The door at the end of the building was open and some light spilled out onto the ground outside. He could see the shadows of at least two people in the building.

Further on, past the shutter door, he could just make out the outline of a figure standing at the end of the wharf. From the way he was standing, Palmer thought it looked like he was facing out across the estuary, watching for something. That was two guards accounted for, which left two more hidden in the yard – assuming he had got his count right at the farm – plus Wallace, Brad, and Riley to find. Riley was unlikely to be one of the shadows inside the workshop, those shadows would belong to Brad and Wallace. The two other guards were missing.

Palmer looked back across to the security hut. The guard in there was relieving his swollen bladder out of the open door. When he had finished, he turned round. It was Quinn. That confirmed it. Palmer now knew for sure that they were in there.

He left the building site and hurried across the road to the fence that surrounded the boatyard. It wasn't a high security fence; it was mainly to deter opportunists and kids from causing any damage. Anything of value was securely locked inside the brick building. The fence was of low-grade chain link about three metres high with a single line of barbed wire across the top. Palmer could have climbed it, but that would have made him visible to anyone patrolling the area. The fence was quite rusty in places, so he pulled out a multi-tool and started snipping at the links.

After a few minutes, he had made enough of a hole to scramble through. He paused to check for anyone nearby, then slipped through unnoticed, dragging his bag behind him. He closed the hole to hide it from any casual observers and readied his weapons.

Palmer raised himself up just enough to see through the corner of the window. Quin was sitting back in his chair with his feet up. He had a glass in his hand and a half-empty bottle of whiskey sat on the desk beside him. Palmer took two slow, deep breaths and kicked open the door.

Quinn tipped out of his chair and scrambled around for his weapon, but it had been knocked out of his reach. Palmer stepped further into the hut and edged around the desk as Quinn stood up and made a grab for his assault rifle. Palmer's Glock coughed twice, and Quinn crumpled to the floor.

Palmer closed the door and lifted Quinn's body back into the chair. If anyone saw him from a distance, it would look like he had drunk too much whiskey and passed out. It would cause enough of a delay for Palmer to make an escape. He removed the two-way radio and earpiece that Quinn was wearing and attached them to his own ear, there was no sound. He was unlikely to pick up any useful information, but he might get a tip-off if they were coming after him.

He checked through the window that looked out onto the brick building. There was still no sign of movement. The guard remained at the end of the wharf and the shadows inside the workshop hadn't moved. He opened the door of the hut and crept out into the yard.

The best option for Palmer was to get around the back of the building to where the sentry was standing on the wharf. This had to be done quickly, but he still hadn't seen the other two guards. They could be doing rounds of the yard or be inside the workshop with the others. Palmer stayed low and made it to the corner of the building without being seen.

Riley stamped her feet on the floor of the van to attract the attention of the guards.

One of them walked over. 'What do you want?'

She pointed at the empty water bottles. 'I really need to go to the toilet.'

'Hold it.' He started to walk away.

283

'Please. I'm going to go. I just don't want to go in the back of this fucking van.'

The guard knocked on the office window. 'She needs a piss.'

Brad waved at the guard. 'Okay, whatever.'

The guard turned back to the van. 'Okay, come on.'

Riley shuffled across the floor until her legs stuck out of the door. 'You'll have to untie me. I can't go like this.'

The guard sighed and shook his head. He untied Riley's ankles and wrists and led her to the toilet. 'Be quick.'

Riley closed the door and locked it. The inside of the toilet was disgusting. It looked like it hadn't been cleaned for months. There was one cubicle and a small sink, but no soap or paper towels. She looked around the small room for something she could use as a weapon, but it was empty. There was nothing sharp or heavy she could strike out with and nothing she could use to cut the ropes when they went back on her wrists. She looked up at the tiny window, even if she could reach it, it was too small to climb out of. Her reflection stared back at her from the grimy mirror, she wasn't going to get out of this. All she could do was try and delay them, maybe Palmer was on his way. She held her nose and opened the door of the cubicle, it might be filthy, but she really did need to go.

Chapter 63

Palmer had made it around to the back of the building. The gap between the brick wall and the fence was a place for stacking empty crates. The space that wasn't covered in boxes was overgrown with nettles and had a healthy collection of old beer cans. Each of the workshops had a door at the back which looked like it was supposed to be a fire escape, but some were blocked off.

There was no lighting at the back of the building and no sign of any guards, they must be inside the workshop. He was able to get from one end of the building to the other quickly, with no hold-ups, until he got to the last unit. As he passed the fire escape, a light came on inside, it flooded out of a small window in the brick wall and lit up his position. He dived to his right and landed in a large patch of nettles.

Palmer looked up. The sudden light from the back of the building had attracted the attention of the guard on the wharf. He was now looking over at Palmer's position. The guard pressed the button on his microphone. 'This is Delta Two, I've got movement out here.' He raised his weapon and started to move towards the corner.

Palmer raised his head. The sudden light from the back of the building had attracted the attention of the guard on the wharf. He was now looking over directly to Palmer's position. The guard pressed the button on his microphone. 'This is Delta Two, I've got movement out here.' He raised his weapon and started to move towards the corner.

Palmer couldn't take any chances. He squeezed the trigger and dropped the guard, then rolled out of the nettles and sprinted across the wharf.

Riley heard the commotion outside. She opened the toilet door and peered out.

Wallace was on his feet. 'It's Palmer.'

Brad got on the radio. 'Delta Two, come in. Delta Two? Come in.' He signalled to the guards. 'Get out there and see what he's talking about.'

The two guards ran out of the shutter door and into the darkness.

Brad got back on the radio. 'Delta One, leave the gate and get down to the wharf.'

There was no reply.

'Delta One, come in, over.'

There was still no response.

Wallace backed into the corner next to the roller door. 'What's going on? How did he find us?'

Brad was listening closely to the radio. 'Be quiet, Kane, we don't know anything yet. He probably saw a dockyard cat. 'Delta Three, Delta Four, come in, over.'

'This is Delta Four, there's no sign of Delta Two, but the boat is heading our way. It's a few hundred yard–'

The radio went dead.

Brad paused, looking at his radio to make sure it was still working. 'Delta Four, come in over. Delta Four?'

'This is Delta Three. There's someone out here, but I've got him pinned down. The boat's nearly here.'

Wallace unholstered his pistol. 'Where's the woman.'

Riley sneaked out of the toilet and stepped around the pile of weapons towards the fire escape. If she could get out, Palmer could finish them off without worrying about her. She gently pushed on the bar attached to the door and it opened with a metallic clunk. She pushed it, but it stuck. She tried again, but something was wedged behind it.

'Where do you think you're going?'

Brad had left the door and was now walking straight towards her.

Riley looked for another way out, but she would have to get past Brad first. She looked down at the pile of weapons, a semi-automatic pistol sat on top of a pile of boxes containing ammunition. She picked it up and pointed it at Brad. 'Don't come any closer.'

Brad raised his hands. 'I'll bet you're used to working in an office. Never been out in the field. I'll bet you don't even know how to use it, do you?'

Riley pulled back the slide on the pistol. A live round spun out of the ejection port. She took aim again.

Brad was laughing. 'Don't even know how to do a press check and see if it's loaded. Don't forget the safety catch.'

Riley turned the weapon and examined both sides. Where the hell was the safety catch? She didn't know what one looked like. Did it even have one?

Brad took a step forward. 'Not as easy as it looks in the movies, is it, Anna?'

Riley's hand was shaking. 'I'm warning you, stay away.'

Brad took another step. 'I don't think so.' He lunged at her.

287

Riley pulled the trigger, once, twice, the gun jumped in her hand and she dropped it, stunned.

Brad fell to his knees. He looked up at Riley, his expression one of complete surprise. There was a dark red spot on the front of his T-shirt, Riley's first, lucky shot. The spot was growing bigger.

Riley put her hand over her mouth, she had never fired a weapon before.

Brad opened his mouth to speak, but only blood came out. Riley's second, panicked shot, fired after the recoil had kicked back at her hand, had hit Brad in the throat. Blood was now pouring out from between his fingers, soaking his shirt. His eyes began to narrow, and he pitched forwards onto his face.

Riley stepped back, away from the spreading pool of blood, and felt Wallace's Glock against the back of her head. 'Don't move.'

Chapter 64

Palmer was crouched behind a concrete block, it wasn't giving him much cover, but it was just enough. If he moved an inch either way, the guard would be able to pick him off. He loaded a grenade into the launcher that was fastened under the barrel of his assault rifle. The guard had made the mistake of sheltering close to the petrol stowage at the end of the Wharf. One good shot was all it would take.

Wallace's voice echoed across the wharf. 'Palmer. Logan Palmer. I've got Anna Riley here. If you try anything, I'll kill her.'

Palmer knew that Wallace would kill Riley anyway. He couldn't allow him to get her on the boat. If he did, she would be dead and thrown into the sea as soon as Wallace felt safe.

The rigid inflatable from the MV Augustus pulled up alongside the wharf. The driver stood up, beckoning to the guard. He opened fire at Palmer's position.

Palmer rolled sideways, away from the concrete block. As the bullets pinged onto the floor, following him across the ground, he knelt up and pulled the trigger on the grenade launcher.

The blast, as the petrol ignited, killed the guard who had crouched close to them, and blew the helmsman backwards out of the boat. The water was on fire in patches where the flaming petrol ran off the wharf.

Wallace fired two shots, but both missed. 'I'll kill her.'

Palmer knew that the sudden bright light of the explosion would have killed Wallace's night vision. He wouldn't be able to see Palmer, he was just firing blind.

Palmer had kept one eye closed when the petrol exploded, preserving his night vision, and had Wallace in his sights, but all he could see of him was the hand that held the pistol and the side of his leg. It was a risky shot, but he had to take it. He held his breath and pulled the trigger. 'Anna, run!'

Wallace spun to the side as the bullet tore into the flesh of his hip. He tripped and fell onto his back. Palmer aimed again, but the helmsman had managed to climb back into the boat. He was bloodied and out of breath, but he was armed and lying down, giving covering fire. Palmer rolled back behind the block and screamed at Riley. 'Get inside, Anna!' He stood up and returned fire.

Wallace crawled along the wharf and rolled into the boat. The helmsman threw his assault rifle to him. 'Keep him down.' He pressed the button and started the engine.

Wallace emptied his magazine in one trigger pull and looked around for another. 'Where's your ammo?'

'I wasn't expecting a gunfight.'

Wallace dropped the rifle and lay down in the bottom of the boat. 'Go, go, go.'

The nose of the inflatable lifted as the helmsman accelerated.

Palmer ran to the edge of the wharf. He fired the rest of his ammunition towards the boat, but it had no effect. There was no way he was going to let him get away. He loaded another grenade into the launcher and fired.

The first grenade landed in front of the boat and caused the helmsman to swerve left. The second grenade exploded to the side of the boat and forced the driver to swerve right. The third grenade, Palmer's last, was perfect. It landed in the middle of the boat and exploded. It killed the helmsman instantly and fatally injured Wallace. The petrol that sloshed about in the bottom of the boat caught fire and the inflatable exploded, showering the water with metal and rubber.

Palmer was on his knees, he was exhausted. He started to laugh, just a small giggle to begin with, but then a roar that echoed around the boatyard. The laughter then turned to a wracking sob as an image of Nathan flashed into Palmer's mind and the bottled-up grief took hold of him.

Riley got to her feet. Her hands and elbows were bloodied from where she had dived out of the way and skidded across the concrete. She looked around; they were all dead. She walked over to where Palmer knelt, crouched down, and put her arms around him.

Chapter 65

Mick Butler climbed the first two flights of stairs towards the third floor of the building. Three members of his team were behind him, ready to burst into action as soon as they had the go-ahead. Butler had directed two men to cover the roof and another two were climbing the east staircase. They had managed to disable a tripwire linked to a Claymore mine on their way up. Butler had been right about that one. They now crouched outside the entrance to the third floor waiting to breach the door.

Butler pressed the button on his throat mic. 'All call signs, stand by.'

One of the troopers slid the flexible neck of the inspection camera under the door. He switched on a six-inch-wide screen and handed it to Butler. The image on the screen showed Butler what was happening on the third floor. He picked up the headset that was attached to the screen and listened.

One of the guards had his phone to his ear. He lowered it and stared at the screen. 'Voicemail again. What's goin' on? We haven't had an update for hours.'

Another guard sat on a fold-up deckchair. 'D' ya think they've been tumbled?'

'No, the boss is too good for that.'

'But what if they have? What's in this box anyway?'

'It doesn't matter what's in the box. The boss said that the operation ends tonight, and we'll get what's coming to us then. I'll try phoning Brad's number.' He tapped his screen and raised it back to his ear.

Butler waited for the instruction to begin the assault. They were exposed all the time they were on the stairs. There was nowhere to seek cover. If any of the guards came out of the door, it was going to hit the fan.

The voice of Butler's boss crackled in his earpiece. 'Operation is a go, repeat, the operation is a go.'

'Roger that.' He switched his radio back to channel one. 'Team Two, go.'

Butler ran through the timing of the assault in his head. The two SAS troopers on the roof would be lowering their black nylon ropes down the side of the building and starting their descent. Each one making sure that he stayed between the windows to ensure he would not be seen. Each man held an explosive frame ready to attach to the windows. After two minutes, they were in position, just above the third floor. 'Team Two in position.'

'Roger, Team Two.'

Butler checked the screen again.

The guard with the phone checked its screen too. 'Maybe I'm not getting a good signal.'

'Don't be an idiot, if you weren't getting a signal, you wouldn't be getting through to voicemail.' The other three guards laughed at him.

'Fuck you lot, I'm going outside to check anyway.'

Butler realized they were about to be compromised. He pressed the send button on his radio. 'All call signs, go, go, go.'

There was a pause of three seconds then Team Two's explosives detonated and blew out the windows. Four stun grenades were thrown in through the shattered frames. The blinding flash and ear-splitting noise overwhelmed the senses of the guards, confusing them and rendering them helpless long enough for the SAS teams to burst in.

As one, the two men at the windows swung in, weapons at the ready. Butler dropped the camera screen, and his team breached the door at the same time as the two men from the east staircase ran in. The guards weren't expecting any of it, they hadn't even set up sentries at the entrance points. Each of the men who swung in through the window dropped a guard. One of them tried his best to run away from the noise, but the men entering from the east staircase took him down. Butler, at the head of team one, shot the last of the guards. It was all over in less than a minute. Butler had overestimated the guards' abilities and their preparedness. He was relieved.

The SAS team checked the rest of the floor for any guards they had missed, Butler sent four of them to carry out a sweep of the building, but they didn't find anyone else. He got on the radio. 'Control, Team One, all tangos down, repeat, all tangos down.'

Butler's team packed up and descended to the car park.

Butler's boss was the first to approach the team. 'That went a lot easier than we expected.'

Butler took off his gloves. 'Yeah, something wasn't right about it. It looks like they didn't know what they were guarding and didn't expect anyone to come after them.'

'You think they were kept in the dark?'

'Wouldn't be unusual to keep the details of the op from the

foot soldiers. Bearing in mind they were in a building with a nuclear device, the only other options are that they were very dedicated and willing to die, or very stupid.'

Chapter 66

On the third floor, the bomb disposal technician put on his protective suit and slowly approached the carbon fibre box that sat against the wall at the far end of the room. He was fully aware of what this was and knew that no suit existed that would protect him if this thing went off. If he got this wrong, everyone was dead.

The second bomb technician watched his colleague from the door, linked to him by a cable that carried his communications signal. 'Take it easy, Dave, they had a Claymore on the stairs, they might have booby-trapped the case.'

'Roger.' Dave checked all around the case for trip wires, pressure pads and micro switches, but there were none. Not on the outside anyway. He inched the case away from the wall and checked behind it, nothing. He checked underneath the pallet it was sitting on, all clear. 'I'm opening the lid.'

'Roger.' The other bomb tech held his breath. This was a delicate part of the operation. If there was a booby trap, it was most likely rigged to blow when the lid opened.

The bomb tech unfastened the catches on the front of the case and cracked open the lid a few millimetres. He inserted a plastic wedge into the gap and checked inside the box with a small torch. There was no sign of any switches or wires yet.

Keeping his eyes glued to the widening gap, he gradually eased the wedge further in. He stopped, there was a light coming from inside the case, a red light that blinked every second. 'We've got a light pulsing, could be a timer.'

The other bomb tech lifted his microphone. 'Okay, Dave. It's the kind of thing we would expect. Take it slow.'

As Dave pushed a wedge in under the lid, it lifted a few millimetres at a time. His torch lit up the inside of the case as the gap widened. 'I can't feel anything yet. I can just about get my fingers in . . . Wait.'

'What is it, Dave?'

'There's a wire.'

At the front of the case, attached to the underside of the lid, was what looked like a piece of fishing line. The plastic filament was reflecting the red light that was flashing inside the case. Dave had a dilemma. He didn't know whether this line was designed to pull something and set off the bomb, in which case he needed to cut it. Or if it was keeping tension on a switch, in which case cutting it was the last thing he should do.

'I'm going to maintain the tension on the wire and then cut it.'

'Roger, Dave. Go easy, mate.'

Dave inserted a pair of pliers into the gap and clamped them onto the fishing line. With his other hand, he slid a small pair of snips into the case and cut the wire. Nothing happened. He could feel the sweat running down his back. Keeping tension on the fishing line with his pliers, he gripped the edge of the lid and eased it open.

Mick Butler's team had loaded all their equipment into two

black Land Rovers and were waiting for clearance to get back to their base when Dave appeared at the entrance to the building, his T-shirt soaked with sweat. He threw his tools into the back of his van and walked over to Lancaster. 'False alarm.'

'What? What do you mean, false alarm?'

Dave held up a circuit board with wires hanging off it. 'The case had three grenades in it. A piece of fishing line was tied to the pins and attached to the lid. It would have done some serious damage to anyone who went poking about inside.'

'What's that?'

'This board had a red flashing light on it, so it looked like a timer. Someone's idea of a joke.'

Lancaster took the circuit board. 'No way. Four men died protecting a box that had nothing in it. This isn't someone's idea of a joke. This was specifically designed to slow us down. This is a decoy.'

'It certainly looks that way.'

'Thanks, guys. You need to get out of here.'

The bomb technicians closed their doors. 'If you do find a real bomb, let us know.' They got into the van and drove away.

Lancaster ran over to where Thomson was standing talking to Butler. 'It's a decoy. There's no bomb here.'

Thomson's mouth hung open. 'What do we do now?'

'We minimise the casualties as much as possible. Get on the phone. Evacuate everyone you can. Tell the police to block all the roads.'

Butler had walked over to the Land Rovers to brief his team. Lancaster joined him. 'You and your men should get as far away from this as you can.'

Butler looked across at his team. 'We've had a chat. Four of the lads have got young families, they get out. The rest of us will hang around for a little while, you might need us.'

'It's much appreciated, guys, if we find the bomb, we'll need all the help we can get.'

Butler's team shook hands and wished each other luck. The four that were leaving got into their vehicle and, reluctantly it seemed, left the rest of their team behind.

Butler waved them off then turned back to Lancaster. 'So, I've just got one question.'

'What's that?'

'Where's the bomb?'

Chapter 67

R iley stood up and helped Palmer to his feet. He was covered in dirt, sweat, and greasy cam cream. There was blood seeping from various cuts and scrapes he had picked up at the farm and in the boatyard. Riley pulled a couple of nettle leaves out of his hair. 'Logan, we have to stop the bomb.'

Palmer was snapped back to reality. In the chaos of the last hour, his focus had been on finding Anna and stopping Wallace. Now he had to disarm the bomb. 'Right, is it still in the van? We need to try and stop the timer.'

'It's not here.'

Palmer was stunned. Disarming the bomb was going to be hard enough. He was no bomb tech or explosives expert. Now they didn't even know where it was. 'What? It has to be here. Find Wallace, find the bomb.'

Riley grabbed his arm and pulled him towards the workshop. 'I'll show you. This way, quickly.' She led Palmer back inside the building and retrieved Wallace's phone from the back of the van. 'He kept looking at the screen, he showed me it. It displays the bomb's location and has a timer.'

'Jesus, where is it?'

Riley turned the screen to Palmer. 'He planted it two days

ago. It's on a party boat on the Thames, heading upriver towards the London Eye, to watch the fireworks.'

Palmer took the phone. It showed a detailed map of central London. Buckingham Palace, The Houses of Parliament, and The London Eye were all labelled. In the middle of the screen, a small red circle was gradually making its way along the winding ribbon of blue that was the river. The party boat was unwittingly carrying Wallace's nuclear device right into the heart of London.

Palmer looked at the timer, sixty minutes to get into central London and find the boat. He was transfixed by the digits ticking down, was it even possible? After everything they had done, to get this close only to fail now. No, he had to try. He looked at Riley. 'Get the van out of here and up to the gate, I'll get it open.'

Riley closed the side door and jumped into the driver's seat. She started the engine and threw the gears into reverse. As she accelerated, she slammed into a bag full of money that one of the guards had dumped beside the door. Probably ready to take with him. As the wheels ran over the bag, it burst and spilled thousands of pounds in twenty-pound notes out onto the wharf.

Palmer set off running back to the security hut where he had left Quinn's body. He must have the keys for the gate on him. His heart was thumping, the adrenaline pumping through his body was the only thing keeping him moving.

Palmer jumped the two steps outside the hut and kicked open the door. Quinn's body had slipped down onto the floor, blood oozing out of his wounds. Palmer jumped over the desk and landed beside the body. Quinn's coat, the actual security guard's coat, was loaded with pockets. Palmer started searching them. 'Come on, come on. You must keep them handy.'

The van screeched to a halt outside the hut just as Palmer felt a bunch of keys in one of the pockets. He pulled them out and ran out to the gate. His hands were shaking, he steadied his breathing and looked for keys that were obviously for a padlock. There were two. The first one didn't fit, it never did. He tried the second one, bingo. He removed the padlock, slid back the steel bolt, and swung open the gate.

Riley pulled the van forward and Palmer climbed in beside her. He looked at the phone, fifty-five minutes to detonation. Palmer wondered if it would be better if Riley put her foot down and got them as far away from London as possible. Riley pulled out onto the road and floored the accelerator. The back of the van skidded and swung as the wheels tried to find grip on the slippery road. She swung the steering wheel left and right as she fought to control it. Palmer held on and watched the phone as the circle that tracked the party boat inched its way across the map.

Riley slammed on the brakes. There was a queue of traffic ahead of them that didn't look like it was clearing out of the way any time soon. The roads that were closed for the new year celebrations had caused some tailbacks, but this looked more like there had been an accident somewhere. This wasn't just caused by vehicles trying to navigate a way around the crowds. Riley leaned on the horn and flashed the lights, but no one was paying attention, they were all stuck in the same queue.

Turning the wheel to the left, full lock, Riley put her foot down, and the van mounted the pavement. The other cars sounded their horns, some of the drivers got out and shouted at her as she shot past them. The van squeezed between bits of street furniture, lampposts, concrete benches, and post boxes. They were making good progress, but then the inevitable happened. They got to a crossroads where pelican crossings and crash barriers had been fitted. Their route was blocked.

Riley turned the wheel a sharp right and dropped back onto the road. The suspension creaked and clunked as it bottomed out. The van bounced and smashed the wing mirror off a car as it went. She threaded the van between two more cars, taking out another wing mirror. Drivers were now getting out of their vehicles and waving, trying to flag her down, trying to stop her reckless, headlong, flight. People dived out of the way as she careered along the road, denting doors, and ripping off wheel trims. As they neared the front of the queue, the van came to a halt. Directly ahead of them, they could see what the hold-up was. A truck, making night deliveries, had tried to make a three-point turn to get around the road closures. It was now wedged across the road.

With the van at a standstill, some of the drivers started to run towards them. Some of them looked angry, menacing, they obviously had dark intentions in mind. Palmer opened the door and stepped out, firing two shots into the air. At this point, the other drivers all seemed to remember somewhere else they had to be.

Palmer checked Wallace's phone. There were forty minutes left. He handed his own phone to Riley. 'Get hold of Lancaster. Tell them what's happening. Get someone to the boat.'

'What are you going to do?'

'I'll get past this truck and grab another car.'

Riley grabbed his arm. 'I'll see you again, Logan, I know I will. I can feel it.'

Palmer nodded and smiled. 'You need to take care of yourself now, Anna. Whatever happens now, whatever happens to me, you get out of here and get on with your life.' He closed the door and ran off up the street.

Chapter 68

Thomson and Lancaster were both franticly speaking into handsets. They each had a group of people that they had to get clear of the approaching catastrophe. The King had already been sent to Balmoral. The PM and the Cabinet were on a plane heading for Manchester along with the heads of the military and various civilian organisations. Their job would be to set up a command-and-control headquarters to deal with the aftermath. Thomson was talking to the Met Commissioner, all cars had to be turned around and sent out of London, some might get far enough away to survive. The people on the streets had no chance. That included her and Lancaster, they were about to become collateral damage, names in a book of remembrance.

No sooner had Thomson ended that call, than another come in. She didn't recognise the number, but this wasn't a time to be selective over who she spoke to. She pressed answer. 'Hello, Thomson speaking.'

'Vicky, it's me.'

Thomson waved Lancaster over. 'Anna, where are you? Tell me you aren't in London.'

'I'm stuck in a traffic jam a few miles from the river. We know where the bomb is.'

Thomson put her phone on hands-free. 'How do you know? What's happened?'

'Wallace told me where it was, it's on a boat that's going down the Thames to watch the fireworks. It goes off at midnight.'

Lancaster looked at his watch and waved Butler over. 'Where's Palmer?'

Riley was out of breath. She was rambling, trying to get all the information out as quickly as possible. 'Logan killed Wallace, he killed everyone, he's heading for the boat now, on foot. It's called the Eliza J, you need to get people there, get them there now. We can still stop this.'

Butler ran back to his Land Rover and jumped in to call the bomb disposal team and tell them about the boat, leaving it up to them whether they diverted to the river or not. The bomb techs swung their vehicle around and headed back into the centre of the city. Two police cars pulled out in front of the special forces' vehicle and, with blue lights flashing and sirens wailing, they all took off towards the river.

Lancaster and Thomson got into another police car and followed on. Thomson put the phone back to her ear. 'Anna, listen to me, get away, get as far away as you can in the time you've got left.'

Riley sounded panicked. 'I can come with you. I . . . I don't want to be on my own.'

'No, Anna. You've done all you can. You need to be the one who tells everyone what happened. Tell them the truth, tell them about Logan and what he did. There's no more you can do here.'

There was a long pause. Thomson knew that Riley would be trying to think of a reason why she needed to be with them, but there wasn't one. Not one that would sound rational anyway. There would be a lot of people trying to cover their own backs after this. There would be recriminations and finger pointing. The people who were dead would be most likely to get the blame. Someone had to survive.

Riley sighed. 'Okay, I'll go now. Thank you, Vicky. Thank you for everything.' With her voice failing, she hung up.

Chapter 69

Once Palmer was past the stranded truck, the road was deserted. With the road blocked off and many people safely at home or downing a few drinks in the pub, there was no one driving around. He considered stealing one of the cars parked at the side of the street, but it wasn't as easy to hotwire a modern car as they made it look in films. There was no guarantee he would be able to get it started and he would just be wasting his time, so he kept running.

As he closed in on the cordon that had been put in place to keep traffic away from new year's revellers, he started to get held up by pedestrians. People were heading for the city, keen to welcome in the new year to the sound of Big Ben. Palmer tried to swerve between them and ran along the road, but, as the crowds grew, it was only a matter of time before he ran into someone.

Palmer could see the man up ahead, staggering down the road, acting the fool for his friends and the women with them. More than a few beers had passed his lips and he was plainly drunk. Palmer tried to avoid him but the man staggard to his left and stepped straight into Palmer's path. The collision was a crunching one and sent them both tumbling into the road.

Palmer landed on his back and was momentarily stunned

by the impact. His head was spinning. He lay in the road and caught his breath for a few seconds then rolled over and climbed to his feet. The drunken man he had run into wasn't in as good a shape and was still flat out on his face, but Palmer didn't have time to hang around and check on him. The man's friends had other ideas. They took an instant dislike to Palmer and grabbed him, forcing him back across the pavement and up against the wall of the bar they had just fallen out of.

The biggest of the man's friends stepped up to Palmer, getting right in his face. 'What the fuck are you doin'?'

Palmer pushed him away and tried to leave but his other two friends held him back. Explaining that he was in a hurry wasn't going to work, Palmer needed to get away from them. He pulled his head back and butted the first guy square in the face. The man went down on his knees clutching his broken nose. That freed up Palmer's arm and the second man got two short jabs to the solar plexus that doubled him over. Egged on by the women who were with them, the big guy decided to come back in for another go, but Palmer already had his pistol pointed at the man's head. 'Back off.'

The big guy immediately went into reverse and backed away from Palmer, as did everyone else anywhere near the commotion. Two of the women helped the drunken man, that Palmer had run into, back to his feet. He was none the wiser and was still happily trying to play the fool.

Palmer held up his hand. 'I'm Sorry.' He didn't know if he was apologising for running into him, or because they would all be dead in thirty minutes.

A fast-food courier on a bright red motorbike had stopped on his delivery to watch the argument. He lifted the visor of his helmet, kicked down the stand, and dismounted just as

Palmer turned around to run off. Palmer looked at the bike. It was small and looked like it had an engine the same size as a lawnmower. It wasn't exactly a machine that would be seen racing around the roads on the Isle of Man, but it would be faster than running. Palmer pointed his weapon straight at the young man and again apologised. 'Sorry, mate, gonna need your bike.'

The courier held up his hands and stepped back out of the way. It wasn't his bike anyway, and it didn't look like he wanted to risk his life for the three sixteen-inch pizzas that were in the top box. Palmer straddled the bike, kicked up the stand, and accelerated away.

Palmer steered one-handed as he took out the phone and checked the progress of the red circle on the screen. The Eliza J was still ahead of him. He was now riding parallel to the river, but he had to get ahead of the boat. He put the phone back in his pocket and willed the bike to go faster.

He approached the road closed sign at the edge of the cordon. No vehicles were allowed beyond this point, not even pizza delivery bikes. Ahead of him were three people in hi-vis jackets, but he couldn't tell if they were police, community support officers, or stewards. It didn't matter. He wasn't going to hang around to find out or explain where he was going anyway. He mounted the pavement and headed for a gap in the barrier. The three sentries spotted him and came together in a human, hi-vis barricade, but Palmer accelerated, blowing through them before they could stop him. One of them, a young woman, managed to grab Palmer's jacket and knocked him off balance. The front wheel wobbled, and the bike went down, spilling pizzas across the road. It skidded for a few metres then crunched to a halt jammed under a van.

Palmer rolled and was on his feet quickly, sprinting along the pavement. The young police officer who had brought him down gave chase. She was fresher than he was and was gaining on him. The only chance Palmer had was to lose her in the crowd. He turned himself sideways and slid through the middle of a group.

The crowd was large and slow-moving. Most of them had already realised that they weren't going to make it to the London Eye and were picking spots that gave them a good view. Palmer side-stepped and zig zagged his way through the throng, hoping that the police officer was having the same trouble. He turned around to check, but she was no longer following him. She was standing in the middle of the road talking on her radio, and, judging by her body language, she wasn't happy.

As Palmer franticly pushed his way through the crowd and made his way towards the river, he checked the phone again. He was now in front of the Eliza J, all he had to do was get on board. The map showed that the Millennium Bridge was just up ahead. That was his only chance. He edged his way out of the tightest part of the crowd and sprinted towards it.

Chapter 70

The crowd on the bridge was almost packed as tightly together as those on the street. Palmer pushed his way to the centre of the middle span, then out to the guardrail. Most people on the bridge were facing the opposite way, towards the Houses of Parliament, as they waited for the celebrations to begin. No one was that interested in what he was doing.

The red circle on the phone was almost at the bridge, and the timer said seventeen minutes. Palmer looked away from the screen and along the river. Heading straight for him was the Eliza J. It was lit up like a Christmas tree and he could hear the thumping music even over the noise of the crowd on the bridge. The phone dropped from his hand. He didn't need it anymore. Either he got there in time and stopped the bomb, or everyone here died, there wasn't a Plan B.

Palmer swung his legs over the guardrail and positioned himself to make sure that he had a clear drop to the water.

He noticed a middle-aged woman watching him from the back of the crowd. She left her friends and walked over to the rail, stopping two steps away from him. 'Are you okay, love? You don't want to go out there, it's not safe.'

Palmer didn't take his eyes off the Eliza J. 'It's okay, thanks.

Just go back to your friends and enjoy the time you have.'

The woman stepped forwards and put her hand on Palmer's arm. 'You might feel like this is the solution to whatever is going on in your life, but there are people who care. There really are. This time of year affects people in different ways. Why don't you come back over this side, love? We can have a chat about things.'

Palmer smiled at the woman. Surrounded by people who were focused on celebration and partying, all she could think of was his welfare. The world needed more people like her. 'Thank you, but I'm not planning to kill myself. Not if I can help it. If this goes to plan, you'll understand.'

The boat had just reached the bridge. Palmer looked down. The New Year's Eve party was in full on, bouncing, noisy, swing. The Eliza J looked like an old coal barge that had found a new lease of life as a sightseeing boat for tourists. At the front of the upper deck was a flat triangular area where bollards and ropes that were used to secure the boat to the docking bay were kept. At the stern of the boat was a folding gangway that would be raised and lowered to allow passengers to get on and off.

Between the two functional areas of the Eliza J, the rest of the upper deck had been turned into one long entertainment area surrounded by wrap-around windows that would give the passengers front row seats to the firework display. Even the arched roof was made of glass and made the Eliza J look like a moving greenhouse.

Palmer let go of the handrail and gritted his teeth. This was going to hurt. The woman screamed and lunged towards Palmer, trying to grab him, but she was too late. Palmer stepped forward and disappeared.

Chapter 71

Inside the Eliza J's glass bubble, the DJ waved her hands above her head as the crowd danced, or in some cases staggered, in time to the music. One person was standing on the rear deck throwing up and three looked like they were asleep in the soft chairs that were dotted around the dance floor.

Palmer hit the roof of the boat with a loud thud. He was right about one thing, it fucking hurt. Most of the revellers partying below didn't notice, but two of them looked up and screamed. Palmer was lying spread-eagled above the dance floor trying to avoid sliding off the roof. The glass started to crack, and everyone cleared out to the edges of the room. Palmer pulled out his 9mm and fired through the roof.

The guests scattered. The bullets that Palmer had fired had shattered the glass and he was now in the room with them. If any of the passengers had thought quickly or weren't already drunk, they could have taken him out right there. Palmer lay on the dance floor surrounded by bits of the broken roof. His whole body was screaming, and he could taste blood. The sharp pain when he inhaled pointed towards a couple of broken ribs and one of his knees felt like it had been hit with a cricket bat. He rolled over and struggled to his feet. No one was trying to tackle him or to help him. They obviously didn't know what to think or do. This was probably way beyond any experience they had ever had.

The DJ killed the music, and an eerie silence filled the room. The quiet was broken by Palmer. He waved his weapon around for effect. 'Everyone off the boat.'

No one moved. They just stood around staring at each other in drunken disbelief.

Palmer fired a shot into the air. 'Now! This boat is about to explode.'

Someone screamed and there was a mad rush for the exits. People threw themselves off the boat and swam for the shore. Boats belonging to the River Police were zeroing in on the area and started to pick up the passengers.

Palmer tested his injured knee then hobbled to the wheel-house, leaving a trail of blood behind him, and pushed open the door.

The captain turned around. 'What was that noise? Did something hit the roof?'

Palmer stood in the doorway. Blood ran down his face from a cut high up on his forehead and another gash had soaked through the arm of his jacket. He had his weapon pointed straight at the captain. 'Yeah, that was me.'

The captain put his hands up. 'What do you want?'

'Your passengers have decided to swim home. I want you to get us away from the people on the bridges, there's a bomb on board.'

'I . . . I don't understand.'

Palmer stepped into the wheelhouse and aimed his gun at the man's head. 'Do it now, Captain. This isn't a fuckin' drill.'

The captain accelerated away from the bridges and stopped

in the middle of the river. He turned and looked at Palmer. 'Now what?'

Palmer was close to collapsing. His body had taken too much punishment and he was losing blood. 'Is there anything on board that isn't normally here? Something that was brought here in the last two days. Something that could be a bomb.'

The captain scratched his head, thinking.

'Quickly, Captain. We have less than ten minutes.'

The captain pointed to the front of the boat. 'A new locker was fitted up for'ard. It's locked. We were told not to open it.'

'That's good, Captain. Now, get off the boat.'

The captain rushed out of the wheelhouse and threw himself off the back of the boat.

Palmer opened the external door of the wheelhouse and stumbled out on to the fore deck. At the back of the deck, behind a pile of ropes, was the new locker that the captain had told him about. It was freshly painted and stood out. He looked around for tools, he would have given anything for a large sledgehammer. Under the ropes was a long wooden pole with a brass hook at the end. That would have to do. He picked the pole up and held it like a spear, smashing the brass end into the lock. Once, twice, three times, his strength was leaving him. On the fourth strike, the padlock shattered.

Chapter 72

The emergency services had reached the river and were directing the passenger rescue. People in small boats were helping to pull survivors out of the water and were giving them first aid while the river police stopped anyone approaching the area.

TV news cameras from all over the world, there to film the fireworks, swung their lenses onto the river, everyone was now aware of the unfolding drama. It wasn't likely that they understood the threat they were under though.

The boat was now floating in the middle of the river, drifting with the current. A police helicopter hovered over the scene, its Nightsun spotlight illuminated the whole area and reflected off the shattered glass roof of the boat.

Palmer opened the lid of the locker. Sitting inside it was the carbon fibre case that contained the bomb. It didn't look like something that would level an entire city. At least, Palmer didn't think so. He unfastened the catches on the front and lifted the lid.

There was no time for him to worry about booby traps, there were only six minutes left.

The timer clicked over, there were now five minutes remaining. Palmer tried to remember what the Russian had told him.

'You must unscrew the plutonium core. Without it, only the primary will explode. There will be no nuclear reaction.'

He had no idea what he was doing, but next to the timer was the top of a cylinder just as Chernov had said there would be. It was fastened in with four screws. Palmer pulled out his multi-tool from the pouch on his belt and opened out the screwdriver.

The screws were large but turned easily. Palmer unscrewed them until they felt loose enough to remove with his fingers. The first one was easy, the second one slightly tighter, the third was stuck. 'Shit.' He got his tool out again and loosened it off.

There were three minutes left.

Screws three and four finally came out. Palmer grabbed the D-shaped handle on the top of the cylinder and started to unscrew the whole thing. It took two complete turns until the core came free and he carefully lifted it out of its housing. Slowly, slowly, inch by agonising inch. Then it caught on something.

There were two minutes left. 'Jesus.'

Palmer looked at the bottom of the cylinder, there were two thin wires attached to it. What was this? No one mentioned wires. How could someone miss that out of the instructions? What did he do now?

He looked at the timer, one minute remained.

This was it, all or nothing, live or die.

Palmer took a solid grip on the cylinder and planted his feet. His injured knee was barely moveable and his hands were wet with blood and sweat.

Thirty seconds remained.

He took one last breath and, in a single movement, ripped

the cylinder out of the case and rolled backwards off the boat.

The shockwave from the explosion and the huge fireball ripped through the boat sending glass, pieces of metal, and large burning chunks of wood high into the air at the same time as Big Ben rang the chimes of midnight, and the firework display began.

Everyone ducked and ran away from the riverbank as the flaming debris started to return to earth. The surface of the water burned as the ruptured fuel tank of the boat emptied out into the river and debris set fire to it.

Chapter 73

The explosion had been spectacular, but Thomson knew that they had survived the main threat. Palmer had done it. Somehow, he had disarmed the device before it had caused a nuclear reaction. None of the onlookers or journalists understood what had really happened, it was possible that they never would, but every single one of them owed Palmer their lives.

Thomson stood beside Lancaster and scanned the surface of the water for any sign of Palmer amongst the wreckage. Lancaster waved the police boats in closer, but they were carrying rescued passengers and couldn't afford to put them at any further risk. Out of the small armada of rescue craft, one unmarked boat pushed forward and weaved its way through the patches of burning fuel. It was being driven by one of Butler's men.

Butler watched over the side, searching the surface of the water with the light from a large torch. The boat was within twenty feet of the burning remains of the Eliza J's hull when Butler held up his hand. He leaned over and reached into the water. When he came back up, he was dragging Palmer onto the boat.

Thomson took off her shoes and waded into the river, her

background as a military nurse could keep Palmer alive until the paramedics arrived. If he wasn't dead already. The SAS trooper driving the rigid inflatable guided it into the shallows and beached it on the riverbank. Thomson grabbed Butler's hands and climbed aboard.

Palmer was unconscious. He had blood dripping from gashes on his face and hands, but he was alive. Thomson checked his pulse. It was fast but strong and his breathing was normal. She felt around his body for any serious wounds or broken bones. His legs and arms weren't broken, but she couldn't rule out other fractures. She took off his jacket and felt his ribs, at least two were broken.

Palmer opened his eyes. 'If you're going to touch me up, you're supposed to ask first.'

Thomson let out a deep sigh. 'Were you just pretending to be unconscious?'

'It's been a long day. I was trying to have a nap.'

Thomson shook her head. 'Look at me. These are my best trousers, you dick.'

Palmer looked at Butler. 'Charming. Is this the thanks I get for saving everyone?'

Thomson started to chuckle. By the time the paramedics had arrived and started to treat Palmer, they were all in hysterics.

Palmer winced. 'Don't make me laugh, I ache all over.'

The paramedics strapped him to a back board and put a neck brace on him. Together with Butler and the SAS trooper who had driven the boat, they lifted Palmer onto a stretcher and wheeled him to the waiting ambulance. As Palmer was being strapped in and the worst of his wounds were being dressed, Lancaster appeared at the door. 'Well done, Logan. Good job. Don't worry about anything, just concentrate on getting better.'

Palmer nodded. 'What about Ruby? Is she okay?'

'We don't know all the details yet, Logan. As soon as we do, I'll come and see you.' He closed the door and the ambulance drove away through the crowd, lights flashing.

Thomson looked at the myriad of TV cameras that were filming the burning wreckage of the Eliza J. These pictures would be shown in news reports all across the world, for everyone to see. She knew there was a call she needed to make.

She picked up her phone and dialled the number that Riley had called her on earlier. Riley answered. 'Logan?'

'No Anna, it's me. He's alive. Logan's alive.

Chapter 74

Saint Mary's Church was originally built, in its current location, sometime in the twelfth century. In its nine-hundred-year history, it had burned down twice and fallen into disrepair once. It had been rebuilt and remodelled to the extent that none of the original buildings had survived. Most of the existing structure was late eighteenth century when it had been rescued by a local philanthropist. The dry-stone wall around the graveyard was the oldest part of the church, having been built from stone left over when the original structure collapsed.

The gravestones that surrounded the church dated back to seventeen eighty. The most ornate burial plots belonged to a handful of families who had contributed the most money to the rebuilding of the church after the last fire. In the 1990s the graveyard was effectively closed to all but the most ardent supporters of the parish. Burials were rare here now, only three people had been interred there in the last twenty years. Most of the funeral services that took place were completed at the nearby crematorium. Ashes were now scattered in a new memorial garden and a plaque added to a wall in the corner of the graveyard.

A lot of favours had been called in and strings pulled by

many people in the local community for the funeral that had happened that day. It was a small, quiet service with only family and close friends in attendance. In Palmer's case, that narrowed it down a great deal. Lancaster and Thomson had turned up to pay their respects but had to leave as soon as the service was over.

Palmer shook hands with Nathan's friends and thanked them for coming. The landlord of the Coach and Horses was there and had put on a small spread back at the pub. Palmer promised to drop in for a pint later, but he had no intention of going, he wasn't in the right frame of mind for it.

The rain was getting heavier, and most people were returning to their cars to get out of it. Palmer didn't even feel it. He stood at the graveside with his hand on the headstone. He didn't want to look at the name that had been chiselled into it. Maybe, in time, he would be able to, but not today.

Debbie's parents waved to him as they got into their car. They had never really got on, but Nathan was their grandson and that was more important. They had had Debbie cremated and scattered her ashes close to their home. Palmer had wanted to attend, but he was still in hospital at the time. It was probably for the best. It wasn't just her parents that he didn't get on with. Debbie's brothers didn't like him either. The last thing palmer wanted to do was cause any trouble. Debbie's family didn't deserve that.

Riley walked over to where Palmer stood and held her umbrella over him. 'You're getting soaked.'

Palmer shook his head. 'I still can't get my head around this. I can't get the image of Nathan dying out of my mind. I see it every night.'

'I know some people who could help you with that.'

324

Palmer knew he wasn't the only person who had been torn apart by the events of the last couple of months. 'How are you doing?'

'I'm staying at Yardley Manor for a while, until I get my head together. I've been sober for five weeks. I'm feeling much more positive about everything.'

Palmer smiled. 'That's good to hear. I'm sorry you got dragged into all of this.'

Riley turned to face Palmer. 'Stop blaming yourself, Logan. None of this happened because of you. It was Wallace that caused all of this. It was Connor Harris who got so far into debt that bad people went after his family, your family. There's nothing you could have done to prevent it.'

'You might be right, but Nathan needed me, and I wasn't there. He died on his own, away from the people who loved him. I was his dad, and I should have protected him.'

Riley lifted Palmer's chin and looked into his eyes. 'You still are his dad. You did everything you could have. If you'd been with Nathan, you'd probably be dead too, along with thousands of other people. You stopped Wallace.' She looked around and lowered her voice. 'You stopped a nuclear explosion.'

'I didn't do it on my own, I was lucky. A lot of other people deserve to be recognised for what they did.'

'They will be, but it's hard when the operation didn't officially happen.'

Palmer nodded. 'I get it, it's how the game works. Those involved in these jobs don't do it for the plaudits and the recognition.'

'What will you do now?'

Palmer shrugged. 'I want to go and see Jerry and Subha.

I've got some apologising to do. They've had their baby now. Maybe I'll spend some time chillin' out in the sun. Sort my head out.'

The rain had stopped, and the sun began to break through the clouds. Riley shook the water droplets off her umbrella and folded it away. 'You know that there's a job waiting for you with Edward Lancaster. He looks after people who help him. He has a reputation for picking up waifs and strays. That's why he took me on.'

'Don't put yourself down. He took you on because you're good.' Palmer pressed his fingers to his lips then placed them on the headstone. 'I like Edward, I think he's one of the genuine good guys.' He looked around the graveyard and put on his gloves. 'But before I do any more work, even before I go and chill out with Jerry, I've got a promise to keep.'

Chapter 75

Connor Harris sat at one of the casino's many blackjack tables and stared at his cards. How could anyone be this unlucky? That was another nine grand he had blown, fifteen more on roulette. If his luck didn't start to change soon, the money he stole from Wallace wasn't going to last long.

Harris had grown accustomed to the luxury lifestyle, the expensive suits, and the fast cars that came with money. He enjoyed the doors that it opened and the women it attracted. The thought of going back to his old way of life, struggling to get by, just another nobody, filled him with dread.

The high rollers who were sitting around him would be out of reach once the money ran out. Compared to them, he was a pauper anyway. They had the real wealth. Hundreds of millions, even billions of dollars behind them. His relative pittance was only enough to get him in the door. He was hoping to break into the lucrative private security market that looked after people like this, but it was hard without contacts. Disappearing meant he had to change his name and, because no one knew him, he couldn't get close to any work.

Harris left the blackjack table and walked back over to the roulette wheel. One more bet and then he would call it a night, win or lose. He had one thousand left. Two chips, five hundred each. He rolled them around in his fingers, waiting for inspiration to strike. Red, today felt like a day for red. He placed both chips on the table and stood back.

'No more bets.' The croupier spun the wheel and set the ball running around its rim.

Harris watched as the ball bounced around, looking for a slot to drop into. He chanted his good luck mantra inside his head, red, red, red. He shook the ice in his drink against the sides of the glass as the wheel slowed.

The ball stopped and the croupier announced the result. 'Twenty-six red, ladies and gentlemen, twenty-six red.'

'Yes!' Harris couldn't help himself. It was the first time he had won in over a week.

The other high rollers looked at him and laughed, he had only won a grand, nothing to get excited about. They probably spent more than that on a bottle of champagne.

Harris drained his drink and picked up his winnings from the table. Maybe his luck was changing for the better after all. It was about time.

He walked across the casino floor and cashed in. Two grand. He had had twenty-five when he walked in. Tomorrow would be better, he was sure. Things were on the up. As he waited for his winnings to be counted out, he looked at his watch, it was 3 a.m. The stubble on his face and his crumpled jacket made him look like a vagrant. He was tired and felt rough, perhaps he would have the day off. He collected his coat, put his money in his pocket, and headed for the door.

The streets outside the casino were deserted at that time of the morning. It was mid-week, and all the bars were closed. Most everyday people were tucked up in bed. They had to get up for work in a few hours. Harris looked up and down the street, there were no taxis in sight, and no trams were running. It was two miles back to his hotel and he would have to walk. He pulled up his collar, plunged his hands into his pockets, and set off.

Harris was all about appearances. The hotel he was staying in was expensive. He couldn't really afford it anymore, but if he were going to get security work from some of the high rollers and the places they stayed, he had to look the part.

The Belvedere Hotel was expensive, not just because it was luxuriant, but because it was secure. It frequently hosted heads of state and various royalty which made it the hotel of choice for the super-rich. Most of them had chauffeurs. The fact that he was walking marked Harris out as an outsider.

The gate to the hotel's grounds had a security barrier and sentry position at the end of a long driveway that led up to the front door. As Harris approached the gate, the security guard recognised him, he made a point of it.

The guard swung the gate open. 'Good morning, sir.'

Harris mumbled his response. 'Good morning.'

The gravel on the driveway crunched under Harris's shoes as he made his way up the incline. The hotel's ornate entrance sat at the top of six wide marble steps with several national flags hanging above the door, fluttering in the wind.

Harris climbed the steps and stopped at the door where he paused and turned around. He looked across the river at the lavish façades of the mansions and luxury apartments that sat there. That was the world he belonged in, a world of never-ending luxury.

The high-velocity bullet that struck Harris in the head had been fired from the other side of the river. It was a shot that very few people could even have attempted, but the man on the other end of the rifle wasn't just anybody.

Logan Palmer watched through his scope as the staff from the hotel rushed out through the entrance. The security guard from the gate was already on the radio summoning help. Palmer didn't need to watch any longer, he knew Harris was dead. He dismantled his rifle, picked up the empty cartridge, and placed it all in his backpack.

When he reached street level, the blue flashing lights and sirens were already making their way along the opposite bank towards the hotel. By the time the authorities figured out where the shot came from, he would be long gone.

Palmer walked round to the alleyway that ran between the buildings. A nondescript car, nothing too new or too expensive, was parked at the end of the alley, away from any streetlights. He opened the boot, placed his backpack inside, and got in the passenger seat.

Finn started the engine. 'Are we good?'

Palmer nodded. 'Let's get out of here.'

THE END

Acknowledgements

This book wouldn't have been published without the support of my friends and my readers. I'd like to say thank you to the following people.

Thank you to Mike Craven, Matt Hilton, Graham Smith, Ann Bloxwich, all my friends at Crime & Publishment, and Moffatt Crime Writers+. Too numerous to mention here, but you know who you are, and I couldn't have done it without you. Without your unending support and freely given advice, my books wouldn't exist.

I would like to thank Jerry Scarlett for joining my cast of characters. We joined up on the same day and have been friends ever since.

As always, and most importantly, I would like to thank my wife, Ruth, and my sons, Luke, and Daniel, for always supporting me and pushing me on. I love you.

About the Author

L J Morris was born in Cold War, West Germany, but grew up in the North of England. During his childhood, books were always an important part of his life. He read everything he could get his hands on but found himself drawn towards the Thriller genre at an early age. At 16, eager to see the world he had read about, he left school and spent most of the 80s and 90s serving in the Royal Navy.

After his military service, he continued to live and work across Europe, The USA, and Southeast Asia for several more years. It was during this time that his love of storytelling resurfaced. He jotted down ideas, using the locations he found himself in as a backdrop and added details from his own experiences to make the stories feel authentic.

He now lives back in the North of England, with his wife and two sons, where he still works in the defence industry.

L J Morris is deaf and uses hearing aids. Although he is able to lip-read, the wearing of masks during Covid made that impossible. He recently began learning British Sign Language (BSL) and is planning to include his experiences with hearing loss in more of his work.

You can connect with me on:
- https://ljmorrisauthor.com
- https://twitter.com/LesJMorris
- https://www.facebook.com/LesJMorris

Also by L J Morris

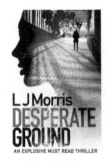

Desperate Ground

When the secrecy of a nuclear weapon agreement is thrown into doubt, a disgraced intelligence operative is recruited to find out if the deal is still safe...

Ali Sinclair, wrongly convicted and on the run from a Mexican prison, is enlisted to infiltrate her old friend's inner circle and find the evidence.

The only people on her side are an ex-Cold War spook and the former Royal Marine that was sent to find her. Together they discover that the stakes are much higher than anyone knew, and the fate of the world is at risk...

But when you've lived in the shadows who can you trust?

"This is an assured and well-crafted debut in the mold of Tom Clancy or Frederick Forsyth. It's intelligent but also has enough pace and action to keep the pages turning long after it's time to turn off the light." – *M W Craven*

"Morris knows his 'stuff', his insider knowledge of an industry that is alien and not a little frightening to most laymen shines through, but never in a way that slows this fast-paced, rollicking action thriller." – *Matt Hilton*

Hunting Ground

L J Morris
HUNTING GROUND
AN ALI SINCLAIR THRILLER

Freed from prison and back in Europe, Ali Sinclair has one job... find Frank McGill.

The information he has is vital if they are to end the conspiracy that threatens to bring down the Government and push NATO to the brink of war.

With terrorist attacks increasing and a mole at the top of the establishment, Sinclair and McGill will need to use all their skills to follow the clues across the continent in a deadly treasure hunt that drags them back towards London.

But when you're being hunted by assassins and the authorities... going home isn't always the safest option.

"Ludlum, Clancy, and DeMille have competition at last" – *Nigel Adams*

"Wow! Wow! Wow! A brilliant opening sets the novel up perfectly for the action-packed read ahead." – *Crime Book Junkie*

"In short, 'Hunting Ground' has to be one of the best books I have read so far this year. Who needs James Bond when you have Ali Sinclair?" – *Ginger Book Geek*